WHAT SHE MISSED

A JOHNSTON & FLETCHER THRILLER

KJ KALIS

This is a work of fiction. Names, characters, places and incidents either are the products of the author's imagination or are used fictitiously. Any resemblance to actual persons, living or dead, or locales is entirely coincidental.

Copyright © 2024 KJ Kalis, BDM LLC

eISBN 978-1-955990-51-6

ISBN 978-1-955990-52-3

All rights reserved

Without limiting the rights under copyright reserved, no part of the publication may be reproduced, stored in or introduced into a retrieval system, or transmitted, in any form, or by any means (electronic, mechanical, photocopying, recording, or otherwise including technology to be yet released), without the written permission of both the copyright owner and the above publisher of the book. The content is not to be used for AI training without permission.

The scanning, uploading and distribution of this book via the Internet or via any other means without the permission of the publisher is illegal and punishable by law. Please purchase only authorized electronic editions, and do not participate in or encourage electronic piracy of copyrighted materials. Your support of the author's rights is appreciated.

Published by:

BDM, LLC

ALSO BY K.J. KALIS:

New titles released regularly!

If you'd like to join my mailing list and be the first to get updates on new books and exclusive sales, giveaways and releases, click here!

I'll send you a prequel to the next series FREE!

OR

Visit my Amazon page to see a full list of current titles.

OR

Take a peek at my website to see a full list of available books.

www.kjkalis.com

1

"Bella! Bella!"

Logan Fletcher yelled at the top of his lungs. His mouth was dry, his heart pounding in his chest. His eyes frantically scanned the area behind his house, but he didn't see anything moving.

Nothing.

The air around him smelled damp, the spring rains pouring down out of the sky as though someone had turned on a faucet full blast and had forgotten to turn it off. It had been raining for hours, the type of lingering precipitation that only areas that had been bound by a long winter, like where he lived in Upstate New York, experienced. It was a cleansing storm, as if the drops were cleaning the landscape from the harsh winter that had just passed, the clouds heavy and low in the sky, no breaks in them as the sun dipped low over the horizon.

It was getting dark. He was running out of time.

The realization only made the situation worse. "Bella!" Logan raced out into the rain to the edge of the backyard, hoping to find his daughter playing on the swing set or gathering newly revealed rocks that had been hidden by the winter snow. The wind blew gently at his face, the drops of rain running down his cheeks.

Still nothing.

Logan spent the next couple of minutes racing back and forth in the yard, his tennis shoes getting completely soaked, the sweatshirt he wore not shielding him from the rain, only soaking it in.

Logan ran back to the house and opened the back door. His German Shepherd, Riggs, tan with black markings and big brown eyes, charged out the back door with a single bark, his eyes searching as if he knew there was something wrong. Logan looked down at the dog as he dodged inside the doorway. "It's Bella, Riggs. I can't find her," he said, barely able to get the words out, as if he expected Riggs to be able to understand every word that was coming out of Logan's mouth. In some ways it wouldn't surprise Logan if his K9 did.

Logan stepped into the house just for a moment, tugging off his soaking wet sweatshirt and tossing it with a splat on the floor, the wet fabric slapping against the tile. He replaced it with one from a pile of dirty clothes that were stacked by the back door ready for the washing machine, ones he hadn't gotten to yet. He pulled it on, not caring what it smelled like, pulled his tennis shoes and socks off and grabbed a heavy rain slicker and a pair of waterproof boots. He shoved his phone into his pocket and yelled for Riggs, expecting him to come running from somewhere in the house. Logan opened the door again, to the whipping of the wind. "Riggs!" The words came out more sharply than he intended. It wasn't Riggs's fault Bella was lost. All Logan was doing was confusing his dog.

The dog's face emerged a moment later from behind a stand of bushes. Logan shook his head. *Get it together, man.* Logan had put Riggs outside in the driving rain and forgot in his panic.

Quickly zipping up the jacket, Logan charged out the back

door, tugging the hood up over his head. "Bella!" Logan scanned the wood line again, hoping to see Bella's form moving. But aside from a fat black squirrel with a puff of a tail that darted up a tree at the sound of his voice, there was nothing moving.

Logan spent the next few minutes searching every inch of the backyard again. He glanced back at the house. Had he missed Bella? Was she somewhere inside with her headphones on or curled up on the floor of her closet like she loved to? Logan ran back to the house, his chest tight with worry. He held the door open long enough for the big shepherd to make his way into the house first. Riggs had his nose to the ground, sniffing as if he knew that Logan was looking for something, but he was unable to figure out exactly what it was.

Logan didn't bother to pull off his boots, not caring at that moment whether he tracked mud all over the tile of the normally clean small house where he and Bella lived or not. Mud could be cleaned up. Losing a five-year-old wasn't as easy to fix as a couple of swipes with a mop. He had to know where his daughter was. Another quick search of the house revealed nothing. Frantic, Logan ran back outside one more time, grabbing a shirt of Bella's from the stack of laundry. He held it up to Riggs's nose, kneeling down in front of the big dog, searching his brown eyes. "Find, Riggs. Find."

Logan watched as Riggs sniffed at the shirt. Was he confused by being asked to track someone who lived with them? Logan hoped not. "Find" was a game they had used in training a million times. Logan would give Riggs a scent, and then Riggs would find it. The cycle was followed by a heavy reward at the back end — usually a treat or a tennis ball or something else that Riggs loved. Riggs touched his nose to Bella's shirt. It was white, with long sleeves and appliqued yellow flowers on the chest, one of her favorites. Riggs sat, signaling he was ready. He knew what he was looking for.

Riggs walked out into the rain from where they were standing under cover near the back door, putting his nose down to the dirt. Logan couldn't do anything except hold his breath. "C'mon, boy. You can do this," he muttered under his breath. Riggs moved around the yard for a few minutes, circling. It looked like he was wandering aimlessly. A lump formed in Logan's throat. That wasn't a good sign.

A minute later, Riggs came trotting back to Logan and sat right next to him, staring at the woods. He hadn't been able to find Bella's scent. Riggs had failed to locate his target. Logan's hands began to shake, and he dropped the shirt onto the wet, muddy ground.

If Riggs couldn't find Bella, Logan didn't know what he was going to do.

2

Logan made four more passes through his yard with Riggs by his side, screaming and hollering for his five-year-old daughter, Bella, who had disappeared into thin air before he ran for cover under the edge of the roof where the shingles overhung the narrow concrete patio. It was empty, devoid of any patio furniture or pots of vegetables or flowers, the way his wife liked it to look. Then again it was early in the season. The patio furniture was still stacked haphazardly against the side of the house, the pots untouched for the last several years.

Logan used the back of his rain-soaked sleeve to wipe streams of water from his face and cheeks. It didn't help, given the fact that his coat was soaked as well. The rain hadn't let up a bit. In fact, if anything, it had become louder. The skies had darkened as well. Whether that was because they were heading towards sunset or the dense cloud cover had just made it even worse, Logan wasn't sure. He glanced down at Riggs, who had laid down next to him on the wet concrete, his mouth slightly open, a long pink tongue hanging out. Every few seconds,

Logan saw Riggs look up at him as if he had questions about why Logan seemed so anxious.

Staring through the sheets of rain as they crossed his backyard, Logan set his jaw and shook his head. His mouth had gone dry. If the sun set before they found Bella, there was no telling what could happen. Bella lost in the woods overnight?

It was unthinkable.

From the back pocket of his pants, he pulled out his phone, nausea clenching his stomach. The screen was damp with rainwater. He rubbed it on the inside of the dirty shirt he was wearing to try to dry it off. He quickly opened it and dialed Zara Walsh. As he did, he saw Riggs get up and pace back and forth, the German Shepherd's head low to the ground, his tail pinned. It was as if he knew, somehow, that Bella was missing, but he wasn't sure what to do about it.

That made two of them.

"Hello?"

"Zara?"

"Logan? What's going on? You aren't on duty, are you?"

"No."

Zara snorted. "Be glad you aren't. This rain is flooding the roads. I've been getting calls for the last two hours. We're having a heck of a time with cars off in ditches."

"That's not why I'm calling." Logan could hear the hardness in his own voice.

"What's going on?"

Logan could tell by her tone that she knew Logan's call was serious. Zara Walsh had been the Chief of the Highmill, New York police department for the last five years. Logan had been there three years when the stubborn, red-headed new police chief had arrived at the office for her first day. Logan could picture Zara in his mind as she sat at home — her round face, long, thin hair and narrow chin. Logan had discovered quickly that people either loved Zara or they hated her. Maybe it was the fiery red hair that matched her personality. Maybe it was the tough exterior that women in law enforcement had. Logan didn't know. At that moment, he didn't care.

"What's wrong?"

The question nearly knocked the breath out of him. It was one thing for him to know that his daughter was missing, something completely different to have to admit it to someone else. "It's Bella." The words came out in a voice so soft it was barely above a whisper.

"Did you say Bella? What happened to her, Logan? Where are you?"

"I'm at the house. I came in and took a shower after my shift. By the time I got out of the shower, she was gone. Zara, I've been looking for her for the last hour. I can't find her. I have no idea where she is."

"What about Riggs? Has he been able to help?"

"No. I tried. The rain —"

"Is tamping down the scent." Zara finished his sentence for him. "I'm on my way."

Logan hung up the phone without bothering to say goodbye.

3

Dr. Skye Johnston was sitting on her favorite chair in the small living room of her house on Orchard Street on the edge of the city of Highmill. She'd gotten home exactly ninety minutes before, after going into the office on a Sunday afternoon to update patient notes. Such was the life of a psychologist who happened to own the practice. There was always work to do at Seneca Counseling Services.

After changing into a comfortable pair of leggings and an oversized sweatshirt that she'd gotten while she was at a concert the fall before, she promptly plopped down in her favorite chair. It was positioned by the window where the outdoor bird feeder was, a spot where she could watch with her cup of tea and a good book.

She had hunkered down for the evening, ready to dive deep into a story by one of her favorite authors when a number popped up on her phone. Frowning, she stared at the screen, pushing a lock of long brown hair behind her ear. The number wasn't one she recognized. After it rang twice, she silenced it and settled her shoulders back into the chair taking another sip of her tea. Then the phone rang again. She glanced over at it. It was the same number. "Well, someone has something to say," she muttered under her breath. Flipping her book over upside down onto her lap so she wouldn't lose her page, Skye picked up the phone. "Hello?"

"Is this Skye Johnston?"

Skye pressed her lips together. She hated conversations that started that way. If someone wasn't sure who they were calling, then perhaps they shouldn't make that phone call in the first place. "Yes. Speaking?" she answered formally.

"This is Dispatcher Reynolds with the Highmill Police Department. The chief called. She needs your assistance."

Skye scowled. "My assistance? With what?"

"I'm not at liberty to discuss that. All I can tell you is there's an officer sitting in a car outside the front of your house."

A shiver ran down Skye's spine. The idea that someone had been sitting outside of her house watching and waiting for her gave her the creeps, even if it was a member of local law enforcement. "Um, okay. Do I have any choice in the matter?"

"Well, we can't exactly force you to go, but Chief Walsh needs your help, ma'am."

Zara needed her help? Had gravity reversed itself when she wasn't looking? "Well, you can inform Chief Walsh and the officer in the driveway that I'll be outside in a moment."

Against her better judgment, Skye got off of her chair, taking a quick moment to fold her blanket and put it back on the footstool. She slid a bookmark into the spot where she'd stopped reading, feeling slightly disappointed that she wouldn't be able to finish the story that she had started. She made a quick stop in the bathroom, removing her glasses and setting them on the edge of the sink, quickly applying a coat of peachy pink lipstick and then grabbing a jacket that was hung by the door as well as a set of tall rain boots. Spring in Highmill could be wet, as evidenced by the torrential rain that had been pouring down all day. By the looks of the heavy cloud cover before the sun had set, it wasn't interested in stopping anytime soon.

Outside in the dark, Skye tugged her hood up over her head and trotted to the police car that was sitting, thankfully, only with its hazards on in her driveway. Though her neighbors were kind, like anyone anywhere, they were on the nosy side. They were always interested in what was going on with everyone else. Skye was sure that Mrs. Corbett, who lived three doors down on the other side of the street, had already spotted the fact that there was a Highmill police car sitting in her driveway. There would be questions. Not that she'd answer them, of course. What she did was her business. Mrs. Corbett wasn't going to be the only person with questions. At that moment, Skye was a little more than curious about why she'd been called away from her comfortable chair after a long day.

As she approached the car, the officer behind the wheel jumped out and opened the rear passenger side door. "Sorry to put you in the back, ma'am, but I've got all my gear up front. Hope that's okay."

Skye gave the young officer, a lanky young man with a fringe of blond hair sticking out from under a Highmill PD baseball cap, a nod. The nameplate on his jacket read, Hauser. "As long as it's warm and dry, that's fine with me."

Skye slid into the backseat as Officer Hauser closed the door behind her. Country music played on the radio at the front of the cruiser, the music interrupted every few seconds by radio traffic from the department. There was a call for a tow truck on I-59, then another on Highmill Road in the center of town. Then silence. Neither of those were a reason to call her out from her house on a stormy night. Skye's curiosity was piqued. What was Zara up to?

Officer Hauser slid behind the wheel slamming the door and shaking the arms of his raincoat off like she'd expect a dog would after coming in out of the rain. "This rain's enough to make me think I should start building an ark," the young officer grunted. He put the car into gear and looked over his shoulder, backing it out of the driveway.

Skye arched an eyebrow. "A little rain? This isn't too bad, Officer. Now, do you have any idea why you are dragging me away from my warm, dry home this evening?"

Skye had more questions at that moment than answers. It wasn't usual for her to be called away from the house, that was, unless she had a patient that was in trouble. That had to be it, she reasoned.

"Not sure, ma'am. There hasn't been any radio traffic about anything other than cars off the side of the road in some flooded streets. I'm not sure exactly what to tell you. We'll be at our location in just a few minutes, so just hang tight."

Hang tight? Skye scowled. All Officer Hauser had to do was deliver her to a location? Did he really have no information? Skye could smell a lie a hundred miles away. Officer Hauser knew what was going on but had been told not to tell her. The secrecy had the fingerprints of Zara all over it. Skye bristled. What was she getting herself into?

4

Skye sat patiently in the backseat of the cruiser as it wound its way across the wet roads of Highmill. She glanced out the window, forcing herself to stay relaxed, though she couldn't ignore the niggling of irritation in her gut at being dragged out of her house on such a rainy, cold, damp evening. All she wanted was to be left alone.

But that was the nature of the job, at least sometimes.

As a psychologist, she frequently got called in when one of her patients had a problem that the police thought they could handle without handcuffs. Skye understood that. In her mind it was a better, although annoying solution to call her in and have her help deal with someone that she already knew relatively well than throwing someone who was already mentally on the edge in jail and adding legal issues to the life circumstances they were already struggling with.

People had enough to deal with. There was no reason to add more trauma to the mix.

Twenty minutes later, after weaving their way through the abandoned, rain-slicked streets of Highmill, Officer Hauser pulled onto a dark, rain-soaked residential street and up the curb onto a driveway, the tires bumping up and jostling her as she sat in the back seat. The wipers screeched against the glass of the windshield as the cruiser's headlights cut across the property. From where she sat in the back seat of the cruiser she could see a small, older ranch house with brown siding. With the low angle of the roof and the small windows, it looked like it had been built decades before. It wasn't rundown, but even in the darkness Skye could tell it could use a little TLC. There was a newer black pickup truck parked in the driveway next to a blue SUV that had the logos and emblems of the Highmill Police Department plastered all over it. Skye's stomach tightened.

Zara.

"Here we are," Officer Hauser said.

Before he could tell her anything else about why she was there, someone ran out to the car, a male figure by the shape of their frame, Skye could tell, but their body and face cloaked by a long black raincoat. Her door opened, the blast of cold air and damp filling the space around her and cutting through the thin pair of leggings she had on. Skye shivered and frowned. Then got out of the car.

"Thanks for coming," Sergeant Kevin Mills said, waving her forward. His tall frame was not much more than a lanky silhouette shrouded by a full-length black raincoat in the dark and the rain. There was only a fringe of his blonde hair sticking out from under the hood.

At least it was Kevin that greeted her and not Zara. Skye blinked. "Not like I had a choice. You people are persistent."

Kevin looked back over his shoulder, his eyebrows raised, as he led Skye towards the house. "Duty calls, Dr. Johnston."

Skye tried to think of a sharp retort but couldn't come up with one at that moment, so she stayed silent, pressing her lips together.

Following Kevin into the house, she stopped just inside

the doorway, taking in what was in front of her. It seemed every light in the house was on, the scene so bright after being outside she nearly had to cover her eyes. Several officers milled about, the hum of low, serious conversations in the background, none of them doing much more than giving her a quick look and then going back to what they were doing. The house was warm, not just in temperature, but in the way it was presented — though dated, it was well cared for and seemed friendly with worn, but clean furniture, the tile swept and kept mud free even in the storm. Skye stood in the doorway not sure exactly what to do. Kevin waved her forward. "This way."

Skye trailed Kevin through the interior of the house and out the back door, where he waved for her to run across into the garage next to the house where one of the bays was open. Skye tugged the hood up over her head once again. The rain was pouring down, the noise of the drops against the ground sending a low vibration throughout the air.

Skye stopped just inside of the garage and looked around. The garage was pretty standard — a smattering of tools here and there, a silver sedan parked off to the side covered in what looked like a layer of dust. A child's pink bike was resting on its side nearby, as if it had been left there after an early spring ride through the neighborhood. Skye looked down in time to see an enormous German Shepherd trotting toward her. She froze. A man came running up behind the dog. With a shout he commanded, "Leave it!"

Kevin Mills, the sergeant that had met her at the door, shook his head as he looked at Skye. "Dog won't hurt anybody, not unless he's told to." Kevin looked over at the man who'd run up from behind the dog. "Skye, this is Logan Fletcher. He's the reason we dragged you away from your cup of tea."

Skye narrowed her eyes. "How did you know I was drinking tea?"

Kevin rubbed his chin and grinned. "I don't know. I think you told me that one time."

Skye shot Kevin a look. Maybe she had. But either way, the fact that he knew made her feel slightly paranoid.

"Anyway, you're here because of Logan. He's got a five-year-old daughter."

Logan interrupted. "Bella."

Kevin nodded. "Bella, who's been missing for the last couple hours."

"Where's Zara?"

Kevin shook his head. "Not here. She's back at the office. I have her truck."

Skye felt her shoulders relax a tiny bit. "Your daughter's missing?"

"Yeah," Logan said, turning his gaze to Kevin, his nose wrinkling. "I don't know why you bothered calling her. We need to do a grid search and canvas all the neighbors. Having a psychologist here is a waste of time. Bella's out there, alone. We need to get moving!"

Skye raised her eyebrows. "Okay, well if that's how you feel, I'd be more than happy to go back to having a quiet evening at home."

Kevin reached out and grabbed her arm. "Not so fast. Logan here was in the shower. When he came out, Bella was gone. We don't have any idea if this was foul play or if she just went outside when she shouldn't have."

"Foul play? What are you talking about?" Logan spat.

Skye narrowed her eyes. Anytime there was a child missing, there were always questions, and worse yet, realities that the parents didn't want to deal with. Which one this was, she had no idea, but they wouldn't know unless they could find Bella.

Correction, if they could find Bella.

5

"How long has your daughter been missing?"

As Skye asked the man in front of her the question, she noticed things that probably other people wouldn't. They ended up being cataloged in her mind like a list — his eyes were slightly wider than she would have expected them to be, his hands were gripped into fists, and she could tell by the rapid rise and fall of his chest that he was breathing shallowly. All classic signs of stress.

Her training took over. She needed to get him to talk in order to get him to calm down. He'd be of no use to her if he didn't focus. No detail at this point was too small. "What happened?"

Skye saw the slightest flicker in the corner of Logan's eye, as if he instantly resented her question.

"Kevin already told you."

Skye looked down at the giant dog that had positioned himself between Skye and Logan. He was pretty, tall with a thick tan coat, black markings and brown eyes. "Can you move your dog away, please? She's making me nervous."

"He. His name is Riggs." Logan stared at the dog for a moment. "Riggs, back."

The dog looked up obediently at Logan and moved away. Skye watched as Logan gave him a few hand signals. The dog looked at her for a moment and then back at Logan, as if he was arguing, and then laid down on the other side of the garage with a grunt. Logan held his hand up like a stop sign. The best that Skye could guess was that was the dog's signal to stay put. She could only hope that would be the case. She wasn't a dog person.

"Let's get back to it, here," Kevin said, shoving his hands in his pockets.

Skye cocked her head to the side. "Start from the beginning. What happened?"

Logan looked at the ground for a second, his face sagging. When he looked up, all Skye could see on his face was sorrow. It was etched deep into every muscle and wrinkle on his face. Not that there were many wrinkles, just a few creases at the corners of his eyes as if he had spent a lot of time outside in the sun fishing or biking or hiking. What he did with his time off, she had no idea, though she could tell he was fit. And if she had to guess, probably not just from the job. He looked like the kind of guy that liked to be active and on the move.

"I picked up Bella on my way home from work and got her settled. I told her I was going to go take a shower and set her up in front of her favorite television program.

"Which is?"

Logan shot a look at Kevin, who shrugged as if he wasn't about to answer.

"She likes watching *Say Yes to the Dress*."

Skye nodded slowly. A little girl that dreamt of wedding gowns wasn't all that unusual, though at five it spoke of a soul that was looking for romantic, happier times and possibly stability. Maybe Logan wasn't the only one with sorrow etched on his face. "And then what happened?"

"I came out from my shower. Was ready to make dinner and she was gone."

"And you have no idea where she went?"

Skye watched as Logan's face reddened just slightly, his lips pressed together, thinning out. "If I did, you wouldn't be standing here in front of me, now, would you?"

Kevin shot Logan a look. "Easy, buddy. She's here to help."

"What kind of help is this?! I'm not sitting in a psychologist's office needing help because my mommy didn't treat me right." He pointed outside. "My daughter is probably outside in the rain somewhere. She could be lost. With the chill in the air, it's not going to be too long before she's hypothermic. I'm scared to death. I'm not here to play twenty questions. I need to find my daughter."

Skye ignored Logan's tantrum; it was typical for people in a traumatic situation. If she reacted to it at all, all it would do is add gasoline to an already burning fire. That wouldn't help them get anywhere. "I'm assuming you tried to use your dog to track her?" Skye nodded at the big shepherd who eyed her up from behind Logan.

Logan nodded. "No luck. The rain has tamped down the scent. He's not trained at search and rescue anyways."

Skye furrowed her eyebrows. "What's he trained for then?"

"Bomb and drug detection."

"Oh, great." Skye stuck her hands in her pockets. Asking Logan questions was not getting her anywhere. "Where's your daughter's room?"

"Over there," Logan answered shortly. "Back of the house, on the opposite side of the kitchen."

Skye had started moving before Logan finished the sentence. She pulled the hood up over her head and darted back out into the rain. The early spring temperatures, hovering in the upper forties, did nothing but cut through her. Logan was right, if Bella was out in the elements, they didn't have long before she froze to death unless she could find some shelter. And that type of decision-making for a five-year-old was asking a lot. Heck, that type of decision-making for anyone who was lost and scared would be a lot.

As Skye made it to the back door of Logan's house, she pulled down her hood and stomped the raindrops off of her boots as she stepped inside. She didn't bother taking them off. Striding through the kitchen, she made her way through two throngs of police officers. Even though she recognized a few of them, no one asked her questions, and no one addressed her. That was fine with her.

As she made her way through the house, she soaked in what was around her. There were a few toys scattered on the floor in front of the television, which had been turned off. Logan had clearly set Bella up with a little play area before he went to get a shower. The kitchen was clean, minus a few dishes in the sink. There was a smattering of small appliances — a toaster, one of those smoothie makers that generally gathers dust in people's kitchens, and a bowl full of bananas and oranges pushed up against the backsplash. The refrigerator hummed along in the background, running through its cycle as though nothing was going on.

There was a short hallway off the kitchen. Skye nosed into each one of the rooms. The first one was an unused bedroom with a twin bed. It had a plaid comforter draped over top of it. By the lack of personal items in the room, it was clearly unused, a treadmill pushed up against the wall. There was a set of dumbbells on the floor next to the treadmill. The faint smell of sweat in the room told her that was where Logan worked out. As she took two more steps down the hallway, she found a full bathroom and a larger bedroom at the end of the hallway with an attached bathroom that looked like it was in need of updating, pale yellow floral wallpaper curling at the edges in a couple of places, the white scalloped vanity sporting rust stains in the sink. The scent of soap hung in the air. It was evidence that supported Logan's story that he'd been taking a shower. Skye wrapped her fingers around the towel that had been draped over the shower door. It was damp. More evidence to support his story.

Skye didn't like liars.

Back out in the hallway, Skye found Bella's room. She pushed the door open and looked inside.

Everything about Bella's room looked just as she would expect a five-year-old's room to look. There was a pink comforter on the bed, two pillows stacked neatly at the head, both with daisies printed on the front of them. There was a matching rug that covered old beige carpeting on the floor and a small, child-sized white desk pushed up against the wall. There was a single dresser and a closet. Everything was arranged in the space to allow room in the middle of the rug, probably for Bella to play. As Skye stood in the doorway, she felt someone behind her shoulder. She looked over toward them, twisting, preparing to tell Logan to go away and let her work when she saw Kevin. She asked him only one question. "Where's Bella's mom?"

"She died a few years back. Cancer."

Skye nodded. That made sense. It fit with what she was seeing. The room held the touches of a woman's hand. Now she could only hope that Logan could keep it together long enough for them to find his daughter.

At least then he'd still have one woman left in his life.

6

Every nerve in Logan's body felt like it had been charged with electricity. He would have been more comfortable if he had thrown himself into a pot of boiling oil than he was at that moment. Skye Johnston, the most well-known psychologist in Highmill, had shown up at his door unannounced. It was clearly the work of Zara, who had texted she was stuck at the office helping with dispatch and would be along as soon as she could. Such was the life of a small police department.

Logan shook his head. After his first conversation with Dr. Johnston, he wasn't too impressed. She treated him like he was on display behind glass at the zoo without a shred of compassion that he could see. "Some kind of psychologist she is," he muttered under his breath.

Skye and Kevin had left the garage a couple minutes before, Kevin trailing after her after she asked where Bella's room was. What good was poking around in Bella's room? Logan had waited, consoling himself by looking out towards the back of the yard, hoping to spot something in the darkness that might be Bella finding her way back. He'd turned on every light the house had, hoping that if she saw the lights of the house blazing, she'd run toward the house. He was trying to give her a beacon to find her way home.

Just thinking about Bella being lost in the dark and the rain sent a shiver through the small of his back.

Logan knelt down. As soon as Skye and Kevin had left the garage, his K9 had made his way back to his partner, sitting next to him. Logan ran his fingers through Riggs' thick fur, leaning into his dog. "We have to find her, boy. We have to."

As Logan stood up, his stomach sinking, Riggs followed suit. He couldn't just stay in the garage petting his dog. He needed to do something.

Tugging the hood on his raincoat up over his clipped brown hair, Logan ran the short distance between the garage and the house, making his way into the back door to the pitying stares of some of the other officers that were hanging out at his house. It was like they were sitting in a vigil, like they would if one of their own had gotten injured on duty and they all were hanging out in the hospital waiting room, nervously sipping cups of coffee.

But this time there was no coffee and the only one that seemed to be overly nervous was him.

Irritated by the thought, Logan stormed down the hallway to find Kevin hanging out in Bella's doorway, Skye wandering aimlessly around in Bella's room, still wearing her muddy rain boots. She didn't even have the courtesy to take her boots off at the door?

Riggs stayed on Logan's heel as he made his way toward Kevin. "What are you looking for?" Logan demanded, his arms crossed in front of his chest.

Skye looked over her shoulder for a moment, then back at the desk where she seemed to be examining Bella's things. "I don't know. I'll find it when I do." Her tone was even, not concerned at all, as if she was simply taking in the sights.

Logan threw his hands in the air, staring at Kevin. "Why is she here? Why don't we have teams of people in the woods? We need to get people outside searching. This isn't helping!"

Kevin held both hands up. "Take a breath, Fletcher. You know why. We don't have any idea exactly where Bella went off to. We're running on a skeleton shift with the rain and the flooding. Unless you can tell me definitively that she's in those woods, we can't send people out looking. Plus, there's the fact that you and Riggs already went out there. If the two of you didn't find her, how are we gonna do it?"

Logan shook his head, trying to fight off the urge to punch Kevin in the mouth. It was a lame answer and an even worse excuse. Even if Logan didn't like it, he understood what Kevin was saying. They could send teams of people into the acres of woods behind his house, and Bella could have walked out the front door and been down the street the whole time. It was a waste of manpower until they at least had some idea where Bella might be. All of it made sense in Logan's mind, except for one fact: Bella was a child. His child.

And he had no idea where she was.

Logan stood frozen at the doorway for another minute, anger nipping at his gut. He watched Skye as she sat down on the floor, looking like she was taking all the time in the world to dig through Bella's room. She paused for a second, looked around, and then rolled on her side, searching underneath the bed.

What was she doing? Logan shook his head, stammering. Waiting for Dr. Johnston to come to some useless conclusion was painful. "I can't... I can't watch this. I'm going back outside," Logan grunted.

Logan stormed past the other officers that were in his kitchen and back out to the garage, Riggs on his heels. Instead of going toward the garage, he went out into the middle of the yard and yelled for Bella again. "Bella! Bella!" He could only hope that she'd hear the sound of his voice and wander back toward it. Logan stood stock still and listened, but the only thing he could hear was the patter of raindrops on the hood pulled up over his head. He hadn't thought to look inside the closet to see if Bella had grabbed a coat or not. If she didn't, her tiny little body would be exposed to the elements. Honestly, he wasn't sure what terrified him more — the idea of Bella being lost or Bella being cold. A knot formed in his belly, the muscles tightened at the back of his neck. They were supposed to be eating dinner. They were supposed to be playing Legos or coloring or reading a story right now. They were not supposed to be doing this.

Logan charged back toward the house and then thought better of it. He wasn't sure he could deal with the stares of the other officers and watch as Skye Johnston fruitlessly dug through his daughter's bedroom. Instead, he veered back toward the garage and stepped into the dry space where his truck was usually parked. He stared out the door one more time, then felt the boil of anger grab hold of him. Without thinking about it, he charged at the wall, putting his fist through the drywall. He felt it give, the surface offering a loud crunch under the power of his arm and shoulder. Pain surged its way up his arm from the contact with the hard surface, but he didn't care. He set his jaw and looked down at the ground. Riggs sat nearby, studying him. "What do you want? Logan barked. The big dog turned and walked away.

Logan was rubbing his hand a second later when the side door to the garage opened. Kevin entered first, followed by Skye. She had something in her hands. As she pulled the hood off her face, Logan noticed for the first time how pretty she was. Brown hair, green eyes, the cool of the air pinking up her cheeks. She had a soft, intelligent look to her, similar to the look his wife Rachel had, at least before she got sick. Logan looked away for a second. When he looked back, he saw Skye's eyes rest on the hole in the drywall and then moved to his hand. She didn't say anything.

Kevin spoke first. "Skye thinks she might have found something."

Were they serious? Logan sucked in a sharp breath feeling his gut tighten. "What?"

Skye held a picture out to Logan. "I found this in her room. It was in a stack of drawings on top of her desk. Do you know where that is?"

Logan clenched his teeth together. How was a random drawing going to help them find Bella? "Yeah. There's a set of caves at the back of the property. Bella and I hiked out there a couple weeks ago. We built a snowman before the snow melted. I took hot chocolate with me, and we sat inside the cave and had a picnic. She thought it was really fun." He looked away. Would he ever have any more of those memories, or would today be the day those ended, like the day that Rachel died?

Skye nodded. "That's exactly the vibe of the drawing. The bright colors, the smiling faces. Bella clearly interpreted this as a very positive experience."

Kevin raised an eyebrow. "And you think maybe she tried to make her way back there?"

"I don't see any indication from anything in her room that she went in any other direction. I think it's worth a shot."

Logan narrowed his eyes. That was the best the famed psychologist of Highmill could do? Grabbing a random drawing off of his daughter's desk and claiming that that's where she was? "I can't imagine that she tried to go the whole way out there by herself. She never does that kind of thing. We have rules. I run a tight ship."

"It's hard when you're a single dad, Logan," Skye said softly.

He shot her a look, but she didn't flinch. "Don't you lecture me about being a single dad."

"I'm not. I'm simply saying that it's a difficult job. And you don't have to be perfect. What we do have to do, though, is try to find your daughter."

No kidding. Logan sucked in a breath to say something, but Kevin interrupted. That was probably for the best. Logan might have regretted the next words out of his mouth. "I think this is the best lead we've got so far. There's nothing in your house that indicates she was taken by force."

Logan wished they would stop talking about that. He knew he was in law enforcement and that he could become a target for retribution, but his five-year-old daughter? That seemed to be a bit extreme for the fact that he worked in Highmill, New York. This wasn't New York City, after all.

Logan let out a sharp sigh. At least the cave drawing was something. "It's going to take a little while to get there in the rain."

Skye shrugged. "I have my boots on."

Something about the way that Skye answered surprised Logan. She was actually willing to go out in the mud and the dirt and try to find his daughter?

Maybe there was more to Skye Johnston than he initially thought.

7

"Are you sure about this?" Logan stared at Skye, the drawing that Bella had made of the cave at the back of the property still in his hand.

Skye drew in a deep breath and rubbed the pad of her thumb and index finger together. It was a habit she'd developed when she listened to her clients talk. Somehow it helped her focus and organize her thoughts. She stared at Logan. "Children have a different communication style than adults do. They tell us a lot by behavior because they don't have the words yet to deal with all of their thoughts and emotions. I think this is your best bet to finding your daughter."

Logan shook his head. "I can't imagine Bella would try to go the whole way out to the cave by herself. She knows better."

Skye watched Logan struggle with the idea that his daughter might have tried to go so far from home all alone. She could tell he was frozen in some respect, wanting to do everything, but afraid of making the wrong decision, scared to death for his daughter, and yet terrified to do more than just stand from the backyard and scream her name in the rain. If Skye had seen it once she'd seen it a million times. Under pressure, people did one of only a few basic things — they ran, they fought, or they froze. It didn't take a psychologist with a PhD to figure out that that's exactly what Logan was doing at that moment. He was frozen in fear. Skye narrowed her eyes and looked at him. "Do you have a better idea?"

"No."

"Then what do you want to do?"

Skye had clearly hit the ball onto his side of the court. It was up to Logan to decide what the next step was. Skye waited, holding her breath. She couldn't even imagine what he was going through. A child at ten or twelve or fifteen who might be lost at least had some survival instincts that were built into them. They had some skills that had been loaded into them by their parents. But a five-year-old? Not so much. At five years old, kids were barely responsible for the basic things in their life, like brushing their teeth or taking a bath. Many of them couldn't write their names or even tell an adult where they lived.

All of a sudden, Logan looked up from the drawing that Bella had made. He glanced towards Kevin, who was standing nearby. Kevin gave an almost imperceptible nod of encouragement as if he was telling Logan that he needed to go, that he needed to trust Skye.

Skye knew the truth. He didn't.

Sighing, Logan relented. "Alright. Gear up. Let's go on a wild goose chase. At least we'll be doing something."

A brief discussion ensued as to who would go and how they would handle things. It was quickly decided that Sergeant Kevin Mills would stay back at the house in case Bella somehow showed up there. Kevin was a frequent visitor and Bella would be calmed by his presence. That left Logan and Skye to do the reconnaissance. Skye glanced at Riggs. The big dog was imposing and, if she were going to be completely honest, somewhat terrifying. "And the dog?"

Kevin answered before Logan had a chance to. "Riggs can stay here with us. It's one less thing to get lost or injured in the woods."

Skye tried not to breathe an audible sigh of relief. Dogs were not her thing, hadn't been since she was a kid. She turned toward the door that led to the backyard and zipped up her coat a little bit higher. Behind her, out of the corner of her eye, she saw Logan struggling with changing out his jacket. He slipped off the black raincoat he had on and pulled on a bright fluorescent orange one that read police across the back in black letters. He handed her a short version of the same jacket. "Here. Put this on over your coat. It'll make it easier for me to see you in the dark."

Slipping into the jacket, Skye tried not to laugh. She felt like she was being dressed in a clown costume, the bright orange a stark contrast to the dark outfit she had on. As she slid the fabric over top of her already zipped-up raincoat, she could smell the fabric. It had a faintly musty, manly odor.

The first steps out into the rain were the worst. If the deluge had lightened up at all, it was only by an imperceptible amount. As Skye took her first steps through the soggy turf of the backyard, she felt the squish of mud and water under the tread of her thick-soled rain boots. Logan handed her a flashlight and told her to stay near him. "Now don't go wandering off," he said, glancing over his shoulder. "And tell me if I need to slow down."

Skye narrowed her eyes. "Slow down? What if you're holding me back and I want to go faster?" Skye couldn't help but challenge him a little bit. Logan seemed like the kind of guy that had all the answers. That was, except for one, and that was where his daughter was at that moment. As they walked, Skye noticed they fell into a rhythm after just a couple of minutes. They crossed the sodden grass of his backyard, past the shadowy hulk of a swing set that glistened with rainwater when

Skye shone her flashlight on it and crossed into a densely wooded area behind the house. The rain was coming down so heavily it was running down the bark of the trees in rivulets. There was no other noise she could hear except for her breath and the patter of the rain on the hood and shoulders of her jacket. The cold was soaking into her so quickly that she was surprised she couldn't see her breath in the beam of her flashlight. Skye looked over her shoulder, trying to get her bearings, looking for the lights of the house, but they had already disappeared in the dark. She felt the vertigo of being almost instantly lost. She'd looked around for a moment when Officer Houser had brought her to Logan's house, but in the dark, it was hard to see. She'd noticed a few homes on the street, spread out a little bit more than the houses in the development where she lived. At that moment, those houses were cloaked by the storm. The only thing in front of her was Logan in his orange raincoat and what looked to be acres and acres of woods.

Skye swallowed, shoving her hands into her pockets and thinking about the drawing she'd found in Bella's room, wondering if she was right. Was it a lead? She knew it was. Was it a good lead? Only time would tell.

She could only hope they had enough time to save Bella.

8

The only thing that Skye could hear other than the slap of her boots on the mud was the raindrops tapping away at the hood on her jacket as they made their way deeper into the woods behind Logan's house. She followed his orange-draped frame in front of her. Logan was considerably taller than she was, probably at least six feet, which was a good six or seven inches taller than she was even on a good day. Despite the fact that he was taller and had longer legs, she was having no trouble keeping up with him.

Skye picked her way among the rocks and sticks and mud that had been left in the woods. Based on what she could see with the glow of her flashlight, Skye thought they might be on some sort of an abandoned hunting trail. It was nothing more than a thin slice in the middle of an otherwise thick woods, the trees still bare from the winter, logs and sticks from storm damage scattered like confetti over the ground after a New Year's Eve celebration. She picked her way carefully behind Logan, trying to pay attention as best she could to the direction they were going, but after a few minutes, she realized that she was completely disoriented. She had her cell phone in her pocket, but she had no idea if she'd be able to get any service out in the middle of the woods if she was the next one to get lost. Her stomach clenched at the thought. She lifted her eyes, double-checking that Logan's orange frame was in front of her. Supposedly, she was following someone who knew where he was going.

Or at least he said he did.

She'd taken off into the woods in a massive rainstorm, following a man she didn't know. What was she doing? Could Logan Fletcher be trusted? She could only hope. Skye shook her head at her naivete. What if…?

Skye shook the thought from her head and focused on the path in front of her. She comforted herself by thinking about the facts. Zara had called her. She knew Kevin Mills from a few other calls she'd been on, and Logan was with the same department. Was she feeling uneasy because of how suspiciously he'd acted toward her or because of her own background?

There was nothing she could do about it at the moment.

Twice as they walked, Logan looked over his shoulder, glancing in her direction. She gave him a slight nod and they kept moving. The conditions — the driving rain, the sloppy, slippery, muddy trail, and the fact they were navigating in the dark made conversation almost impossible.

Not that she would have wanted to talk anyway.

Skye followed Logan down a gradually sloping hill and then up the other side, reaching out to a nearby tree branch to help her steady herself on the slick surface. As they started to climb up the other side, Skye lifted her eyes. In front of her there was nothing but blackness, just rain and the smell of mud and damp leaves in her nose. Although she was dry under the two jackets she wore, the chill in the air had soaked through. She shivered as she walked, thinking about nothing more than the hot cup of tea she'd abandoned at her house.

Skye and Logan walked in silence for another five to seven

minutes in her estimation. Skye didn't want to risk pulling out her cell phone to check the time and take a chance at having it damaged from the pouring rain. As she trudged along behind Logan, she guessed they'd been walking for at least fifteen or twenty minutes. Up ahead, Logan stopped. He shone his flashlight down at the ground and looked back over his shoulder at Skye, waving her forward. "I keep looking at the ground," he said. "Thought I would find some footprints from Bella's shoes or boots. But I don't see anything. I hope this isn't a wild goose chase."

Was he attempting a guilt trip? It was his kid that was lost, not hers. A wave of doubt washed over her. "What do you want to do?"

The fact that they hadn't found any evidence of Bella out on the trail wasn't a good sign, though how much of a footprint a five-year-old would leave running through the woods, Skye wasn't sure. In this weather, it wasn't likely she'd drop her coat — if she had one.

If.

Skye's eyes settled on Logan again. He shrugged, the beam from his flashlight illuminating the streaks of rain on his cheeks. "We might as well keep going. With all this rain even if someone had walked this way, their footprints could have gotten erased."

Skye was certain he was right about that. The rain had been at it for hours. Skye turned and looked behind her. Even in the footsteps she'd just left, the top layer of the soil was so watery that the boot prints she'd left behind had almost all already dissipated back into the trail already.

Logan tilted his head to the side. "Let's keep going."

"You sure don't want to go back?"

"We're almost there. Might as well check and see if your theory is correct, just so we know."

Skye couldn't tell, but his answer almost sounded sarcastic.

Skye followed Logan as they hiked up and over a small rise, the muddy trail slipping away under her boots. She almost fell once, but grabbed a tree limb in time to right herself as Logan turned back and offered his hand. She waved him off. She didn't need help from a man she didn't know.

The land flattened out and then dove downward again. Logan looked back at her. "The cave is right over there. This way!"

Skye kept moving, trying to keep up with Logan, who had increased his speed as they walked. She couldn't blame him. It was a natural reaction when someone was getting close to meeting a goal or finding the answer to their question. The body and the mind provided a last burst of adrenaline to push things forward.

The only question was, would they be elated or disappointed once they entered the cave?

By the time the thought hit Skye's mind, she decided that it didn't matter. She would just be grateful to get out of the pouring rain for a moment. Even with her insulated jacket and the hood up and an extra jacket over the top, the cold rain had soaked into her bones, the kind of chill that could only be taken away by a hot bath and an even hotter cup of tea and a good snuggle under blankets. She thought back to where she'd been just a few hours before, curled up on her favorite chair reading a book after a long day at work. Listening to people's problems all day could be draining, especially when they didn't want to make any real changes in their life. Sighing, she realized she probably would have preferred to be snuggled under her blanket in her chair at that moment rather than out in the pouring down, freezing rain. Maybe it was selfish, but then again, Logan Fletcher didn't seem all that grateful for her help, not to mention the fact that he had that giant, terrifying dog...

Skye didn't have a chance to finish her thought. Logan pointed, jogged forward, and then ducked his way inside what looked to be a black hole cut into the side of the hill. The mouth of the cave. They had found it. Relieved, Skye followed, happy for any break from being out in the weather.

The opening to the cave itself was about the size of a standard doorway, perhaps a little lower, a hole naturally formed by rough limestone. That said, it was plenty wide enough for her to walk through comfortably, only catching the sleeve of Logan's coat because she, frankly, wasn't thinking about the layers she had on. Rough rock was on either side of the entry. As soon as she made it inside, she saw the area widen out.

Surprisingly, the space was quite large, probably a good ten feet by ten feet in her estimation. Aside from the beams of their flashlights, there was no light inside at all. It was as dark of a place as Skye had ever been, maybe darker, the blackness absolute in a way that was creepy. There was dampness in the air, the sour smell of some sort of mildew growing nearby. Skye blinked. As she glanced around the space, she heard a breathless shout from Logan. "Bella!"

Skye lifted her flashlight in time to see Logan darting toward his daughter. Bella was hunched up on a rock at the back of the cave, her knees pulled to her chest, her arms wrapped around her knees. Skye could tell immediately that she was cold. Very cold. Her skin was pale and her lips almost blue, her body shaking violently from the cold. Logan immediately ripped off his raincoat and wrapped Bella in it, scooping her up in his arms. "Bella! What are you doing out here? You scared me to death!"

"I was waiting, Daddy."

"Waiting for what?"

Skye could see the confusion on Logan's face as if he couldn't believe the words coming out of Bella's mouth. Bella had a completely serious expression on her face, as if she was on a mission. Bella was clearly trying to tell them something. But what? Skye frowned. Something had kept Bella in the cave and Skye wasn't sure it was just the rain. Before she could ask, Bella spoke.

Bella pointed at Skye. "Who's that?"

"That's Skye."

Bella looked back at her dad, her small eyebrows furrowed as Logan pulled a metallic survival blanket out from a small pouch in his pocket and wrapped it around Bella's shoulders. "That's a funny name."

Skye took a couple steps forward. "Hi, Bella. I came out here to help your dad find you. You left us a good clue with that picture you drew in your bedroom. It was very pretty."

Through chattering teeth, Bella smiled. "I'm glad you liked it."

Logan knelt in front of Bella, grabbing her face in his hands. "Are you okay?"

"I think so, but I'm a little cold."

Skye watched as Logan patted every inch of Bella's body as if he was checking for broken bones. He looked up at Skye. "The only thing I see is a little scrape on her wrist. Other than that and being cold, she seems like she's okay."

"That's good. I'm glad we found her."

Logan's eyes met Skye's. "Me too. Now let's get her out of here."

Bella stood up and didn't move. "But Daddy, we can't leave yet."

"Why?"

"Because the man is sleeping. He'll be scared if he wakes up and there's no one here. He'll be all alone. It's very dark. I need to show him the way home."

Skye frowned. What was Bella talking about? Skye walked over and knelt in front of Bella. "Bella? What man are you talking about? Can you show me?"

Though Skye didn't have any children or a husband of her own, she had done a rotation as part of her PhD program with a child psychologist. She knew that sometimes kids processed things differently than adults did. Bella was the correct age to have an imaginary friend. Maybe that's what she was referring to?

Undaunted, Bella grabbed Logan's hand and pulled him deeper into the cave, just beyond the wash of where their flashlights had been. Skye followed, tracing their steps with her flashlight. Around an outcropping of stone that led to a smaller room, Bella pointed. "The man. He's over there. He's been sleeping the whole time I was here. I was gonna bring him back to our house for hot chocolate. But he hasn't woken up yet." She looked at Logan and held her tiny pink finger to her lips. "Shhh, Daddy. Don't wake him up. He's sleeping."

Skye furrowed her eyebrows together. A sleeping man? She pointed her flashlight at the ground. What she saw knocked the breath out of her lungs.

Face down on the ground was a body. By the way it was sprawled, Skye knew instantly that whoever it was, he was dead. She grabbed Bella by the shoulders and moved her back towards the entrance of the cave without asking Logan's permission. There were certain things that would scar children for the rest of their life. Certainly finding a dead body was one of them.

Skye stood for a moment at the cave entrance waiting for Logan. It didn't take him long to reappear. He fished around in his pocket and pulled out a black walkie-talkie. Lifting it to his face he pressed the call button. "Kevin? Can you go to channel five?"

"Copy that."

Skye watched as Logan coolly switched the channel on the radio and held it up to his mouth again. She could tell his training was kicking in. It was eerie. He seemed too calm and too in control in her mind. His daughter had been lost and now he was just going to play cop?

She knew what he was doing — compartmentalizing. People who worked in high-pressure situations did it all the time. They'd put each part of their experience in an individual bucket. It allowed them to stay under control. It could be a powerful tool, but the problem was, from Skye's vantage point, that the mind didn't work that way. The mind was like a river. It would flow where it wanted to. The same situation applied to people. Eventually, their memories would bust out of the carefully constructed boxes they were put into and rush like a tsunami toward the rest of the person's life, destroying large chunks of it like a tidal wave. Skye licked her lips, watching Logan with his radio. Had the tsunami burst in his life yet?

"You there, Kevin?"

"Yup. Go ahead."

"We have Bella. She's unharmed. But we also have another issue." He gave Skye a knowing glance as if to say they weren't going to talk about the body in front of Bella. "I'm gonna need the coroner out here."

There was a pause before Kevin answered. "The coroner?"

"Copy that. I'm gonna light up the beacon on this radio so you know where we are."

"Copy that."

By the strain in their voices, Skye could tell that Kevin had questions for Logan that he wanted answers to, and Logan wanted to share those answers, but in the company of a fragile five-year-old, it wasn't the time or place to do that. Logan looked at Bella. "We're going to have a talk about this later. There's no going out past the grass without me, you know that."

"Sorry, Daddy." Bella looked at the ground.

Logan looked at Skye. "There's an access trail about a quarter mile from here. I didn't suggest coming that way earlier because of how much mud there is, but now we don't really have a choice given the situation. We're gonna have to use it to get Bella and," he glanced down at her, putting his hand on her head, "the sleeping man out of here." He picked up the radio and keyed it up again. "Kevin?"

"Go for Kevin."

"Sergeant, there's an access road just north of my location. You're gonna have to bring the trucks out that way. It's gonna be swamped. You're gonna need four-wheel drive. Don't let the coroner bring his van on the trail. He'll get stuck and we'll never get him out."

"Copy that. We're on our way now."

Skye stood near the mouth of the cave, a trickle of fear running down the back of her legs. What was she doing? She was in the middle of a rainstorm with a man she didn't know and a dead body. The good news was they rescued his daughter. Skye looked at Bella. She was adorable. Dark hair like her dad, a round face with bright eyes. She seemed to be unharmed except for the very real possibility of trauma given the fact that she'd been babysitting a dead body for the last several hours.

Bella, and Skye, should have stayed home.

Skye looked at the ground and shoved her hands into her pockets, fighting off the damp and the cold. She glanced at Logan, who had knelt in front of Bella again, checking her over, tugging the survival blanket even tighter around her and then taking off his own coat to put on her. Bella waved it away with a flick of her hand. Skye raised an eyebrow. She was spunky. Skye liked that.

Despite the horrific weather, and what they had found, at least they had managed to save Bella. That was the good news. Blinking, she realized she was using one of the techniques she prescribed for her clients, reframing. How many times had she said, "Okay, how could you reframe that into a more positive perspective?" Funny how many times she needed to take her own advice, the advice that she got paid well to dole out to people who were often in circumstances they deemed miserable, but not nearly so if they were to take a look at them under the harsh light of truth.

Thinking about it as she stood there, as much as people wanted to say that the truth was relative, in her book it wasn't. The sky was blue, and the grass was green. There were some truths that were immutable — probably more than people would like, that was for sure.

And the harsh truth at that moment was that as much as she would like to be home in her comfortable chair, under her blanket, drinking her hot tea and reading a book, she had done a good job helping Logan find his daughter. But there were questions now, questions that needed to be answered.

The first one was, who was the dead man in the back of the cave?

9

Looking back on it later, Skye would reflect on the fact that the few minutes between when they had found Bella and the mysterious dead body abandoned in a cave seemed like a full day and seconds passing all at the same time. It could only be explained as the way the brain processed stress and overwhelming emotion. Time hurried and stood still at the same time, her senses trying to catch up and create a story around what was happening.

It had been a long time since she had felt that way. Very long.

Skye stood near the mouth of the cave, the thin light from the moon overhead barely lighting the clouds as the storm passed. The rain never abated, its steady thrumming sounding like splashing at a water park just outside the entrance of the cave as they waited for Kevin. With the weather, it was taking a little time to marshal the resources from the Highmill Police Department to get Bella away from the scene and insert law enforcement and the medical examiner to deal with the dead body they had found.

Logan stayed protectively with Bella and Skye as they stood, waiting at the mouth of the cave. It was probably no more than twenty minutes or so before Skye heard shouts and saw the beam of flashlights being waved in the darkness, a group of people charging toward them wearing bright orange rain gear. Logan stepped to the mouth of the cave and waved his flashlight into the darkness to give the officers a chance to see exactly where they were located.

And then everything became controlled chaos.

Two officers, one of them being Sergeant Kevin Mills, both of them dressed from head to toe in heavy rain gear along with their duty belts, tactical vests, and heavy boots made their way to the mouth of the cave. The second officer with Sergeant Mills quickly pulled off a backpack, wrapping Bella in another metallic survival blanket and then a wool blanket. She looked like she had been wrapped in tin foil. Kevin looked at the two of them. "We'll get Bella back to the house. I have a car waiting at the top of the trail to take her straight there."

Logan's expression was grave. "She needs to get looked at. I didn't find anything but —"

Kevin held up a hand. "The ambulance is already parked in your driveway. The medics are inside. They're ready for her as soon as she gets there. If they see anything at all they will take her right over to Woodland Medical Center, lights and sirens, no questions asked. Don't worry, Logan, we've got this."

Skye watched the tense conversation between the two of them. Clearly from the clipped way they talked with each other, they'd spent a lot of time together. Skye understood Logan's need to have Bella looked at, but in some respect, she thought it was overkill, the pendulum swing of relief and protectiveness going back the other direction. Logan had lost Bella and now he was going to make sure, without a doubt and beyond any question, that she was okay, even though the only evidence of injury was a scraped wrist and exposure to the cold.

The man in the other part of the cave was another story.

Within a minute, Bella had been bundled up, every inch of her small body covered. The officer in charge of taking her back to the house, a stout man with arms the size of hams and narrow eyes whose name badge read Crenshaw, had scooped Bella up into his arms. Logan called behind them. "Radio me when you get to the car and radio me when you get back to the house."

The officer nodded as he stepped outside. "Copy that."

With Bella safely out of the cave and on her way back to the house, Skye felt like they had completed at least one of their missions for the evening. It was a good feeling to have Bella's location resolved and in a positive way. In her career, Skye had sat with more than one family who had lost a child. The grief could be overwhelming, suffocating to the point that the people barely had any life left in them. Given the fact that Logan had already lost his wife, she was glad, for his sake, that Bella was on her way safely back to the warmth of her house.

Kevin's voice interrupted her train of thought. "So what do you need the coroner for?"

"Bella was guarding a body," Logan said grimly.

By the light from their flashlights, Skye could see Kevin's mouth drop slightly open. "What? I thought you were kidding me when you said we needed a coroner."

Logan shook his head. "Why would I kid about that? This way."

Logan led Kevin to the back area of the cave where Bella had found the body. Skye followed.

"You weren't kidding, were you?" Kevin mumbled, shining his flashlight on the corpse.

Logan shook his head. "I wasn't. I haven't turned him, but I felt for a pulse. There's nothing."

Skye stood behind the two men as they talked casually about the body. Much of the tension had left now that Bella had been safely found and whisked back to her house, despite the fact that they were standing in front of someone who was dead. Logan's radio crackled to life. "Bella's en route to the house."

Logan nodded and held the radio up to his lips. "Copy that. Thanks."

Kevin knelt over the body and looked up at Logan and Skye. "Any idea who this guy is?"

Logan shook his head no. "I haven't checked yet. Was just trying to get Bella out of here safely."

"That's fine. It's not like this guy is in any hurry to go anywhere, is he?"

Skye tried not to smile at the haunting sense of humor that the two officers were using to cope with the circumstances. It was a hallmark of people who saw tragedy. They'd make light of it, so it wasn't such a serious attack on their soul every time they saw something horrific. Skye sighed, mainly at herself. Did she have to evaluate everything in terms of a psychological reaction?

Skye took a couple of steps toward the body and then pointed to a lump in the man's back pocket. "That looks like a cell phone or a wallet."

Logan gave a nod and reached into the pocket, pulling out a wallet. He flipped it open, Kevin pointing the flashlight at the interior contents. Logan worked quickly. "Well, this clearly wasn't a robbery. There's several hundred dollars in cash and all the credit cards are in here. The wallet looks undisturbed." He thumbed through the contents for a moment. "Here it is." He pulled out a driver's license. "Victim is one Ian Dunn. Lives here in Highmill."

Kevin shook his head. "Never heard of him."

"Me either."

Skye looked at the two officers kneeling over the body and

the way the newly identified Ian Dunn was sprawled on the ground, face down, his arms up over his head, the hood on his jacket pulled up covering his face. Questions started to form in her mind.

Who was Ian Dunn and how had he ended up dead?

10

It didn't take more than another fifteen or twenty minutes for the radio to crackle again with two bits of news — Bella was back at the house, already sipping hot chocolate and getting checked out by the paramedics, who were unable to find anything wrong with her other than she was cold, dehydrated and had a scratch on her wrist. The second piece of information was that the coroner was slogging his way into the cave.

"Well, this is kind of a new development, isn't it?"

Skye stood back as a forty-ish-year-old man dressed in a brown raincoat with white letters on the back that said coroner stepped into the cave. Behind him was a man that could have been his brother, clearly a few years younger and clearly disgruntled by the fact that they were out in the middle of a horrendous rainstorm dealing with a dead body, his narrow face stony. The coroner stopped and looked at Skye, offering his hand. "Jay Chapman. I'm the county coroner. You are?"

"Skye Johnston."

"Nice to meet you, very nice." A smile crept across his face as he pushed his glasses up on his nose. "Clearly, I'm not here for you, though?"

Skye raised an eyebrow at the coroner's joke. She wondered how many times he had used that on someone at a scene. "No, I'm alive and kicking. Thanks for asking, though."

"You are most welcome."

"Over here," Kevin called.

Dr. Chapman looked over his shoulder. "Jeff, let's fire up the lights, the big lights. Can't see a doggone thing between the rainstorm and this cave."

Skye watched in fascination as Jeff reached into a duffel bag that he had lugged with him through the rain and the mud to get to the cave. She'd never been to the scene of a murder before. Helping out when one of her clients had a breakdown, that was one thing. A dead body in a cave? That was something else entirely.

Jeff withdrew two small lanterns that didn't seem to be much bigger than the size of an oversized mug that she might use for coffee. He pulled straight up on the first one. It expanded like an accordion, doubling in size, the light flickering on. A brilliant white light suddenly cast sharp shadows throughout the cave. As he turned on the second one, Skye quickly clicked off her flashlight and stuffed it in her pocket. The lanterns were so bright they nearly made her feel like they were standing in the sunshine.

"That's much better," Dr. Chapman said. "What do we have?"

Logan cleared his throat. "We found Bella here, just on the other side of the wall. She thought that the man had fallen asleep."

Dr. Chapman looked at Logan and then looked at Skye. "We?"

"Dr. Johnston found a drawing that Bella had made of the

cave. To be honest, I thought she was crazy to think Bella would try to hike out here all by herself, but she was right."

Skye watched the interaction with interest. Logan had carefully skipped the part about how his daughter had gotten away from him. It was likely the truth was too hard for him to face even though the result had been positive.

Dr. Chapman tapped the side of his head. "Never doubt a woman's intuition, never ever, Officer Fletcher. It has been the downfall of more than one man throughout history."

Logan scowled but didn't answer.

"How did the body get here in the first place? Any thoughts on that?" Dr. Chapman asked, not addressing the question to anyone in particular.

"That's what we don't know," Kevin said.

Dr. Chapman started by circling the body. "Jeff, let's get a body bag out. I'll do a quick initial assessment. The weather is really rough, rougher than I imagined, so let's see if we can take a few pictures and we'll get this guy bagged and tagged and get him out of here. Any idea who the victim is?" he asked, looking at Kevin and Logan.

Logan handed over the wallet he'd found on the body. "According to this, Ian Dunn."

Dr. Chapman flipped open the wallet after pulling on a pair of gloves. He read from the driver's license. "Ian Dunn, resident of Highmill, New York, aged thirty-seven. That's a good age. Thirty-seven. A person knows enough but not too much."

Dr. Chapman handed the wallet to Jeff, who slipped it into an evidence bag and secured it, adding it to the equipment in the duffel bag. Dr. Chapman put his hands on his hips. "Alright, Mr. Dunn, let's see if we can figure out what happened to you." He stopped, cocking his head to the side. "Anybody else notice this guy's clothes? They look like the kind you'd wear to a business meeting, like he was heading home from work or something."

Skye nodded but didn't say anything. She'd noticed the same thing, but they'd been so concerned with getting Bella out of the cave and away from the body that she hadn't bothered to mention it to Logan. After all, she wasn't a police officer. What did she know? She was simply a psychologist along for the ride.

Ian Dunn was wearing a pair of black pants and dark leather shoes with laces, the kind someone would wear to an office. He had on a hooded jacket, not necessarily a raincoat, but one in a dark khaki color that looked to be water resistant, but definitely not the kind that you would wear out in the middle of a torrential rainstorm like they'd had during the last twenty-four hours. Was that a clue about the timing of the murder? Ian was face down on the stony dirt of the cave, his arms outstretched in front of him, his face shielded by both his arms and the hood from his jacket. Whether the hood had been pulled over his face intentionally or had just flopped there, Skye had no idea. He looked like Superman out of uniform, stretched out, face down on the ground.

Dr. Chapman took a look at his body while Jeff took a few pictures. "Well, there's no obvious cause of death on this side of the body. How about if we flip him over and see what we can find?"

Jeff put down his phone and his camera long enough to pull on a pair of gloves and find a spot near Ian's legs. Together he and Dr. Chapman turned him over. As soon as he did, Skye sucked in a breath, hearing groans from Kevin and Logan at the same time.

Dr. Chapman clucked under his breath. "Well, isn't that most unfortunate, quite unfortunate, really. At least we can be assured that his death was quick."

Skye looked away, a wave of nausea catching her by surprise. In the place of what had been Ian Dunn's face was nothing but a bloody, shattered mess. The way his face had been blown apart, it was clearly not the result of a beating but of multiple gunshot wounds to the face. Only his right eye remained intact. It stared lifelessly upward. Ian's teeth were shattered, the whole left side of his face opened into his brain. Her stomach lurching, Skye covered her mouth with her hand. The only thing she could think of was that she was so grateful that the hood had covered Ian's face. She couldn't imagine the trauma Bella would be facing if she had seen Ian's face. Luckily, Bella's childlike imagination had protected her, simply telling her that the man who'd been left at the back of the cave was sleeping, taking a nap like nothing had ever happened.

But based on what Skye saw, it was far from just a nap.

Ian Dunn, whoever he was, had been brutally murdered.

11

With Bella safely out of the way and the coroner working on the body, Skye excused herself and walked toward the opening of the cave. She took a deep breath in. It wasn't as if there was any odor coming from the body, at least not yet. If she had to guess, the cold, damp air had slowed down the rate of decomposition. Around her, the cave smelled like a combination of dirt and fresh rain. But that didn't erase what she had seen. Logan and Kevin had stared at the body as if it wasn't anything more interesting than a package of meat at the grocery store. But it wasn't hitting her that way. She swallowed. The scene was grisly to be sure. The only positive was that Bella hadn't seen it. The hood, whether left that way intentionally or unintentionally, had protected her young mind from seeing the way that Ian Dunn's face had been ripped apart.

That single happenstance might have protected Bella from a devastating emotional trauma.

Skye's stomach lurched again. In her line of business, she dealt with the mental and emotional carnage left behind by trauma, not the physical damage done to people.

She looked toward the back part of the cave where the lanterns were lighting up the crime scene. Part of her wanted to walk back into the cave, call for Kevin, who seemed to be slightly more reasonable than Logan, and ask for a ride back to the house. She'd done her job, hadn't she? But she paused. A part of her was curious too. What would make someone basically demolish another person's face? Her curiosity getting the best of her, Skye turned and walked back toward the section of the cave where the coroner was working on the body.

Dr. Chapman was taking a few last pictures of the body while Jeff rolled a black body bag to get the remains of Ian Dunn out of the cave when she heard a voice behind her.

"Zara?" Skye managed to mumble. The chief of the Highmill Police Department brushed past Skye and then stopped and turned, her expression blank.

"Thanks for your help, Skye. I appreciate you getting Bella back where she belongs. I'll have Kevin get you out of here." Zara stared at Skye as if she expected Skye to challenge her. Her green eyes nearly lost against her pale skin, only the rim of her red hair sticking out from underneath her hood.

Skye paused, ready to argue. She could stay. Maybe she could be of help. But something in her decided not to. Zara was, after all, the chief of police for Highmill. Swallowing, Skye simply nodded and waited for Zara to take charge like she always did. Skye shoved her hands in her pockets and watched from the periphery. Zara flipped her hood back and stood at the feet of Ian Dunn and looked him over, shaking her head. She glanced at Kevin. "Sergeant, how about if you take Dr. Johnston back to her house? We should limit the number of civilians here. I've got this."

Dr. Chapman looked up from where he was kneeling in front of Ian Dunn's body, pushing his glasses up high around his nose. "We're almost done here, Chief."

Zara nodded, her expression blank. "I figured. Nobody

wants to be out in this weather, I'm sure not even him," Zara pointed at what was left of Ian Dunn. She looked up and gave another nod to Kevin. Kevin started moving toward Skye, ushering her toward the mouth of the cave and the storm outside.

Skye could tell it was time to go. Zara didn't want any civilians, even ones she had called away from their homes, to be at her crime scene.

Typical Zara.

As Kevin walked towards her, Skye glanced back at Logan. He mouthed a quick, "Thank you," and then got back to work. Skye felt Kevin's hand touch the back of her shoulder, nudging her forward. She could cut that tension in the air with a knife. It was probably better if Skye got out of Zara's way. Zara was like a black hole. She tended to suck everybody in who got close enough.

As Skye stepped out of the cave and back into the rain, she tugged her hood up over her head again, shoving her hands down in her pockets. The rain hadn't abated at all. Sheets of it were still pouring out of the heavy gray sky above. The only light available was the headlights of a few emergency vehicles that had made it out through the muddy access road to the cave site.

Angling for Kevin's cruiser, Skye stepped in a puddle and nearly slid off her feet, the mud slick underneath her boots. Kevin extended a hand, grabbing her by the elbow and steadying her. She gave him a nod as he guided her back toward one of the SUVs marked with the Highmill PD logo, opening the door for her, helping her inside.

Inside, Skye took a deep breath and flipped the hood of her jacket back off of her face, watching rivulets of water run down her sleeves, mud collecting on the floormats of the SUV. A second later, Kevin was inside, starting it up. She watched as he shifted it into four-wheel drive. He glanced back at her as he navigated back out onto the access road. "Thanks again for helping with Bella. If you hadn't found that drawing in her room, I'm not sure what we would have done."

There was no mention of Zara. That was probably better. Skye wasn't sure he'd picked up on the strain between the two of them, but even if he had, at least he had the sense not to get involved. Skye looked up, forcing herself to let go of any anger she had lurking in her gut. She hadn't gone to the call to please Zara. She'd gone because there was a job to do for the community. This time, it was finding Bella. There was no telling what it would be next time. "Yeah, I'm happy I could be of help."

Skye looked at her hands for a second. From the glow of the instruments and the onboard computer in front of her, she could see that they were pale white, the fingertips nearly blue from the chill in the air and damp. Kevin must have realized how cold they'd both gotten standing out in the rain. He turned up the heat. A second later, Skye felt warmth start to soak into her wet clothes. She licked her lips. "I know the chief wanted you to take me home, but could we maybe stop at Logan's house? I just wanted to check on Bella before I head back. Purely professional reasons. She's been through a lot today," she added hastily.

Kevin glanced at her and gave a nod. "Of course. I'm sure Logan would appreciate that."

After twisting and twining away down the access road, navigating what felt like a river of mud and water that had covered the path back to the paved streets, they finally pulled into Logan's driveway. There were still two cars left in the driveway — police cruisers — both of them dark, neither of them with any emergency lights on.

Skye had been so focused on why she had been dragged away from her house that she hadn't really taken time to look at where Logan lived very carefully when she first arrived. Now, knowing Bella was safe, she did. It was a ranch home, covered with brown siding and a matching chocolate-colored roof, not unlike the house that Skye had grown up in. In the darkness, it looked a lot like a cabin someone might buy up in the mountains. The detached garage was closed and dark, but the house had warm lights coming on from the inside, casting a friendly glow out into the yard. Skye could see shadows of shrubs lining the front walk. It looked like they were in need of a trim.

As Skye got ready to jump out of the car and head back into the storm again, she tucked the hood of her jacket up over her hair. She turned toward Kevin. "You said that Logan's wife passed away?"

Kevin doused the lights on the SUV and reached for the door handle. "Yeah. It's been a couple of years. Been hard on Logan, but he seems better now. Beth Ann – that's my wife – we help out when we can."

Skye had a million questions but decided not to ask them. People's experiences and history were what intrigued her. That was one of the reasons that she had gotten involved in psychology in the first place. That, and the ability of people — including her — to overcome difficult circumstances.

Skye jumped out of the SUV and trotted up the front walk, following Kevin. He pushed the door open in front of her and then waited while she walked inside, his tall frame nearly blocking the doorway. As Skye squeezed past, she could hear the television on in the background, the chirpy, happy voices of some sort of children's program. She smelled coffee, the musky smell of a freshly brewed pot hanging in the air.

Stopping at the door, Skye pulled her boots off, not wanting to track mud and water all over Logan's house now that they had found Bella. Kevin took her borrowed jacket from her and hung it on a hook by the door, then her own jacket. Skye blinked. By the way Kevin moved around the house, he had clearly been there quite a bit. She pushed her hair away from her face, a few damp strands sticking to her cheek. Skye knew that law enforcement often acted like a surrogate family for the officers. Police officers went through experiences that couldn't be replicated anywhere else, the stress of the job only surpassed by possibly surgeons, firefighters, and the military. Because of that, those shared experiences bonded the people in a department together like nothing else. It was unique to those careers. Sure, other industries had teams or tried to build them, but there was nothing like the bond between people that served together in a way that could require the ultimate sacrifice. So, that said, it didn't surprise her when she saw two officers manning Logan's house. One was standing in the kitchen, hovering over a stack of boxes of pizza and pouring a cup of coffee for Kevin as he walked in the door, and another sat on the floor with Bella, her tactical vest off to the side, playing some sort of game that involved a set of pink unicorns. Bella was focused on the game, then giggled with delight when the unicorns all toppled over as if it were the funniest thing in the world.

At the edge of the small family room where Bella and the officer were sitting on the floor playing was Riggs, Logan's enormous German Shepherd. Skye stopped in her tracks as the dog lifted his head and looked at her. What the look meant, she wasn't exactly sure, but she didn't move from her spot. Kevin came up behind her. "Don't worry about Riggs. He's harmless. He's just looking out for Bella right now."

"If you say so." Skye didn't move from her spot, eyeing the dog.

Kevin raised an eyebrow. "Not a fan of dogs?"

Skye didn't take her eyes off of Riggs. "Don't have a lot of experience with them, especially not one that has been trained as a K9 officer."

Kevin cocked his head to the side. "Well, the fact that he is one should give you confidence. Riggs knows what his job is.

Unless someone tells him to come after you or you decide to act threatening, you're fine. I promise."

Skye wasn't exactly sure about that, but it wasn't as though she could stay glued to her spot on the floor forever. She pressed her lips together and took a couple of steps forward, lifting her head to the police officer who was playing with Bella in a silent request to spend some time with Bella. As the officer stood up, she looked at Skye. "She seems fine to me. Happy and laughing. You'll probably know better, but she isn't acting any different than my kids do."

Skye gave a nod. "Thanks. I'm hoping that's the case."

But if Skye knew anything after being a psychologist for a decade, the only proof was time. Only time would tell.

12

It was another forty-five minutes before Zara dropped Logan off in front of his house. There were pictures to be taken of the crime scene, a list of questions from Dr. Chapman that he wasn't sure exactly how to answer, and a few initial report forms to start filling out on a tablet that Zara retrieved from her SUV.

By the time he got back to the house, Logan was exhausted, the kind of tired that can only be solved by food, quiet, and a lot of rest. As he stared at his driveway, seeing multiple Highmill PD cruisers in the driveway, he realized none of that was going to be immediately possible.

A quick count revealed three police cruisers in the driveway in addition to his black pickup truck. He sighed. As he started to slide out of the passenger seat of Zara's vehicle, she waved. "I'm going to head home. I'll see you in the morning. When you get in, start working on the case. You can take the lead since you found him."

Logan didn't say anything but nodded in relief, partly that he had been given the case and partly because Zara was leaving. At least that was one fewer person to interact with. All he wanted to do was go into his house, check on his daughter, and lock the doors. He and Bella were due for a talk. A long one. He couldn't lose her. He couldn't. Not after...

Logan pushed the thoughts of Rachel's death two years before out of his head, pulled his jacket around him, and ran to the front door, pushing it open. Inside, he could hear the chuckles of a conversation going on. Somewhere in the house, the characters from one of Bella's television programs were laughing in the background. He heard the tap of dog nails running toward him on the wood floor. Riggs came around the corner like a wild beast out of control. Riggs plopped his butt down in front of Logan, his tongue hanging out, his eyes bright, his tail wagging in sweeping motions as if he was using it to dust the floor. Logan reached down and scratched the big dog behind his ears. Sometimes he forgot how goofy Riggs was. Sure, he was a working dog and an important part of the Highmill Police Department, one that had cost the department a lot of money and cost Logan a lot of his time spent in training, trips to the vet, and certification classes, but seeing how happy Riggs was, it was worth it. Logan bent over. "How you doing, boy? You good? How's our girl?"

As the big dog trotted off, letting Logan know that everything was fine in the house, Logan glanced around. Two officers, Maggie and Paul, stood in the kitchen, each of them with a piece of pizza in their hands. Kevin stood nearby, watching, looking into the family room as if there was something going on. Logan frowned. It had been a long time since he'd had that many people over at his house at once. Probably since Rachel's funeral. Logan scanned the rest of his house. He spotted Dr. Johnston sitting on the floor with Bella. Hadn't Zara told Kevin to take her home? She was sitting cross-legged on the floor, stacking up blocks with Bella and then watching her knock them over, a broad smile on her face.

Logan started to frown and then cocked his head to the

side. Skye was pretty — long brown hair, high cheekbones, green eyes, pale pink lips. Even with no makeup on, she was a stunner. He glanced at her left hand, which rested in her lap. No wedding ring. What was her story? As if she had sensed his presence, Skye looked up, noticing Logan standing at the edge of the family room. She looked back at Bella and held her hand up, her palm open. Bella gave her a high five and then plopped back down on the ground, looking at Kevin. "Uncle Kevin! Come play blocks!"

Logan watched as Skye got up and gave Kevin a nod as they changed positions. She walked toward Logan, standing next to him, staring back at Bella. As Skye stood next to him, he thought he could smell the faint scent of some sort of floral perfume. He breathed it in deeply and then looked at her. Despite the hike in the torrential rain, she smelled good. "I thought you were going home."

Skye shrugged. "I wanted to check in on Bella before I headed out. I hope that's okay?"

It wasn't as if Logan could argue, especially given how he'd treated her. Skye had saved his bacon in a big way. He should have been more accepting of her help when she'd arrived, but then again, his child had been lost. He pushed a tinge of embarrassment away. How was he supposed to act?

"Yeah, sure. How is she?"

Skye stiffened just slightly as if she was assessing the situation. "For the moment, fine. You are asking my professional opinion, right?"

Logan nodded.

"I'm not a child psychologist. It's not my area of specialty, but I did do a rotation in the field. Whether Bella is able to tell you or not, she went through something significant tonight. Her little brain is trying to process all the pieces. I asked her a series of questions while we played. She seems calm and not distracted. Those are all good signs, but you might want to have her visit with a child psychologist a couple of times just to make sure there's no long-lasting issues. Things like this can cause problems down the line."

Logan's stomach tightened. Bella had seen a psychologist after Rachel died. The nightmares she'd had about losing her mom were probably more terrifying to Logan than they had been to Bella. He could only hope they didn't resurface after her trip to the cave.

"What should I expect?"

Skye shook her head. "I can't say exactly. She could have bad dreams, just seem extra clingy, or be concerned about you being out of her sight." Skye looked around at the other officers. "But the good news is you have a great support system here. If you need the name of a child psychologist she can see, call my office. I'll have my assistant get you a name."

"Thanks. I might do that."

Skye called to Kevin. "Can you give me a ride home?"

Kevin stood up, unfolding his long frame from where he had been sitting on the floor with a surprising amount of speed. "Sure, and then I'm gonna head home too."

Logan nodded. He folded his arms across his chest, glancing at Bella. She had plopped down in front of the television, sitting in a cross-legged position. She was staring at the screen, hugging a pillow to her chest, watching the characters on the television scamper around and sing and dance.

All was well.

Or was it?

It was only a moment later when it seemed like everyone had made their way to the door. Maggie and Paul snagged one of the pizzas to take back to the department. There was too much for Logan and Bella to eat. Kevin disappeared with Skye, the door closing behind them. Riggs made his way over to Logan's side, sitting right next to him. Logan looked down at him. Since Rachel died, he had taken up talking to Riggs as if he could understand what was going on.

"Well, boy, looks like everything is back to normal," Logan muttered under his breath.

That was true, except for the dead body of Ian Dunn Logan still had to deal with. And, given the fact they lived in a sleepy town in northern New York state, there wasn't anything normal about that at all.

13

Toby Graham had spent the better part of the last two hours pacing in front of his computer, shooting it accusing glares. He was sure that if he looked down at the floor at the path he'd followed, he'd be calling an interior decorator to have his carpet in his office replaced the next day. He stopped, putting his hands on his hips and then walked over to the angled drafting board that was against the opposite wall. It was an old-fashioned contraption, something that had belonged to his father. He'd been an architect just like Toby. On it was taped a set of initial drawings for an amazing project that Toby had worked for a lifetime to get the privilege to work on — a new academic building on the Cornell University campus.

The problem was what they were asking was impossible. Toby had spent weeks attempting to come up with a concept that would work for the Board of Trustees at Cornell and excite the donor. Their desires didn't fit what was even close to possible. Every idea Toby had floated had gotten shut down. So many of them had been rejected, he was concerned that if he didn't come up with a working concept, the donor would pull the contract from the firm Toby worked for and award it to someone else. That couldn't happen.

Toby stopped his pacing again and turned back toward his computer. The problems with the project were numerous. The piece of land that the university had allotted for the new building was too small for the square footage they wanted. Dreadfully so.

While Toby had explained to the Board of Trustees and the donor about the impossibility of fashioning a building that would work, the donor had come up with their own suggestion — build it taller. In any other case, that strategy might have worked, except for the fact that the Cornell Board of Trustees had very specific ideas about how their campus should look to potential, current, and alumni students. Given the fact that they wanted the new building to match the Romanesque Revival style of the rest of the campus, their only other option was to build a skyscraper. But no one put pointy towers on a twenty-floor building. It just wasn't right.

Frustrated, Toby flopped down on his desk chair and jiggled the mouse on his computer. The two enormous monitors on his desk flickered to life. They immediately went to the project he was working on, a stark reminder of the fact that he hadn't made any progress. Toby leaned his elbows on his desk, pulled his glasses off and set them off to the side. He rested his face in his hands. How he was ever going to get this project to work, he wasn't sure. Even if he did manage to come up with a concept that pleased the trustees and the donor, he just knew he would be committing his life for the next two to three years of nothing but pain and anguish as they argued about every aspect of the project.

Such was the life of dealing with clients.

Some clients were easy to work with. Some were not. This group was definitely not. It always seemed like the more money a project cost, the more demanding the clients became. Toby shook his head and closed his eyes, leaning his face into his hands, trying to come up with an idea — any idea — that would work. After a minute of resting his eyes, Toby looked up and put his glasses back on his face. In the reflection of one of the monitors, he caught his own image. There was a tiny bit of stubble on his chin that needed to be shaved off — he preferred a clean look — and blond hair that was trimmed close to his head, combed carefully to the side. He could see the collar of his dress shirt, the kind he always wore to the office. He had them sent out to be washed and ironed by a professional service, so he looked presentable. Even at that late hour, he had the cuffs buttoned.

Toby wrinkled his nose, seeing there were a few wrinkles amassing at the elbow of his shirt. He tried to smooth them out but realized it was futile, given how many hours he'd been wearing the shirt. It had been a long day. Many of his colleagues have started showing up to the office looking like they were headed to the grocery store wearing nothing more than jeans and a sweatshirt. Toby wasn't that way. He was a professional. He dressed like one.

From the corner of the desk, Toby grabbed the insulated cup that he kept nearby, hearing the ice cubes inside jiggle. He took a sip of the cold water, which stung his teeth and gums. He grimaced as he set it down, shaking his head. Water wasn't going to do it, not after the day he'd had. He reached into the bottom drawer of his desk and pulled out the whiskey that was there. He pulled out a small crystal glass he kept for such an occasion and poured what he estimated to be exactly two ounces in the bottom. Maybe if he loosened up a little bit, solutions would start to flow for him. He'd solved more than one major architectural problem over a couple of drinks.

Toby shook his head. The Cornell project was different. It was a career-maker, one that would launch him into the upper stratosphere of architects in the United States. Sure, there were a lot of people designing large buildings, but to have one with your name on it at Cornell was a whole new level. He rubbed his chin, staring at the drawings in front of him, feeling the warmth of the whisky settle into his belly. Something else settled on him too — the idea that maybe the project wasn't possible. He was brilliant. He knew that. If he couldn't come up with a solution, then there wasn't one to be had. Toby slugged the rest of the whiskey from the glass and leaned back in his chair, lifting his arms overhead and weaving his fingers behind the nape of his neck, his elbows jutting out. He stared at a lone cobweb on the ceiling of his dark office. He would have to remind the cleaning people that they needed to remove cobwebs in addition to dust. Given how late he was at the office, he might have a chance to remind them of just that.

As his eyes settled back down on his desk, his gaze settled on a picture he'd added a few months before. It was him and Naomi, his girlfriend of six months. They'd met on a project — Naomi was the construction manager for a large office building that Toby had designed on the other side of Highmill. It certainly wasn't as prestigious as the Cornell job that he was working on, but after meeting Naomi, he was glad that he had accepted the commission.

And even the projects he didn't love kept food on the table.

He and Naomi had talked on and off for weeks without meeting, confining their discussions to the construction that was going on at the Oak Park Business Complex, then finally met at the site when they were getting ready to break ground. Naomi worked for a large commercial construction firm in Highmill, Pearce Construction. She'd shown up at the site wearing a tight pair of jeans, construction boots, and a hard hat, driving one of the company's white pickup trucks. She unrolled the blueprints like she had been working on construction sites her whole life, flipping through the pages and asking Toby specific questions about the design and things they needed to focus on, scratching notes on the pages with an old rectangular carpenter's pencil, the kind he hadn't seen in years.

Toby had fallen madly in love.

Two more trips to the site and two dinners later, they were dating. The whole relationship had been a whirlwind, but one that had been amazing for him. Toby loved her with everything he had. If he could just get past this Cornell project, then maybe he could concentrate enough to get her a ring and see what life would be like with a wife. He pressed his lips together. She would certainly say yes, wouldn't she? Toby felt a flutter in his gut. Whether it was from the thought of proposing to Naomi or the frustration of dealing with the Cornell project, he wasn't sure.

Feeling a surge of energy, Toby popped up from where he was sitting and started pacing again, crossing his arms in front of his chest and staring at the floor, counting his steps. One. Two. Three. Four. Every time he turned on his heel, he glanced toward his picture of him and Naomi, their arms around each other. He paused for a moment, staring at his phone then narrowed his eyes. Where was she? He'd sent her a couple of texts, but she hadn't responded yet. Maybe he should surprise her and go over to her house. Maybe that would calm him down. Maybe Naomi would give him an idea that would rescue the Cornell project. Maybe she'd see a solution that would save his career and their future.

He didn't like maybes.

14

Naomi Fraser had been sitting in her car in the rain in front of Ian Dunn's house for two hours. The wipers on her SUV hadn't stopped the entire time. Every few seconds, she would look up from her phone, squinting into the darkness hoping to see movement, something that would encourage her to get out of her car in the torrential rain, but there was nothing. There were no lights on at Ian's house. Not one. Naomi frowned. That wasn't like him.

She sighed, wondering where he was. As she did, she glanced at her phone again. She had sent him a bunch of texts over the last twenty-four hours but hadn't heard from him. It was the weekend, so it wasn't like he was missing from work or anything. She dropped her phone on the seat next to her in frustration. As much as she wanted to call their boss and find out if he had heard from Ian, the last thing she wanted to do was alert the owner of the company that she and Ian were interested in each other.

Naomi looked out the side window of her SUV into the darkness and the rain. What was she doing? She was already in the middle of a relationship with Toby. Everything about Toby was great. He was a successful architect, handsome, and treated her well. He'd just landed a big project, one that could propel his career for years to come. Unlike many other guys she'd dated before, he took her out on actual dates to restaurants and theater productions that required her to put on a dress, something she hadn't done regularly in a long time.

Thinking about it just made Naomi wonder even more about what she was doing sitting sentry in front of Ian's house. Toby was a gentleman, always holding her car door for her or pulling out her chair, his lopsided grin drawing her in even though he always wore khaki pants and a buttoned-down shirt. Naomi pressed her lips together, thinking. They had dated for a month before she finally asked him if he had owned a pair of jeans. He did not. His wardrobe ranged from pressed khaki pants and Oxford shirts to workout clothes. Even his workout clothes were formal. No ratty T-shirts, only fitted professional-level gear he used when he went mountain biking or running.

After the first night Naomi spent at Toby's house, she looked in his closet. There were suits in every color, each of them narrowly cut and tailored to fit him perfectly, a rainbow of button-down shirts in every color from white to black, with everything in between, arranged by color and sleeve length. There was a row of pressed pants lined up above his shoes. Even when he was relaxing at home, he wore designer pieces as leisure clothes — things that he had gotten for himself at Lululemon or from the Nike store. He was fancy, that was for sure.

Naomi was not.

Naomi looked towards Ian's window, thinking she saw a light flicker on out of the corner of her eye, her stomach lurching in anticipation. The feeling faded when she realized it was nothing. Pressing her lips together, she stared at Ian's house. Ian was so different from Toby. He was anything but fancy. He had cropped brown hair and typically wore a pair of nice jeans and a polo shirt to the office where he was the Vice President of Operations for the Pearce Construction Company.

Ian was someone who had worked his way up through the ranks. He had started at Pearce as an intern, left for a few years while he went to college, then came back as an intern again, this time with a degree in construction management and business under his belt. He rose quickly through the ranks, working on a variety of commercial projects — everything from a series of large strip malls that have been developed in Highmill to the construction of a new regional hospital at the edge of the county. He was so reliable that he began to work directly with Mr. Pearce, the owner of the company, and had been promoted to operations the year before.

That's when his and Naomi's orbits began to intersect. In the past, Naomi had stuck with the construction team, focusing on what happened at the sites. She was rarely in the office, if at all, usually making her home at a rickety desk in a construction trailer that had been delivered to the site. Her work was exhausting and intense as a construction manager — she was one of the few females certified in the State of New York — and it required a ridiculous amount of attention to detail. Add to that the necessary level of knowledge about construction in addition to being a big picture person, someone familiar with the intricacies of nearly every trade, well versed in safety regulations in addition to inspection requirements, not to mention the financial constraints of the project, and that was Naomi. When she first started working for Pearce Construction, she would go home every single night with a raging headache. With the advice of one of the other construction managers, Naomi started to work out every day after work to get rid of the stress. The headaches soon dissipated.

Amazing how a little movement could eliminate stress.

Five years into her career, she was now one of the go-to people at Pearce. She was handed projects that the other project managers simply rolled their eyes at, knowing how difficult they were. That's how she had gotten to know Ian.

The year before, when Pearce had broken ground on a hospital project, Naomi had been paired with one of the most experienced project managers they had at Pearce. It was too big of a job for only one project manager to handle. The amount of wiring alone that was going into the hospital could have circled the globe twice by her estimation and that didn't begin to account for the millions of screws and nails, the tens of thousands of sheets of drywall, and the truckload after truckload of insulation that had to be delivered to the project and the questions.

The endless questions...

That was the one thing about being a project manager that people didn't seem to understand. The questions never ended. Whether it was from the client or the architect or the engineer, or on the other side, questions from the subcontractors — the excavators, surveyors, concrete finishers, framers, electricians, plumbers, and interior designers — the questions never stopped. Project management was nothing more than an endless flow of questions. Some of them she could answer, some of them she could not.

One day, when the project was about to wrap up, Naomi had found herself in the construction trailer, which had become her own over the last year, sipping a cup of herbal tea late in the afternoon, trying to stay calm while the painting contractor sitting in front of her was explaining why he had to pull his crew off of their project and go work on another when they were scheduled to work late into the night. The subs were like that. If they thought there was a better, more profitable job somewhere, they would bid on that one, get it started and then if you were lucky, come back and finish yours. If you were not, they wouldn't bother coming back, leaving you high and dry and stalling your project, throwing off scheduling, and throwing a wrench in the works in terms of getting the project finished. Delays cost money. Lots of it, especially on a project the size of the hospital.

Ian had walked in in the middle of Naomi dealing with the painting contractor. She had stripped off her white construction helmet and her safety vest and had been sitting calmly at her desk until the painting contractor lit into her with a series of words that no woman, lady or otherwise, should ever have to hear. He stayed in his chair but poked his finger towards Naomi's face, his voice bouncing off the inside of the construction trailer.

Naomi stood up, rested her palms against the edge of the desk, and leaned over it, getting into the man's face. "I don't think you understand what's going on here, Liam. If you leave me high and dry, there will be consequences, ones that you don't like."

Liam wiggled in his seat, puffing his chest out. "Like what? What are you going to do, little lady?"

Little lady? Naomi set her jaw and leaned even farther across the desk. "You think that project managers don't talk to each other, Liam? You think that if I don't send a few emails to a few well-placed people, tell them that you're leaving me high and dry, that you will still get work in this county? I wouldn't do it, Liam. If it were me, I would walk myself out of this trailer and go get your guys working and make sure you finish the job and do it right. Otherwise, those one-star ratings you have on Yelp will be the least of your worries. Whether you can ever get a job in this county again will be. Do I make myself clear?"

Naomi remembered watching the man's face redden, his eyes bulging out from the sockets. He stood up, grunted something unintelligible under his breath and stormed out of the trailer, slamming the door behind him. Naomi collapsed into her chair, closing her eyes and shaking her head.

When she opened them, Ian Dunn was grinning. "That was quite the performance."

Naomi narrowed her eyes. "I meant every word of it."

"I could tell."

Naomi couldn't tell if Ian was busting her chops or not. She sat stiffly in her desk chair. "Well, he better get to work."

Ian glanced out the window and then looked back at Naomi, his eyebrows raised. "Oh, he's back to work all right. I can see him from here. He's waving his hands in the air and his crew is scuttling off to work."

Naomi threw a hand up. "These guys, they don't understand that I might be a woman, but they aren't going to take advantage of me." As soon as she played the woman card, she was sorry that she had said it. But when she looked up, Ian was still smiling. Playing the female card in her industry was distinctly a no-no. You had to be as tough and as strong as the men. Otherwise, you wouldn't survive.

"Well, I for one, am glad you are a woman."

What did that mean?

Ian continued. "I came to ask you a couple of questions, but how about if we do it at the local bar? You look like you need a drink."

Naomi nodded. "That I do."

She and Ian had had a couple of drinks that night, rolling out the blueprints for the hospital project on one of the tables in the back of a local bar named The Rusty Nail. Naomi had quickly answered the questions that Ian had, ones passed on by Mr. Pearce about the project, the timing, and the financials.

And then Ian disappeared for a while, their paths not crossing again while she finished the hospital project and moved onto another one.

Ian popped up in her life again the month before, stepping into a construction trailer at a large commercial office complex that she was working at, the same grin on his face. He had said he had more questions and invited her to go back to The Rusty Nail, where they had repeated what they had done some months before. But this time, something was different. There was a spark between the two of them. She rode back to his house in his car, his hand crawling its way onto her thigh. She'd managed to mumble that she was involved with someone else. The look on his face said it didn't matter.

As Naomi sat in front of Ian's house wondering why the rain hadn't stopped and why Ian wasn't responding to her texts, all she could think about was Ian abandoning her. Even though their relationship had just started, she couldn't stand the thought, her heart clutching in her chest. Were they dating? Naomi frowned. If someone asked, she wouldn't have been able to tell them for sure. She wasn't sure that Ian was the kind to date. At that point, she hadn't even bothered to ask him about past, or current, for that matter, girlfriends. But were they in a relationship? If taking off your clothes a few times a week counted, that got a resounding yes.

Looking at her phone, she realized Toby had texted her half a dozen times in the last two hours, each of them getting increasingly emotional and demanding — "Where are you?", "Why aren't you answering me?", "I expect you to get back to me! Who are you with?" A pit formed in her gut. She needed to break up with Toby. She hadn't told him about what was going on with Ian. He'd be furious if he knew.

Where was Ian?

Naomi glanced at the seat next to her. Her tablet was sitting there, her excuse for making the drive to his house late at night. Her reason for stopping at Ian's was she needed an approval on a structural steel quote to get back to the provider.

But her real reason? She was in love.

And not with Toby.

15

After listening to the voicemail from her sister, Skye sat in her car for a minute and stared blankly out through the windshield. Her heart was pounding in her chest. In clinical terms, Christy Johnston, Skye's younger sister, was nothing more than a narcissist. She was someone who was only concerned with what she needed, when she needed it, and how she needed it. The description was taken from the Greek god Narcissus who spent so much time staring at his beautiful image in a pool of water that he withered away and died, so enamored with his own reflection he forgot to eat or drink.

Christy wasn't much different, although if anyone had bothered to ask, Skye would have suggested that at least Narcissus was probably pleasant.

Christy was not.

While in clinical terms Christy was a narcissist, in layman's terms she was nothing other than toxic. She left a trail of people wherever she went. She burned through people that had been friends with their family, relatives, and even friends Christy had made on her own. It wasn't as if she had just walked away from them. In some cases, she'd left the people devastated and broken in her wake.

Memories of Christy popped into Skye's mind — the time Christy grabbed a silky nightgown Skye had bought for herself and carried it into the kitchen and asked coyly, "Someone left this in the bathroom," in front of their father, who immediately turned beet red. Then there was the time when Christy had demanded that their father purchase her a car, even though Skye had spent the entire summer when she was sixteen working shift after shift at an ice cream stand to afford to pay for her own. Their whole family had been in turmoil until her father finally relented. He offered nothing more than a shake of his head to Skye in apology.

The stories went on and on.

It had been years since the two of them had been in regular communication. Skye hadn't returned to Rochester except to visit after she went to Cornell. It had been better that way — at least better for Skye, who had determined that no contact with her only sibling was better than the alternative, which included regular drama, especially after both of their parents died, their mom, first, of lung cancer a few years before, then their dad, of a heart attack, the year before.

Even their family attorney, a guy who had been hired by their mom and dad when they were kids, had refused to take business from Christy after a while because she was so nasty, throwing his body down on a chair in Skye's kitchen and declaring, "I'm sorry, I know she's your sister, but what's wrong with her?" And George was about as mild-mannered as they came.

Skye pressed a button on her cell phone to listen to the voicemail once more.

"Skye?" The voice was sing-songy and sickly sweet. "It's your sister Christy! Guess what? I'm in town. I bet you're surprised that I'd ever step foot in Highmill again. You know how I feel about this place, but I've come for a visit. I want to get together. I'm so excited! Call me back so we can make a plan!"

Seriously?

Skye shook her head. If anyone who didn't understand the situation listened to the message, they would think that Christy sounded like the friendliest person in the entire world. And she was — but the problem was it only lasted for a little bit. The moment she didn't get what she wanted, things would turn, and not in a good way.

Skye stared at her phone for a second. The sister in her wanted to call Christy back. The psychologist in her was screaming in her head. "Don't do it! You're going to open a door to a lot of hurt!"

And after the way Christy had acted in the past, Skye knew that was exactly the case.

Her stomach in a pit, Skye tossed her cell phone off on the passenger seat and started the car, ignoring the message. She could taste the bile in the back of her throat. Driving away from her office building, Skye knew the reality of the situation — whether she liked it or not, at one point or another she'd have to face Christy and reset her boundaries. But for the time being, she could at least ignore her. Maybe she'd get lucky, and Christy would get the hint and go back to wherever she was living at the time. The last she'd heard, Christy had been living in Idaho in a little town that sported a ski resort and not much else.

The good news was that Skye had moved since Christy had been in town last. Sure, Christy could use property records and try to figure out where Skye lived — which she was just wily enough to do — but it might at least buy Skye some time before an inevitable showdown occurred again.

Skye shook her head as she drove away, wondering when the drama with Christy would ever end. Would she never understand that she couldn't trample over people the way she did and expect to maintain relationships? Skye pushed the thought away. This wasn't the time for clinical assessments. She knew who Christy was. Christy knew who Skye was. And they didn't get along. It was that plain and simple.

As Skye drove towards her house, she realized she needed a distraction. Thinking about Christy was getting her nowhere. She started thinking about the clients she'd had that day, the problems that they had and the solutions she'd tried to lead them to. Her mind drifted to the night before. How was Bella doing? Thinking about it brightened her spirits. Finding Bella safe and sound had certainly been a win. And based on the way that she was calmly interacting and playing with everyone after she'd returned to her house, that was a win too.

But the thoughts brought up more questions in Skye's head.

As Skye turned onto Highmill Road, which ran from one end of the town to the other, Skye dodged a slow-moving box truck and a school bus filled with kids that looked like they were going to some sort of a competition, all wearing matching red hoodies. Skye stared in front of her. Had anyone from the department figured out what happened to Ian Dunn? Skye sighed. The whole thing seemed strange. Ian hadn't been dressed in clothes for hiking and whoever had killed him had certainly managed to do a lot of damage.

Unless it wasn't gunshot damage after all?

Skye wasn't experienced in causes of death, but she considered for a fact that it could have been an animal that went after his face. There was black bear in the area. Northern New York was filled with them. But she quickly dismissed that idea, gripping the steering wheel of her car a little tighter. If a black bear had gone after Ian, there would have been damage to other parts of his body, or at least she imagined that would be the case, claw marks and bite marks on his arms and hands and torso, just not half of his face obliterated. His clothes would have been torn and dirty from running from the bear.

But his clothes had been pristine, as if he'd just left a meeting and someone had caught him unaware.

No, it had to be a gunshot.

The thought landed on her like a ton of bricks. How someone could do that to another human she didn't understand. Not as a person and not as a psychologist. She could have all of the clinical explanations at her fingertips, and it still wouldn't make sense.

As Skye drove down Highmill Road, passing the library, a store that sold candles and crystals, and Sonja's Bakery, Skye realized she was passing a toy store, one she'd gone into the previous summer to buy a gift for the young son of one of the therapists that worked for her. She needed a distraction from Christy and the image of Ian Dunn's face that was burned into her mind. It would be a good idea to go check in on Bella, wouldn't it? Skye blinked and then turned her car into the parking lot, jogging into the store, the chime of a bell ringing as she tugged the door open.

Inside, her eyes were immediately accosted by toys in all sorts of bright colors — pink, fuchsia, orange, a sunshiny yellow, and an array of blues and greens and purples. There was no doubt about it, living in a kid's world was bright and cheerful, even if it was only an illusion that would be broken by age and experience. A young man wearing a red sweatshirt that said "Al's Toy Palace" was sitting at the counter and playing on his phone. He stood up, dropping his phone on the surface like it was a hot potato when Skye walked in as if she'd caught him doing something wrong. He jumped up out of his seat, his eyes wide. "Can I help you find something?"

Skye smiled. "No. I'm good. You can go back to playing with your phone."

The young man looked surprised and then grinned. Skye knew she had just become the coolest customer of the day.

After a pass through the aisles, Skye found a coloring book, colored pencils, and a puzzle that was covered in daisies that she thought Bella would like. The flowers had been all over her room when Skye had been in it the day before. She quickly paid the young man at the counter and watched as he placed the items in a bag and handed it to her. "Have a good night," he said.

Skye tilted her head to the side. "I'll try."

At that moment, it was the best she could do.

16

It wasn't like Skye to show up unannounced at someone's door. Inevitably, when people had dropped in unannounced at her house, it hadn't been good news. The visit she'd had from some of Highmill's finest the night before was just one example in a long line of peaceful evening interruptions that had left a sour taste in her mouth. But, given the fact she had no way to reach out to Logan Fletcher other than through the department, which involved interacting with Zara, or at least alerting Zara to her presence, driving directly to Logan's house seemed to be the lesser of two evils.

After a little bit of getting turned around, Skye eventually found her way to Logan's house. Just as it looked the night before — a black pickup truck parked in the driveway in the same spot, soft yellow lights streaming out from the front windows. It was still raining, more like a drizzle than anything else.

At least that was something.

Skye jumped out of her car, tugging the bag of gifts and her cell phone with her, slamming her car door behind her. She strode to the front door, tugging the collar of her jacket up a little tighter around her ears. Even though the temperature seemed to be a bit warmer than the day before, the air was still damp and ate through her clothes in no time flat.

At the front door, she paused for a moment, suddenly unsure of herself. How would Logan react to having someone he'd only met once show up at his front door? She didn't want him to misinterpret her visit. She was there to check in on Bella. That was it. She didn't know anything else about Logan other than his wife had passed away a few years before and his young daughter seemed to have a case of wanderlust. Skye didn't know if he had a girlfriend or was interested in someone. Not that she was looking for any kind of relationship. The thought made her shiver.

Even though she was trained in managing relationships, she seemed to be way better at helping others navigate them than she was. Having people in her life had, for the most part, been painful for her, painful in a way that she would prefer not to have to deal with.

Deciding that it would look worse to pull out of the driveway without finishing what she started, Skye knocked tentatively on the front door, realizing if Logan was home, he probably saw her headlights in the dark driveway as they crossed his front window. It only took a second before Logan opened it.

"Skye? I mean, Dr. Johnston?"

The light from inside the house silhouetted Logan in the front door, but there was enough of a glow for her to see his face. Everything had been so chaotic the day before, she hadn't even looked at him carefully enough to remember most of his features. But now that things were calmer, she had a chance to study him. He had short brown hair, the stubble of a beard covering his jaw, and wide brown eyes. He had on a pair of sweatpants and a long-sleeved T-shirt, the sleeves pushed up to muscled forearms. His hair was damp. It looked as though he had just gotten out of the shower.

"Hi, Logan. I just wanted to stop by to see how Bella was doing. I brought her something," Skye said, holding the bag up.

Logan stepped back from the door, a grin on his face. "That was nice. Come on in. She's playing over there."

As Skye stepped in the door and Logan closed it behind her, her gaze darted down to her left, seeing movement out of the corner of her eye. Riggs had moved toward her and was sniffing the back of her calf. She glanced up at Logan, a questioning expression on her face. She froze, the back of her neck tingling. He smiled and waved his hand in the air. "Pay no attention to Riggs. He's just curious."

Easy for you to say. It's your dog.

Skye lifted her chin, trying to get her mind off the fact that the dog had taken an interest in her. "How did he get the name Riggs?"

"From the movie? You know, *Lethal Weapon* with Mel Gibson? He played an LAPD officer named Martin Riggs. Always loved that movie."

She knew the name sounded familiar. Had she seen it? She wasn't sure. If he had mentioned a book, she would have known for sure. Television was a waste of time in her mind. Movies were only slightly better. "Sure." She didn't really remember the movie, but something in her told her that Logan probably remembered every bit of it. After all, he almost would have to in order to name his dog after one of the characters.

Their conversation was interrupted when Bella ran over and wrapped her arms around Skye's leg. She looked up at Skye, a smile on her face. "Hi, Skye."

Skye smiled back. There was something about the innocence of a child that tended to wipe away the stress of the day — even the stress of getting a voicemail from your crazy sister. Why hadn't she gone into child psychology again?

Because innocent children who were traumatized at the hands of people who should know better could drain the life out of a person. At least with adults, they were responsible for their own reactions. Kids were not.

Skye shook the thought from her head and squatted down. "I was thinking about you today. On my way home from work, I stopped at the toy store and brought you a little present. That is, if it's okay with your dad?" Skye looked up at Logan. She hadn't even bothered to consider whether it would be okay with him or not.

Bella started to jump up and down. "Dad! Dad! Can I? Can I?"

Logan adopted a stern look on his face. "Well, I don't know," he said, frowning.

"Please?"

His frown turned into a grin. "All right. Just make sure that you say thank you."

Bella yelled, "Thank you!" so loud that Riggs stepped back.

A moment later, Skye found herself being dragged over to Bella's play area in front of the television and told to sit on the ground. Skye handed over the bag from the toy store. She glanced around at the scene in front of her. The television was on softly in the background, a kid's program. The characters were adding pieces of fruit together, clearly an educational show that Logan had found for his daughter. A fire crackled in the fireplace, the heat warming the side of Skye's face. Skye could smell something cooking. What it was, she wasn't exactly sure, but it smelled good.

"What did you bring me?" Bella asked, rubbing her hands together.

"What did I bring you? Let's see," Skye helped Bella unpack the bag. She took one look at the coloring book and hugged Skye, her eyes bright. "How did you know I love to color?"

"Well, I saw all the artwork in your room."

She pulled the colored pencils out of the bag. "These aren't crayons." She pouted.

"No, those are colored pencils. Those are for big girls. You think you can handle them?"

Skye glanced up at Logan, who was standing over her right shoulder. His arms were folded across his chest as if he seemed amused by the scene unfolding in front of him.

"I think so." Bella dropped the pencils and stared back into the bag, pulling out the puzzle. "What's this?"

Skye was sure Bella knew what it was. Kids typically did that when they were searching for the words to a question they didn't have yet. "It's a puzzle. See? It has the same kind of flowers that are on your bedspread in your room."

Bella snatched it out of Skye's hands and ran to her dad. "Look, Dad! Look at the pretty flowers!"

"They're beautiful, honey." He put a hand on her head. "Just like you."

Bella smiled. "Can Skye stay and play for a bit, Dad?"

"Sure."

Skye shrugged out of her coat and laid it on the nearby chair, sitting down on the floor with Bella. Skye glanced over her shoulder. Logan had stepped away, going back into the kitchen. He was stirring a pot of whatever was on the stove. Skye didn't want to overstay her welcome, but she did want to take a few minutes to assess how Bella was doing. For some reason, she felt responsible, as if it was one thing to locate Bella, but another to ensure that her experience going forward would be one of positive development and not one marked by trauma. Skye bit her lip as she focused on the young girl. Unresolved trauma was one thing Skye had seen too much of in her practice. Issues like that could wreak havoc for decades in someone's life, its iron claw grip refusing to let go of its victim, coloring nearly everything that they saw and did, causing them to make decisions that could destroy someone's life.

Would that be the case for Bella?

Bella promptly sat down on the carpet that covered the floor of Logan's family room, pushed the coloring book she'd been working on and the crayons off to the side and ceremoniously grabbed the new coloring book that Skye had brought for her. She handed Skye the pack of colored pencils. "Open, please?"

Skye smiled. "I think you can do it."

Bella scowled. "I don't wanna wreck it."

Skye nodded. "Fair enough. I'll show you how and then you do it, okay?"

After demonstrating how to open a package of colored pencils, Skye closed it and handed it back to Bella. She worked at the flap with her little fingers and managed to pry it open a second later. Part of child psychology was watching children and how they reacted to new experiences — everything from new toys and new environments to questions they hadn't thought about before. Even with their limited vocabulary, they had ways of communicating that were strangely intense and accurate.

Bella handed Skye a blue pencil and took a yellow one for herself. She began coloring, pointing for Skye to start working on a section of the drawing. Skye colored for a second and then looked at Bella. She could tell Bella was trying to get the hang of the colored pencil. Skye was happy Bella wasn't giving up. It said something about her character. "Did you have a good day today?"

Bella nodded but didn't look up. "Yup. Went to school. Came home and had a snack. Now you're here!"

"That's good. I had a good day today too."

Bella looked up, her face serious for a moment. "What do you do while I'm at school? Daddy's a policeman."

"And a very good one, I've heard. I help people solve problems."

"Like when I was lost yesterday?" Bella cocked her head to the side, staring at Skye.

"Yes."

The fact that Bella brought up what had happened was a good sign. Skye set her pencil down and looked at Bella. "Can you tell me what happened yesterday?"

Skye waited. She looked over her shoulder. Logan had turned and looked in her direction, a questioning expression on his face as if he was saying, "Shouldn't we let this one go?" Skye looked away, realizing Riggs had positioned himself right behind her, an eager look on his face as if a game or a treat might appear at any moment. She swallowed, trying to ignore the fact that the powerful shepherd was practically breathing down her neck.

"I wanted to play outside."

"But it was raining yesterday," Skye offered.

Bella shook her head. "That doesn't matter. Daddy goes to work in all kinds of weather."

It was an interesting way of framing her decision making, Skye decided. Bella had clearly justified her actions based on what she saw Logan modeling. "And how did you end up at the cave?"

"It started to rain very hard. I didn't have my raincoat. I remembered the cave. It was dry there."

"Why didn't you just come home?"

Bella looked at Skye as if she was asking the strangest question in the world. "I was having fun."

Skye picked up a green pencil and began drawing it across the page. "When you got to the cave, what did you do?"

"I looked around."

"It was dark, though, Bella."

"No, it wasn't. I had my light with me."

Skye cocked her head to the side and glanced at Logan, who nodded as if he was verifying what Bella had said. "Your light"

"Daddy gave me a flashlight. I took it with me."

Skye narrowed her eyes. That explained how Bella was able to see the man in the back of the cave. Skye had wondered about that. "What about the man?"

"Oh, him!" Bella said, looking at Skye and then looking back down at her coloring. "He was sleeping. I talked to him for a minute, but he didn't wake up. Then I patted him and told him it was okay if he was tired. I would wait until he woke up. Then you came!"

Skye colored for a second without saying anything. She stared at the work that Bella was doing. Given her age, she was doing a good job at coloring inside the lines. She was clearly bright and perceptive, a good thinker who had somehow managed to grab a flashlight, but not a raincoat. Given what she had seen, she'd managed to get through the day before without seeing it as a trauma. From Bella's point of view, she'd helped Ian by waiting with him while he slept. That was important.

Skye swallowed. "Can I ask you a question, Bella?"

"Yes."

"You have friends at school?"

Bella wrinkled her nose as if Skye had asked a crazy question. "Of course! My best friend, her name is Sarah. She has hair that looks just like mine."

"So, if Sarah told you she wanted to go outside and play in the rain like you did yesterday, what would you tell her?"

Bella looked up at the ceiling for a second, pressing her index finger to her lower lip. Then she dropped it and looked at Skye, her expression calm. "I would tell her to wear a raincoat."

17

After sitting on the floor and coloring with Bella for a few more minutes, Skye got up, smoothing her pants. She could see a few flecks of Riggs's fur had found their way to the fabric. She flicked them away.

Logan left his spot in the kitchen and joined Skye. "Sorry about that. The hazards of living with a dog."

"It's no problem. These needed to be washed anyways."

Skye caught Logan's expression. He looked at her and then walked away, seemingly understanding that he wanted to talk to her privately.

As they moved further into the kitchen, Skye crossed her arms over her chest and glanced over her shoulder. Bella had resumed coloring with her brand-new set of colored pencils. Skye sucked in a breath. "I hope it's okay. I wanted to look in on her and see how she was doing. What she went through yesterday was pretty significant."

"And?"

"By all accounts, you have a very strong daughter. She has seemed to arrange the facts in her mind in a way that are nonthreatening and that helps her to feel like she made a good decision. Honestly, it's pretty remarkable."

Logan pressed his lips together. "Hiking the whole way out to the cave in the middle of a rainstorm was not a good decision."

"No, that's not what I'm saying."

"I know, it's just that —" Logan stopped mid-sentence.

Skye understood what Logan was saying. After the loss of someone significant, life could seem fragile. Logan had already lost his wife and the mother of his child. From her experience, Skye knew that Logan was likely still feeling vulnerable from almost losing Bella the day before. Skye bit the inside of her lip. She understood the feeling after losing her parents, though she knew, clinically at least, that losing a spouse was a whole different level of loss. Skye lifted a single eyebrow. Perhaps Logan was the one she should have done the assessment on?

"What I'm trying to say is that Bella had a choice in how she processed the information from yesterday. She could have gone down the path of 'I got lost and I got scared and it was a horrible situation,' or she could have gone down the path of 'these are the decisions I made to go out and rain to go to the cave, and I came back and everything was fine.'"

"You're not suggesting she'll do it again? Are you?" Logan's expression carried an equal measure of fury and fear.

Skye shrugged, ignoring his response. It was better to just tell him the truth. "You have a very strong daughter, Logan. I'm not sure exactly what she will do. But what I can tell you is that she has processed this incident in a way that she was in control. That's good news."

"Is it?" Logan leaned closer to Skye. She breathed in the scent of his soap. It had been a long time since she was that close to a man. "Honestly, I probably would have preferred if she was terrified so that she never did it again."

Skye held up a hand, taking half a step back. "I get it. It can be frightening as a parent when your kids start pushing boundaries. But you seem to have things handled. I'm sure you'll figure out a way to talk with her about this so she doesn't repeat the behavior. It's important to do that in a way that doesn't freak her out, though." Skye closed with the warning.

"Well, I appreciate you buying Bella a gift and checking in on her." Logan looked over at the stove. "Have you eaten?" He raised his eyebrows.

"No, no. I need to get home. I have patient charts to update before tomorrow."

Logan tilted his head to the side. "But that wasn't an answer. Have you eaten?"

"No."

"Well, that's settled then. Everyone has to eat."

Before she knew it, Skye was wrapped up in a flurry of dinner preparations. Not that there was a lot to do. Dinner in the Fletcher household was apparently not a formal endeavor.

On the small table in the kitchen, Logan got out an extra placemat and set a bowl and a plate and some silverware on it, offering Skye a glass of water, which she happily took. A minute later, Logan was calling Bella for dinner, ladling thick soup out of the pot on the stove and putting a basket of hot crusty bread at the center of the table. "Sorry, it's not fancy. I worked all day."

"This is wonderful. It's a lot more than I would have eaten at home."

Bella took a taste of her soup and then stared at Skye. "You don't eat at home?"

"That's not what I meant. What I meant was your dad made a very nice dinner."

Bella nodded. "Oh, okay."

Skye grabbed a paper towel from the roll that was on the table and used it as a napkin. Logan flushed. "Sorry. Forgot to put those on the grocery list last week."

"It's no big deal." Skye took a taste of the soup. It was tomato-based with beans and noodles and chicken in it, plus carrots and celery. Her mom used to make soup, but it never tasted this good. "This is delicious."

Logan wiped his face. "Thanks. It's my version of dump-in-the-pot minestrone. It's usually something we have when I need to go to the grocery store."

"You made this?"

"All by myself." Logan chuckled. "I've had to learn how to cook a little bit more since —"

Logan glanced up at Bella and then looked back down at his soup. He didn't finish the sentence.

Seems like that happened a lot.

Skye could tell by his expression that the pain of losing his wife was still raw. She felt for him. It had to be a nearly impossible situation. It would be bad enough to lose your spouse, but then to be left with the responsibility of raising a small child by yourself had to be horrible.

Skye quickly changed the topic to Logan's work, asking him how long he'd been with the department and how he ended up in Highmill. "I've been with the department for eight years. Grew up here."

Skye frowned. "I'm surprised I haven't run into you before. I've been here for ten years. Grew up in Rochester. Got here after I finished my education."

"Well, I work a lot of day shifts now because of Bella. The chief, she's good that way. She's been helpful."

Skye looked down at her soup and didn't say anything. When she looked up, Logan was staring at her.

"You and the chief have some sort of history?"

"Nothing worth talking about."

The conversation stalled for a minute and then Bella saved it. "I'm full!"

"Alright," Logan said. "You know what to do next."

"I know, I know. Take my dish to the kitchen."

With a great amount of determination, Bella picked up her bowl of soup and carefully carried it to the kitchen, only managing to slosh it twice on the floor from what Skye could tell. Luckily, Riggs was on the job, playing clean-up behind Bella.

The perks of having a dog.

She scampered off, as Riggs cleaned the floor, and disappeared into her bedroom.

Skye took the last bite of her bread and dabbed at the corners of her mouth. "That was delicious. Thank you."

"You're welcome."

As Logan got up, picking up Skye's dish, Skye leaned her elbow on the table and touched the side of her face. "Can I ask if anything has happened with the case?"

"Funny, I was just about to ask if you wanted to hear about it."

"I do."

"Well, Dr. Chapman hasn't come up with a lot yet. Whoever killed Ian Dunn used a nine-millimeter pistol to blow half of his face off."

Skye winced.

Logan's mouth dropped open. "Sorry, that was probably a little too flippant of a description."

"No, it's okay. At least it's accurate." Skye thought back to the condition of Ian Dunn's head when they'd found him. "The thing I wanted to know is how he ended up there. He definitely wasn't dressed like someone who'd been out hiking in the pouring down rain."

"That's true. Our working theory is that the body was dumped there. It's supported by the fact that there's no blood spatter and there are some missing parts of Ian's face that haven't been recovered." Logan shook his head. "Sorry. Not sure exactly how to put that delicately."

Skye stood up from the table, feeling a little irritated. "Listen, Logan, I don't know you very well, but you don't have to tap dance around me. People spend all day long, every single day, telling me the worst part of their lives. I might not see what you do, but I certainly hear about it."

Logan nodded. "Fair enough." He turned back toward Skye, leaning his back against the counter. "Listen, since you got in on the ground floor of this one, I was wondering if maybe you'd be available to do a little consulting?"

Was he making a pass at her? Skye's face reddened. "I don't know about that. I'm pretty busy with work and —"

Logan's phone rang. "Hold that thought." Logan tapped the screen of his phone. "Hello?"

Skye folded her arms across her chest as she listened to Logan. "Okay, wait, hold on. I think Dr. Johnston would want to hear that too. Yes, she's here. She came to check on Bella. Give me one sec."

Logan disappeared down the hallway holding his phone. Skye heard the click of a door. She guessed he was closing Bella's bedroom door so that she couldn't hear what was going on. When he came back, he lifted his chin. "It's Dr. Chapman. He found something."

Skye nodded.

"Okay, Doc. Go ahead, you're on speaker."

"Hey, hey, Skye. How you're doing?"

"Good, Dr. Chapman. How are you today?"

"I'm good, I'm good."

Skye furrowed her eyebrows together. Did Dr. Chapman always repeat himself like that?

A second later, they were off to the races. "So, I just finished the autopsy. It was a lot. A lot. You'd think that finding a dead body in a cave wouldn't be a big deal, but we spent hours sifting through all of the mud and debris, and more debris that had stuck to the victim's clothes to try get some sense of where he'd been before the cave. Well, I'm going on and on and getting nowhere, aren't I?"

Skye raised her eyebrows. Logan smiled at Skye. Dr. Chapman was definitely quirky. Skye tried redirecting him. "You said you found something that you wanted to share with us?"

"Yes, other than the obvious, Mr. Dunn is dead. And those were gunshots to the face. Lots of gunshots. Likely about five, I'm guessing. But hard to tell, very hard to tell given the fact that I don't have all of the pieces of his face to put it back together again. You would need to find the crime scene in order to do that. But what I'm guessing is that it's already been cleaned up and those pieces are long gone. Long gone."

Logan shook his head. "Is there something else?"

"Oh yes, yes. I just got back the series of X-rays we did. That's why I'm calling you, Logan. Pretty typical for an autopsy. We X-ray, and X-ray again. Lots of X-rays to determine if there's any other injuries."

"And there were?"

"Indeed."

"What did you find?" Skye asked, suddenly curious.

"Fractures."

Skye shook her head. "Fractures? What are you talking about?"

Suddenly, Dr. Chapman's tone became serious. "I don't like this, not at all, not at all. As part and parcel of our autopsy, I X-ray them from the tip of their toes to the top of their head. They get the full treatment here in my autopsy room. The full treatment. What I found on your victim's right arm was troubling. Very troubling. Mr. Dunn had a series of spiral fractures on his radius and ulna."

Skye pressed her lips together. The radius and ulna were the two bones that made up the structure of the forearm.

Logan shook his head. "Could he have sustained those in a struggle or fallen or something?"

"Well, the first thing, Logan, is they were fresh. Very fresh. This was no old injury that was partially healed. And spiral fractures don't just happen. It's not generally what we would see with a fall. And there were no defensive wounds on his hands. None. Not one."

"You're saying that Ian didn't defend himself?"

"Or he didn't have time to. Either way, the spiral fractures are the things that concern me."

Skye blinked. "Not the fact that half of his face was blown off?"

Dr. Chapman snorted. "No, no. Bullet holes I can explain. Aside from the fact that he's missing half of his face, that's easily understandable and was the cause of death. We know what bullets do to tissue and bone. But the spiral fractures tell a different story. A spiral fracture is only incurred when an arm is violently twisted, so a bone won't break in a spiral pattern unless it receives a significant amount of torque. You've probably seen on television the compound fracture. That's when the bone cracks in half and pokes out through the skin or bulges just below the surface. It's a devastating injury, but one that's easily explainable. A fall or being hit by a moving object like a car, that would explain a compound fracture. But a spiral fracture is something —"

"That they only see in people who have been tortured," Logan finished the sentence, his face paling.

18

Logan rubbed the stubble on his chin. The idea that Ian Dunn had been tortured by his attacker was a turn of events that he hadn't anticipated. Tortured? This was Highmill, not Kandahar.

He also hadn't anticipated the fact that Skye Johnston, the pretty psychologist that had given him the lead to find his daughter the day before, would be standing in his house when he got the news. What exactly that meant, he had no idea. He pushed the thought away, the bile rising in the back of his throat. Whether that was because of what Dr. Chapman was saying or the rapid way in which his life was changing, he had no idea.

"What are you saying, Doc?"

"It's bad, Logan, bad. I can't tell you if Ian Dunn was tortured, per se, but I can tell you that his body shows signs of significant trauma. Whoever did this wanted something from Ian. Whether that was simply to physically move him from one location to the next and that's how the spiral fracture occurred, or the person was trying to get information out of Ian, I can't tell you. What I can tell you is whatever happened resulted in Ian Dunn's death."

Logan watched as Skye looked away for a moment, her expression pensive. "Did he have any other health issues? Anything that would have sped up his death?"

"Excellent question, Dr. Johnston. Excellent. No. Other than the damage to his face,

he was an otherwise healthy thirty-seven-year-old man. Heart and lungs were in good condition. Good muscle tone. He appeared to work out on a regular basis. Nothing that I can see that would have contributed to his early demise. And no disease markers."

Logan shook his head. Whether or not that was pertinent to the case, he wasn't sure, but he was glad Skye asked for the information anyway. "All right, can you send the report over to Chief Walsh and copy me? We don't have any leads, but we've got to get to work on this and figure out what happened."

"I will, I will. Good luck with this one, Logan. Let me know if you need more information.

Nice to talk to you again, Dr. Johnston."

Logan pressed the end button on his phone and shoved it in his back pocket. He sighed and then looked back at Skye. "Well, that was interesting."

She had a frown on her face. "It was."

Before Logan could say anything else, Skye had moved out of the kitchen and into the family room, picking up her coat, starting to pull it on over her shoulders.

"You're leaving? So soon?"

Skye raised an eyebrow. "I think I've been here for long enough. You and Bella probably have things to get to, as do I."

"Right, patient files."

Skye nodded, avoiding his gaze.

It had been nice having another adult in the house for dinner. Logan realized it had been a long time since any females, other than officers he knew from the department, had been his guests. In fact, since Rachel died, those were pretty much all the visitors he'd had in his house. He looked at Skye. She'd been helpful and insightful on the call with the coroner. He cleared his throat. "Listen, before you go, can I ask you a question?"

Skye turned, her lips parted. "I guess. What's on your mind?"

Logan was surprised at her response. It sounded slightly defensive as if she wasn't sure what he was going to ask her.

"Highmill hasn't had a case like this in probably a decade. Certainly not while I've been on duty. I started to ask you this right before Dr. Chapman called. I was wondering if you might be available to consult?"

Skye shrugged. "I don't know, Logan. I have a lot of patients. I have a business to run. I've got a lot going on."

So much so that you spent time buying gifts for my daughter and eating soup at my house?

Logan took a step forward. "I know it's a big ask. You don't know me. We just met yesterday, but you seem to have a way of getting to the nitty-gritty of things."

Skye didn't move. Her eyes narrowed. "That's my job."

"I get that. But Highmill doesn't have a detective unit. We're too small."

Skye tilted her head to the side. How was that possible? "I didn't realize that. Who will handle the case?

"Probably me and Zara."

"Zara?"

"You know, the chief."

"Oh yes, I know Zara Walsh." Skye sighed.

Logan frowned. Her response didn't surprise him, though the depth of pain on her face did. There was definitely more of a story than she was saying. "You have an issue with Zara?"

"Nothing that's worth talking about. Let me just say I think there's probably enough experience in your department to handle the case without me."

As Skye started to walk towards the door, Logan grabbed her elbow. She wheeled around, fire in her eyes. "Don't grab me like that."

Her tone was stern enough that Riggs, who had been following them, immediately sat and stared at her, at attention. Logan removed his hand slowly and held both of them up in front of his body. "Okay, sorry. I didn't know." He furrowed his eyebrows. Her response wasn't natural. Something had happened to Skye. What that was, he had no idea. But Logan didn't want her to leave, not when they'd had such a pleasant visit. He hated for things to end on a sour note. "Do you have a problem with Zara?" he asked. "I'm sorry, I don't mean to be blunt, but I don't know any other way to get to the heart of the issue."

Skye stood next to the front door, her shoulders slumping. "Yes and no. A few years back, I had a client in trouble. Instead of letting me step in and get her the help she needed, she was arrested. She killed herself the next day."

"I don't understand?"

"Zara threw the book at her, Logan." Skye's eyes were wide, as if she was having a hard time understanding what Logan didn't get. "That's what you have to understand. This poor woman, she was already on thin ice psychologically. Felt like she couldn't do anything right. Felt like she was making no contribution at all to the world. And Zara came in, heavy handed, basically proved everything this woman had thought about her life. She drove herself up to Henderson Lake the next day and jumped off the bridge. Her body was found a day or so later."

"And you blame Zara?"

"No, that's not exactly accurate," Skye said stuffing her hands into her pockets. "I'm pretty circumspect about the behavior of my clients. Time has taught me that the only one who is responsible for someone's action is that person themselves. But there are people who contribute to problems. There are opportunities for each of us to show grace and mercy and compassion to people who are hurting or who have made a bad decision."

"And you think that Zara didn't show those same values to your client when she needed them the most."

"Correct." The word came out sharp as a double-edged sword.

Logan looked at the ground for a second. He could understand Skye's hesitancy based on what she said. Zara could be, for lack of a better word, dogmatic, especially if she was challenged. "Well, like you said, there are times that people need help. What if I need your help on this case?"

Skye's expression only softened a tiny bit. "I'm sorry, Logan, but the answer is no. If you have a question or two, let me know, but I can't get involved, not after what happened." Skye glanced toward Bella's room. "Let me know how she's doing, though, okay? If she doesn't show any behavioral changes in the next week or two, then I would expect the way she's processed the memories have helped. If you notice any changes, you can text me." Skye read off her number to Logan, who put it in his phone.

He sent her a text in return. All it said was, "Logan Fletcher."

"Got it."

"And if you want to come and check in on Bella and have another bowl of soup, let me know." It was an invitation, sort of...

Skye's response was noncommittal. "I will."

As the door closed behind Skye, Logan watched her jog to her car. She'd come in like a breath of fresh air.

And now things felt stale again...

19

Whether on purpose or inadvertently, Skye ended up taking the long way home from Logan and Bella's house. She drove slowly, her thoughts whipping around in her head like a tornado, forcing her to focus in one direction and then dragging her mind in the completely opposite direction. She stopped at a red light and looked out the window at the dark skyline, the trees moving ever so gently in the breeze, only to have the moment interrupted by the impatient honking of a horn behind her. She held a hand up apologetically, noticing the light was green. She eased her car forward back into the flow of traffic on Highmill Road.

What was wrong with her?

She chided herself. If she didn't know the answer to that question then she wasn't a very good psychologist, now was she?

What she was experiencing was what happened to many of her clients. Something, in this case, the disappearance of Bella and the dead body of Ian Dunn, had shocked her system. Her mind was still processing everything she'd seen. Despite her calm demeanor, the lost child and dead body had set off an earthquake in her own life.

Not to mention Logan Fletcher.

The last twenty-four hours had shifted things in her life, areas of questions and concerns and painful memories. They'd started popping up like mental blisters in different parts of her body. It was a veritable game of whack-a-mole. Though Bella had seemed fine, Skye wasn't so sure they were out of the woods yet. There was her sister, and there was the Zara issue that Logan had brought to light. She shook her head, using her tongue to touch a crack in her lower lip. She knew why she was stressed. There were too many individual problems in her own life to deal with, not to mention the issues her patients were dealing with. It was too much all at once.

And then she thought back to what Logan had said. He'd asked her to work on the case with him. "To consult" was the way he put it. That was the straw that had broken the camel's back in terms of her thinking, she realized.

Assisting on a murder investigation? Skye wasn't qualified for that.

She felt a knot form in her gut as she parked her car in the garage and went inside her house, flipping on a few lights. It was never the first thing or the second thing that blew her mentally out of the water. It was always the third or fourth. Her grandmother had always said that things happened in threes as if that was a way to ward off the truth that life could be rotten and overwhelming sometimes. Dragging out some old superstition that would protect the bearer of the information from life's twists and turns wasn't truthful, nor was it helpful in her clinical opinion.

At that moment, two things had happened — Bella had disappeared, and Ian Dunn had been murdered. Where was the third?

Even if the third was Logan asking her to help with the case,

Skye knew better than anybody else that there was no protection from life's twists and turns except for a whole lot of really good coping mechanisms.

She'd spent her life learning them and teaching them to others.

As she changed into her favorite leggings and another one of her oversized Cornell University sweatshirts she kept for evenings at home, Skye felt restless, picking at a loose thread on one of the cuffs. She fought the restlessness by getting busy, hanging up her clothes, tossing her work pants that had Riggs's fur all over them into the hamper, and lining up her tennis shoes back on the shelf where they belonged after wiping them down with a soft cloth she kept nearby to make sure that they stayed white and pristine. Heading to the kitchen, tapping the lever on her electric kettle, she watched as it lit up with blue lights around the base of it letting her know it was in the process of boiling water. From the pantry, Skye pulled out the floor mop and ran it through the kitchen , looking for any crumbs that had escaped onto the floor while she waited for the water to boil.

There were none.

Satisfied that her house was under control even if her thoughts weren't, Skye went and got her laptop and set it up in her family room. She hadn't lied when she told Logan that she needed to work on case notes. She sucked in a deep breath. Patient notes were like kudzu vine. They kept growing and growing and growing. If she didn't cut them back on a regular basis, they would take over.

As she took her computer into her living room and set it on the table next to her favorite chair, the information that Dr. Chapman had provided about Ian Dunn cycled through her head. *Five gunshots. Nine-millimeter slugs retrieved from Ian Dunn's skull. Probably killed elsewhere. Missing anatomical parts. Spiral fractures.*

She froze, every muscle in her back tightening.

Spiral fractures. That was the part that was the most disconcerting.

Understanding physical injury was part of her daily business. Physical injury almost always led to psychological injury. They were forever linked. In Ian's case, the way those injuries were incurred, through force and twisting, said a lot about the mental state of the person who had forced his will upon Ian.

Violent. Angry. Out of control.

Skye walked back to the kitchen and sighed as she pulled a mug out of the cabinet. She balanced her tea strainer on the rim and pulled out her favorite blend of chamomile, measuring the leaves in the palm of her hand and dropping them into the strainer. She poured boiling water over the top and watched as the little leaves and stems, carefully mixed by her favorite tea shop, floated and then sunk. Three minutes later, she pulled the strainer out, dumped the used tea leaves in the trash, rinsed out the strainer, dried it off, and put it back in the cabinet.

"Everything has a place, and every place has its thing," she muttered under her breath as she made her way into the living room. Her nightly tea ritual usually brought her peace at the end of a day. Usually.

Skye grabbed her phone on the way to the living room and eased herself into her chair, pulling her laptop across her knees after covering herself with a blanket.

Ten minutes later, she'd only gotten through a few notes on the patients she'd seen that day. She couldn't help but think about Ian and Logan and Bella. There was more to the story. What had motivated someone to do that to Ian Dunn? And how had Ian Dunn ended up on Logan's property found by his small child? Was it all just a coincidence?

Or was it something more?

Skye pressed her lips together and picked up her phone. She knew how her mind worked. As much as she'd like to turn her back on the questions in her mind, they would keep growing unless she got answers. The best way to get those answers? Help Logan. She found the text that he had sent her, quickly saved him as a contact and sent him a message. "Thanks for the soup. I'll help with the case."

A message came back a second later. "You will?"

By his response, Logan seemed surprised. In actuality, Skye was too. She paused for a moment, then sent a text back.

"I will."

20

The next morning, Skye rolled over in bed as her alarm went off. She reached for it and slapped at the button to get it to stop screeching at her. A murky gray light was pushing its way underneath the curtains in her bedroom. She listened for a second. The rain had stopped; she didn't hear its persistent tapping on the roof above her.

At least that was something.

She rolled out of bed, the cool air touching her warm skin. Part of her wanted nothing more than to crawl back to her warm blankets.

She didn't.

In the bathroom, Skye pulled on her bathing suit, followed by a pair of sweatpants and an oversized orange T-shirt she got from a giveaway in a local park the summer before. She added an equally large gray sweatshirt that swamped her small frame. It said "USA Swimming" on the front of it — a gift after a donation she had made to the US Swimming Olympic Team.

Sitting next to the door to the garage was her bag. She shouldered it, locked the door behind her and went to her car. Starting it up, she blasted the heat, trying to chase the chill off.

She'd been cold since they'd hunted for Bella in the rainstorm. Skye pulled her hood up over her head as she backed out of the driveway. It had been a day and a half, and she still felt like she couldn't get warm. The memories popped up in her head like an unwanted virus. The image of Ian Dunn's face being half blown off, the way that Bella was curled up in the corner of the cave waiting for him to wake up. It wasn't just her clients that struggled with bad memories. Now she had a new set of her own to deal with.

As she started to drive away from her house and through the development, Skye realized most of the homes nearby were still dark, the people inside smart enough to stay in their warm beds. Even though there were days Skye hated getting up early, she never regretted her early morning routine. She never wanted to do much after work. She was always too tired. The pressure of listening to people's issues every day was challenging, enough so that many of the people she'd graduated with had already moved on to consulting practices, giving up daily clinical work.

Skye started thinking about Bella, Logan, and Ian Dunn as the first light only crept up over the edge of the horizon. Her mind began to wander, questions forming in the back of her head and repeating themselves over and over again. Skye blinked. Her own thoughts sounded like Dr. Chapman on steroids. She drummed her fingers on the steering wheel. It was dangerous territory if she let her mind go too far on its own.

Turning on a local radio station where they were talking about the upcoming baseball season, Skye tried to concentrate on what the analysts were saying. Not that she was interested in baseball, but at least some other people talking interrupted the cascade of thoughts in her mind. She had questions. Lots of them.

Twelve minutes later, Skye pulled into the aquatic center at Lakefield Community College. She shrugged her bag up over her shoulder, locked her car doors, and pulled the hood strings tight against the cold breeze that was blowing. Trotting inside, she pulled the door open and was immediately accosted by the strong smell of chlorine.

Without thinking, she walked briskly down the hallway, tugging open the door to the women's locker room. It was empty. The only evidence of anyone in the building were a few wet footprints left on the tile floor. Tall stands of lockers lined the walls and created two sets of center columns. Skye went to the back corner, opening the locker that she used every single morning — number 113 — and stowed her bag inside.

Slipping off her tennis shoes, she tugged off her sweatpants, hanging them on a hook inside the locker. She pulled off her sweatshirt and her T-shirt, revealing a red one-piece bathing suit. She liked it because it reminded her of the kind she used to wear when she was a lifeguard growing up. It was simple and utilitarian, not meant to evoke any particular response from anyone. It was meant for comfort and training, not to show off her physique.

And this early in the morning, she wasn't in the mood to show off for anyone.

Skye grabbed her towel and wrapped it around her waist, tucking the end in so it would stay up. From inside her bag, she fished out a set of goggles and a hair tie, quickly taming her brown hair into a bun at the back of her neck and popping the goggles on, adding a swimming cap over top to protect her hair from the chemicals in the pool. A few weeks before, she tried wearing waterproof earbuds so she could listen to music while she swam, but she found it distracting. Silence was her friend, at least most of the time.

Skye closed the locker door and attached a combination lock, then turned on her heel, walking to the opposite side of the locker room toward the entrance to the pool. The odor of chlorine was so strong, it almost made her eyes water. The air inside of the aquatic center was so thick with humidity. Skye could nearly see it floating in the air, the windows high at the top of the building glossed over with steam. There was no one else swimming that morning, Skye noticed as she walked down the deck. There was only a maintenance man at the other end of the pool vacuuming the bottom of it, standing on the edge with a long pole, cleaning up the bottom of the concrete surface. She gave him a nod. He gave her one back as if to say it was fine to go ahead and swim.

As she pulled her towel off and tossed it on a bench nearby, she noticed the man pulled the equipment out of the pool and switched over to a skimmer, dipping the end of it in the water, using the screen to pick up things floating on the surface that seemed invisible to Skye. The lighting in the aquatic center was pleasantly dim — bright enough for her to see clearly, especially with the underwater lights of the pool, but not so bright that she felt like she was swimming outdoors. It was a calm environment, one where she could focus.

In the summer, when she swam outside, Skye enjoyed the feeling of the sun on her back as she swam her laps. But the summer pools hadn't opened yet. It would be at least a couple of months before they were ready to welcome visitors. In the meantime, the aquatic center was the best she could do.

Some swimming was better than no swimming at all.

Skye walked to the far end of the pool and made her way to the edge, quickly jumping into the shallow end where the water just came up to her ribcage. She sucked in a sharp breath at the cold water hitting her skin. The air seemed to be warmer than the water was. She knew after a few minutes of moving she would start to feel better. But for the moment, it was a shock to her system.

Maybe it was one she needed.

Standing in the shallow end, she did a couple of quick stretches for her shoulders and then splashed water on her face, letting it run down her back. She bit her lip knowing that submerging herself at first would be a shock. Then again, there was no way for her to get her laps done without getting moving. She glanced up at the clock on the wall. It said six AM. "Right on time," she mumbled to herself as she dove under the water.

An hour later, her shoulders and legs aching and tired, Skye pulled herself out from the water, stripping the swim cap and goggles off of her face. She grabbed her towel, rubbing herself down, feeling the heat come off of her skin. In the corner of the aquatic center, a group of elderly women had assembled, ready for their seven AM morning water aerobics class. Aside from the instructor, who wore a bright green one-piece suit, each of the ladies had on some sort of oversized black swimwear. Skye could only imagine that the extra fabric would float like seaweed in the water.

Skye wrapped the towel around her waist and walked toward the locker room. She gave the ladies credit. At least they were doing something. They were out having a good time, being active, and enjoying each other's company. From her perspective, that was a wonderful thing. Too many people were isolated because they had such a hard time being who they were. If they embraced their own quirkiness and got out in the world, Skye would probably be out of a job.

The rest of the morning went relatively quickly. Skye drove home, jumped in the shower and got herself ready for work, spending ten minutes straightening up the house, making sure her bed was made, checking the refrigerator to make sure there was food for dinner that night when she got home in case she needed to make a stop at the grocery store, and putting her mug from her half-consumed tea from the night before in the dishwasher. The last thing she wanted to do was come home to a house that was a mess.

After making sure that the house was cleaned up, Skye went back into the bathroom and dried her hair, pulling it long and straight and letting it cascade down over her shoulders. She tugged on a pair of wide-legged black pants, a white T-shirt, and a red jacket, finishing it off with a set of bright white tennis shoes. She did a quick touch of makeup and then headed to the door. As she walked toward the garage, she caught a glimpse of herself in the mirror that hung in her foyer.

Years ago, she would have worn a full suit to work, complete with heels. Now, most days she wore clothes that were super comfortable with a professional edge. Some of her colleagues had even started showing up at work in jeans. Skye made a mental note to discuss it at the next staff meeting. It was one thing for the patients of Seneca Counseling Services to wear sweatshirts and sweatpants and jeans to their counseling sessions. After all, they wouldn't be in their office if they weren't in crisis. It was something else to have the counselors looking like that. Differentiation was a key component to the therapeutic process. Yes, the patients needed to connect with their therapist, but their therapist needed to also maintain a professional boundary. Clothing was an easy way to do that.

It was definitely a good topic for staff training.

At work, Skye stopped at the reception desk and checked her schedule and also the schedules for her other counselors that day. Seneca Counseling Services — the practice that she had started five years before — now had eight therapists on staff and could definitely use at least two more. They had a backlog of people with mental health issues that needed to be seen. They ranged from everything from relationship issues to addiction to life transition — things like getting married, getting a new job, getting divorced, coping with elderly parents.

Any one of those issues on its own could be difficult to cope with. Skye's team usually saw people who had at least one, if not many, of those issues happening all at the same time in a cascade.

Life could be brutal sometimes.

The realization brought up the mental image of Ian Dunn's face to her mind as well as her offer to help Logan.

What had she signed up for?

Skye checked her schedule for that day. It was full, save for a one-hour block where she could get lunch. However, half of that was taken up by a call with their accountant. Skye rubbed the back of her neck. There was never a dull moment when you owned your own business. Walking down the hallway, she opened the door to the counseling room she used. Without even looking, she knew what she'd see when she got inside — calming light gray walls and charcoal carpet covered with a brightly colored rug in reds, blues, and greens. There was a couch and a chair opposite each other, separated by a glass-topped coffee table that housed a few standard magazines, *People, Good Housekeeping, and Sports Illustrated* — something for everyone. A box of tissues was in the center of the table.

Skye paused at the door, gathering herself. Based on the fact that the door was closed, she knew her client was already ready for her. Skye pushed the door open and smiled, looking at the woman who was sitting in the chair on the opposite side of the room, staring out at the window. "Hey, Naomi. How are you?"

21

As Skye closed the door to the counseling room, Naomi turned and looked at her. The rims of her eyes were red, the edges of crumpled-up tissue evident in the fist of her left hand. It didn't take a genius to know that she'd been crying. A lump formed in Skye's throat. She knew what was coming and it was going to be uncomfortable for both of them.

Almost immediately, the issue of Naomi's love life was a subject of conversation. "I just don't understand," Naomi said, standing up from her spot on the chair and walking over to the window, her arms crossed in front of her chest.

"What don't you understand?" Skye asked evenly, crossing her legs.

Naomi sniffled. "Toby seems like a good guy, but there's just something about him, something that is making it hard for me to connect with him."

Skye adjusted in her seat. "What do you think that is?"

"I don't know. He's just so…intense, but in a weird way. It's like he's fine one minute, then something snaps and he's all over me about stuff."

"And does that intensity bother you? How do you feel about it?" Everything in Skye's gut told her that Toby wasn't a good guy. He sounded like a classic controller, someone who had to have things their way all the time, someone who struggled with a deep well of insecurity. But it wasn't Skye's job to figure that out for Naomi.

"I'm not sure." Naomi turned and faced Skye. "To be honest, it scares me. I know he loves me, but I'm just not sure I feel exactly the same way about him."

Skye wanted to jump out of her seat and wave her hands in the air and yell, "Then break up with him!" but she kept her face relaxed and her tone even, folding her hands in her lap. "Can you see yourself with him for the long term?"

Naomi returned to her chair and sat down. She looked down at her lap and then back at Skye. "I don't think so. I mean, I don't want to hurt him, but I think he's more into me than I am into him."

Naomi paused, dealing with her own thoughts. Skye knew better than to fill the space. When she was a newly minted psychologist, her supervisor told her she was too quick to give her clients answers. It wasn't up to her to do that. Her job was to provide a safe space for them to find their way. The side benefit of staying quiet was that it gave her the time to observe.

Skye cocked her head to the side and waited. It was evident there was something that Naomi wanted to tell her, that she was trying to work up her courage to do it. Skye took a sip of coffee, wrapping her hands around the warm mug and waiting. She felt like she spent half of her day waiting for people to have their revelations. Sometimes they were good revelations, and sometimes not. But they were revelations, nonetheless.

As soon as Skye set her coffee cup down, Naomi coughed and then cleared her throat. "There's someone else."

Skye raised her eyebrows. "Someone else? You haven't told me about this before. How long has this been going on?"

"About a month or so. It's just —"

"Just what, Naomi?"

Naomi stood up from where she was seated and walked back to the window. Skye watched her. There were clients that she had that stayed glued to their chair during their entire session. They would find a seat on their first day and would plop down on that same spot every single time. There were other people that migrated from spot to spot and others that got up and went back and forth between the window and their chair. Naomi was the latter and not the former. It didn't bother Skye. It was a good way for her to manage her shifting mood.

"The problem is, is I know the guy from work. "

"Why is that a problem?"

"You know how they are. I'm working in a male-dominated industry and an office romance could tank my career."

"So, what do you want to do about it?"

"I mean, I would break up with Toby in a second if I thought Ian was the one. But last night, I went over to his house. I've been looking for him for like twenty-four hours, and he's gone. I have no idea where he is. He didn't even show up for work this morning."

Skye sucked in a breath, her heart racing in her chest. "I'm sorry. You said this guy's name is Ian?" She looked down at the notepad that was on the table next to her, picking it up and grabbing a pen, trying to keep her gaze away from Naomi for the moment, hoping Naomi didn't see the look of recognition on her face.

"Ian. Ian Dunn. He works at Pearce Construction with me."

Skye froze as a sheen of perspiration covered her forehead. She scratched a few nonsensical notes on her pad to buy her time to control her reaction. Highmill wasn't a big city. What were the chances that there was more than one Ian Dunn in the community? Not good by her estimation. Ian Dunn wasn't going to be home anytime soon. In fact, his body was sitting at the coroner's office, Dr. Chapman working on getting any additional information he could about the man's brutal murder.

Skye wrapped her fingers together, knitting them in her lap, trying not to move, listening as Naomi continued to talk. Even though everything in her wanted to tell Naomi that Ian was dead, it wasn't her place. Naomi would find out soon enough.

And when she did, Skye would have to help her pick up the pieces.

22

By the time they got to the end of the session, Naomi didn't seem much more committed to breaking up with Toby than she had when she walked in.

That was only problem number one.

Skye, still thinking about the fact that Naomi had fallen in love with a man who was now dead, managed to tell her to work on her journaling, make sure she was following her self-care practices that they had discussed in the past, and that she would see her again in a week. Skye watched as Naomi disappeared down the hallway, her head hung low, using the private exit that Skye's firm provided for all of their counselees.

Turning away, Skye sighed. It was just her luck. What were the chances that Ian Dunn would be involved with one of her counselees? She pressed her lips together as she walked to her office, grabbing the file for her next client. That was the problem with most of the people that came to see her. Very few of them were willing to make any changes in their life. They wanted to come in and complain about their family, their mom or their lover. Certainly, that helped them process their feelings, so that was a win. But in terms of making any actual radical life changes, those were few and far between. The clients that did experience real change were the kind of people who were natural action-takers, who just needed someone to point them in the right direction. Naomi was clearly not one of those.

At least not at that moment.

The rest of Skye's day was relatively uneventful — counseling sessions with a woman whose aging mother was suffering with dementia, a couple where the husband was new to sobriety and they were working on issues of lying and infidelity, and a whole series of women who seemed to be either unsure about their relationships, their careers, their husbands, and even their pets.

Skye flew through her lunch and her meeting with the accountant. All the while, three things kept eating at the back of her mind — Logan, Bella, and Ian Dunn. As soon as her last session was over, Skye gathered up her bag and her notepad, stuffing them inside. She needed to sit down and input notes from her sessions that evening.

As she did, her phone rang. She looked down at the screen. It said one word, and one word alone, "Sister." Skye shook her head, rejected the call, and tossed her phone in her pocket. There was no way that she was going to deal with Christy, not on that day. She had other things to deal with.

23

Toby had been struggling with the design for the new academic building at Cornell University until about mid-morning, at which point he came up with a brainstorm — a brilliant solution in his mind — that would allow for the Board of Trustees and the donor's wishes to come true. He spent the next four hours reworking his design, coming up with three separate conceptual ideas that the Cornell people could toss around.

People liked to have choices, especially those that had millions of dollars to spare to build a monument to themselves.

By the time Toby was done, he was exhausted. He uploaded the images and designs to the cloud server his firm, Schuyler Design & Architecture, used to store large files, quickly copied the link, penned an encouraging email to the clients, and sent it off with not much else than a wish and a prayer. With any luck, one of the three designs would suit the clients and the trustees, at least enough to become a place that they could start working from.

Now all he could do was wait.

Given that he'd worked the majority of the weekend, Toby

didn't feel bad about leaving his office a little early. He was always one of the first ones in and the last ones out anyway. He pulled on an insulated jacket over his buttoned-down shirt, shoved his laptop into his bag, and locked the door to his office, passing a couple of other people in the hallway who seemed to give him a sideways glance as he was leaving. He didn't bother telling them he was done for the day. For all they knew, he was going to finish his work at home or go meet a client or one of their suppliers.

Toby paused in the hallway just past his boss's office, wondering if he should say something, stared at the floor and then heard someone call his name.

Dan, his boss.

Too late. Toby was caught.

Dan was positioned behind his massive oak desk in his office, his shirtsleeves rolled up as if he'd just gotten done splitting a cord of lumber. "Listen, just wanted to connect with you before you leave. You are headed out, aren't you?"

To Toby it sounded a bit like an accusation. "I am. I spent pretty much the entire weekend working on the Cornell project. Thought I would go home and finish work from there, if that's okay with you." Toby hated that he had to ask. He knew he contributed more to the firm than nearly anyone else. He should be managing partner, not Dan.

"Yes, yes, of course. I saw the email that you just sent." Dan was one of those bosses that liked to be asked permission. If Toby was deferential to him, things were fine, but if Toby tried to assert himself, Dan pushed right back. After telling a client that their idea for a two-story lobby in an office building was tired and overdone, Toby had been summarily demoted to a junior assistant on several Schuyler Design & Architecture projects for about a three-month period when the client had taken their business elsewhere. He'd been in Dan's doghouse. Dan was so angry at the loss of revenue, there was little Toby could do to recover but grin and bear the punishment, which consisted of working with a new architect they had just brought in. She was green. Very green.

Even worse, in Toby's mind, she had no talent.

The office scuttlebutt had started immediately. Toby tried to cover by saying that the firm was too swamped with work to accommodate the clients and Dan needed someone to train Caitlyn, but everyone in the office knew it wasn't the truth. He was being punished for bad behavior.

Dan's voice interrupted his thoughts. "Listen, good work on the Cornell project. I like the direction you're headed."

Toby gave a nod. "Yeah, thanks. This one has been a tough nut to crack. The parcel of land they have to work with isn't exactly ideal."

"I can see that. Sometimes these people with tons of money have an expectation that the sky is the limit, but you know as well as I do that trying to meet everyone's needs here is really tough. That said, we do need to make this work. You understand that, right?"

Toby nodded. Didn't Dan just say he liked what Toby had done? He knit his eyebrows together. Something was going on. "Did you have one of the particular concepts you think will work the best for the client?" He tried distracting Dan from whatever it was that he was about to say.

"I'm not sure. I'm going to have to look at them in more depth." The way the words came slowly out of Dan's mouth, Toby could tell that they were good solutions but probably not the ones that Dan would have chosen.

"Well, I can —"

Dan held a hand up. "I don't want you to take this the wrong way, but I think making you solo on this project was probably a mistake. It's an awful lot of stress. Too much to put on one person. I get that. So, from here on out, I'm going to be personally supervising the hours that go into this project. I'm also going to put another architect on the project as well so we have multiple perspectives. I asked Caitlyn to start working on some drawings last week. The stuff she has come up with is really innovative, and I think we can —"

Toby's heart lurched in his chest. Caitlyn was doing concept work on the Cornell project? How was that possible? She was sloppy and her design work was boring as far as Toby was concerned, run-of-the-mill in terms of creativity. She wasn't good at doing much other than drawing up strip centers and boxy office buildings.

Toby looked at the floor for one second, his stomach in a knot, and then looked up at Dan. "I understand. This is a big project and you're right, it's probably too big for one person to handle it on their own. I would be grateful for the help. I should probably have come to you earlier with the same idea." Toby barely managed to get the words out of his mouth before Dan interrupted.

"I'm glad you see it the same way I do." Dan's words hung heavy in the air.

Toby held his breath. He knew what was happening. Adding Caitlyn to the project was code for, "You're on the verge of screwing it up like you did last time and we can't have that stain on our reputation."

Toby blinked. "Yes, I understand. I will be sure to check in with Caitlyn tomorrow morning. Maybe the two of us can put our heads together."

Dan nodded. "That's great. And by the way, I asked IT to pull back the email that you sent to the client. That will give you and Caitlyn a chance to review the work you've done and any ideas she has. Let's see if you guys can come up with some common ground. She's really talented at client communication, so let's have her take the lead in contacting the client. I've also scheduled the three of us for a meeting tomorrow afternoon at —"

The rest of what Dan said sounded like nothing more than a bunch of "blah, blah, blah," to Toby. He nodded and stood still, feeling like a fool. Why had he put so much effort into his job? Who did Dan think he was, even if he was the managing partner, to rip a project away from Toby when he was so close to pulling it off?

Toby would show Dan. He would show all of them. No one would take away what Toby wanted.

No one.

24

Toby did everything in his power to not storm out of the office after the subtly professional dressing down he got from Dan.

Or maybe it wasn't so subtle.

Clearly, Dan had lost faith in Toby's abilities.

By the time Toby made it to his car and got inside, starting the engine, his hands were shaking with fury. What kind of boss assigns a project and then months later rips it away halfway through right after a huge surge of progress? What if other people in the firm found out? What would that do to morale?

Toby threw his sedan into gear and sped out of the parking lot, turning onto Highmill Road and heading eastbound. He needed to see Naomi. He needed someone to help him feel calm and centered, like he was worth something, like there was a shred of good or potential left inside of him. If there is one thing he had learned about Naomi since they've been dating, it was that only she could do that. She had the power to help him, the power to snap him out of his funk and help him feel hopeful again.

And he didn't want her to share that talent with anyone else. She was his girl. His.

The late afternoon streets of Highmill were crowded with traffic, parents picking up their kids from school, those same parents driving their kids to after-school activities like karate and music lessons and basketball practice. Workers who worked the second shift were on their way to work at the steel mill on the edge of the city, one of the few left in the state of New York. All in all, it made for a drive that required more patience than Toby had at that moment.

After twisting and twining his way through traffic, he finally found his way to the development where Naomi lived. Although it was filled with houses that were not the custom variety, much to his surprise there was something about it he liked. Something about it that was very Naomi. The homes themselves were unassuming, but well-constructed. Many of them had been built by Naomi's company, Pearce Construction. Old man Pearce was a legend in Highmill. He'd managed to expand the construction business his own father started into a commercial enterprise that ranked among the nation's largest.

In addition to the work that Pearce Construction did in Highmill, they had satellite offices in other states where they had new construction projects going on all at the same time. Old man Pearce was a genius at reading the tea leaves to see where the newest construction surge was happening and then managed somehow to get himself interjected in those markets just in time to snag the biggest and choicest projects. Toby hoped to be the architect on many of those new projects, but despite his connection with Naomi, none had come his way yet. He'd told her how much he wanted to get in front of Mr. Pearce, but she hadn't set anything up yet.

Why hadn't she done that? Was he not good enough?

Pulling into Naomi's driveway, he noticed the garage door was closed. Not that that was unusual but there were also no lights on in the house. Toby frowned, then realized, given the fact that it was late afternoon, even if Naomi was home and had lights on, he wouldn't see them.

Toby walked to the front door, wondering if there would be a time when he would have keys to her house and find her inside, cooking dinner for them and their kids. It was a small shard of hope he could hold onto. But for now, all he could do was console himself by ringing the doorbell.

Waiting at the front door for her to answer, Toby shoved his hands in his pockets, fighting off the chill. The torrential rain two days before might have stopped, but the wind had kicked up. The cold was cutting through the thick jacket he had worn that morning. He shook his head as he shivered. He knew better. He had lived in Upstate New York for his whole life. The weather could change on a dime. A spring day that started in the seventies could drop into the upper thirties in a space of an hour if a clipper came across the Canadian border and blew its way into town. Toby waited for another second and then peered in the side window. All of the lights were off. He checked the time on his watch. Naomi should be home by now, shouldn't she?

Thoughts thundered in his head as he walked back to his car. Maybe he should have sent her a text before he headed over? But then again, he had been so upset when he left work, that the only thing he could think of was Naomi. He desperately wanted to spend some time in her quiet, cozy home, spilling his feelings to her.

He wanted her to himself.

Getting back into his car, he realized that he had no idea where she was. The thought irritated him. Normally, Naomi got off work a couple of hours earlier than he did. Then again, her work as a construction manager started way earlier. She was typically up at five AM and out the door a half hour later, arriving at the job site by six. Most of the subcontractors that worked for Pearce began their day by seven AM, unless they were working overnight to finish a project. Naomi had told him when they first started dating that she had a rule for herself that she needed to be at the site before any work started. "It's the best way to avoid problems," she had told him a few months before. He found her initiative admirable and not just a little bit sexy.

Toby sat in his car for a second and realized it was getting cold. He turned on the engine and flipped on the heat, sending Naomi a text. "Where are you?"

There was no answer.

Irritated, Toby sat and waited in her driveway for another twenty minutes. When she still hadn't shown up and hadn't bothered to text him back, he threw his car into reverse in frustration, pulled out of her driveway and drove around aimlessly. He considered going home, but he needed to see her. He needed to be with his Naomi.

Why wasn't she responding to him?

At the next stoplight, he stared at his phone. Still nothing from her. What was going on? Anger started nipping at his gut. Did she have no idea the lengths that he would go to protect her and their relationship? He circled his car around and headed back to Naomi's house, driving through the development with probably more speed than was wise, given the number of families that lived in the area, but he didn't care. The urge to see her was suffocating him. He just needed a minute of her attention.

Just a single minute...

25

Naomi stopped dead in her tracks as she saw the blue BMW sedan that belonged to Toby pull up in the driveway. What was he doing at her house? Everything in her wanted to grab her groceries, run inside, and close the door. She would have to deal with him at some point, but today wasn't the day. She didn't have the energy for him, not after work.

After a busy morning dealing with subcontractors at the worksite for the office building the company was in the process of finishing, she'd gotten a call from Mr. Pearce. "Naomi?"

"Yes, sir?" Everyone at Pearce Construction referred to Mr. Pearce with that level of respect.

"I'm afraid I have some unfortunate news. I just got a call from the police department. No reason to tiptoe around the issue, that's what I always say. I know you and Ian Dunn have been working closely on projects. I just wanted to let you know that he's been found dead."

The breath caught in her throat. "Dead? What do you mean?" Her mind raced, thinking about the night before when she'd gone to his house and it had been dark.

Mr. Pearce paused, as if he was composing himself. "They didn't give me any of the details. Said it's an ongoing investigation, but that said, you're gonna be on your own for the time being until I can pull somebody else into Ian's position. It's tragic, but the work has to continue. Here's my question to you — can you handle it?"

Naomi knew she only had a split second to answer. Old man Pearce wasn't a patient man. But he was the kind that would give people a break when no one else would. "Yes, sir. Of course. You can count on me."

"Good. Now, if you have any questions, I want you to come to me directly, at least for the time being, that is. I'm going to help you. We will get you through this project. Nothing to worry about. Nothing at all. We take care of our own."

After eagerly agreeing with Mr. Pearce, Naomi had managed to finish the rest of her day at work, the shock keeping her moving. She felt numb and disoriented. Part of her wished that her session with Dr. Johnston had been scheduled for the afternoon after she had gotten the news instead of that morning.

But the grief was real. Between meetings with subcontractors, Naomi had snuck off to her SUV, finding her eyes filled with tears once again that day, sobs coming from deep inside of her. First, she'd cried about her relationship with Toby, one she had but didn't want. Now, she was crying about her relationship with Ian, one she would never have.

Tears flowed down her face. Luckily, she had at least a little privacy in her car. The last thing she wanted was anyone feeling sorry for her. Dabbing at her eyes with a small tissue from a pack she found inside her glove box, she'd managed to get it together long enough to call Dr. Johnston's practice and leave a message. Maybe Skye could get her in for an extra session?

Then the texts from Toby started. Naomi ignored them as

she went to the grocery store, robotically picking up a few pieces of fruit, a bag of grapes, some chicken breasts, and pasta for dinner. And now he was in her driveway, his sullen look telling her he was disappointed in the fact she hadn't responded. "I'm sorry I didn't text you back," she said as he ran toward the garage and grabbed a couple of the grocery bags, following her into the house.

"That's okay," he said stiffly. "Where have you been?" The way that he said it sounded heavy, as if it was a demand and not a question. Who was he, her father?

"I was at the store. I had a busy day at work. I needed to grab some things for dinner."

Toby stared at her as she set the bags down on the counter. "You look tired."

Naomi looked away. "I am."

"Well, I had a bad day too."

"I'm sorry to hear that." Naomi instantly regretted how sharply the words came out. But at that moment, she didn't really care what Toby was going through. There was no way it was as bad as having a colleague die. There was some part of her that wanted to tell him about Ian, but her lips didn't move, as if he would be able to tell by the expression on her face that Ian had been more to her than just a co-worker. Then it hit her — she could have very nearly lost the love of her life.

Toby stared at her for a second, his mouth open. "Aren't you going to ask me to stay?"

Naomi put the chicken in the refrigerator and closed the door and then turned back towards him. "No. Tonight is not a good night, Toby. I'm sorry. I need a little time alone. I have work to do." Naomi stood still. She saw the bloom of embarrassment flush Toby's cheeks.

"I see where this is going. You only have time for yourself."

Naomi held her hands up. "Listen, I just had a bad day. I just need a quiet night at home by myself to regroup. I have things I need to do for Mr. Pearce. I promise I will reach out tomorrow."

Toby narrowed his eyes, his expression dark. "You know, I thought you were different, Naomi. But you aren't. You're out running around. You won't text me back. You're not interested in asking me about my day." He paused, glaring at her. "I thought we were together, Naomi. Are we?"

"We are. I promise, Toby." Why Naomi was promising anything, she wasn't sure, except that Toby seemed so angry in that moment that all she wanted him to do was to leave her house. The only thing that she could think of was how to make him calm again so maybe he'd go away.

"I'm not so sure about that, Naomi. I don't appreciate being treated this way. I think by now you should know better."

With that, Toby stormed out of her kitchen. The next thing she heard was the back door slamming and then the revving of the engine of his sedan. He pulled out, his tires squealing as Naomi watched from the front window, feeling completely helpless. She ran to the garage, relief flooding over her, closing the garage door and locking the back door.

As she made it back to the kitchen, she leaned her palms on the counter for a second, trying to stop the tears that were streaming down her face in a flood. As she stood up straight, she realized her hands were shaking.

Was it because Toby scared her or because Ian was gone?

26

Toby was furious at the way that Naomi had spoken to him. He needed her. He'd had a horrible day at work, felt completely rejected by his boss, Dan, and basically got demoted to a junior member of a project that he should have owned.

And the woman he loved?

She didn't care.

As Toby drove toward his house, he gripped the steering wheel so tight his knuckles were white. Something was going on with Naomi. There was something he couldn't put his finger on. But over the last month or so, she'd seemed distant, not herself. It was as if something inside of her had shifted gears, as if she had made a decision without talking to him about it.

How dare she...

Toby was dedicated to her. That was one thing that he knew about his personality. Take it or leave it, when he decided he was all in on something, he was. That was how it was when he decided he wanted to become an architect at the age of twelve. Sure, his dad had influenced him, but his dad had also opened doors. He'd spent time every summer working in his dad's office, spent weekends studying blueprints and helping his dad adjust drawings. By the age of fifteen, he was probably a better architect than anyone in his office.

Definitely better than Caitlyn.

And now he'd practically lost a Cornell project to someone who had only a fraction of the experience Toby had. It was hard to imagine.

The one oasis in his life, the one place where he could go and feel calm and satisfied, knowing he was in complete control was within his relationship with Naomi.

And now that had gone awry.

Toby drove aimlessly for the next hour, circling the streets in Highmill, everything in him wanting to go back to his condo, pack a bag, get in his car, and disappear. No one would care. He'd basically gotten the message from his work that he was useless, and now Naomi had done exactly the same thing to him. He pulled into his condo building, put his car into park, picking up his phone, looking for flights to Mexico. Maybe some hot weather would do him good. Would Naomi even wonder where he'd gone if he disappeared? A moment later he threw his phone down in frustration. He shifted his car back into gear and drove back to Naomi's house, parking down the block, cutting his headlights, sitting in the darkness. He sat and watched it for a solid twenty minutes. There wasn't much to see. Naomi had drawn the blinds, only the edge of golden light from inside her warm home teasing Toby from the outside. He shook his head, setting his jaw. He should have insisted that she give him keys to her house. If she had, he could have just walked up to the front door like it was his own, opened it and gone in and gotten things straightened out.

But she hadn't. It was still *her* house and *her* life.

And at that moment, she had made it obvious that she didn't want him to be a part of it.

27

As he sat in his car in front of his condo, Toby couldn't stop thinking about the way that Naomi had talked to him. Was he that wrong about their relationship? He'd pinned all of his hopes on her. He felt heat rise to his cheeks as he drove away. Ten minutes later, he found himself sitting in the parking lot of a local bar he and Naomi like to go to called the Tin Roof.

He gripped the steering wheel, staring ahead of him. In a surge of energy, Toby got out of his car and charged inside, grabbing a seat at the bar. The bartender, a guy everyone knew only as Mac, though Toby highly doubted that was his real name, walked over and tossed a square white paper cocktail napkin down in front of him. "What can I get ya, Toby?"

Toby could barely look up. "A beer and a shot. Make it a double."

Mac gave a nod and returned a minute later setting the amber-colored beer down in front of Toby along with a short, fat glass that had an inch and a half of whiskey in the bottom of it. Toby picked up the double shot, put the glass to his lips and threw the liquid back into the back of his throat. Looking down, he grimaced as the liquid burned his throat. He took a sip of the beer to cool the sensation and then folded his arms on the bar, waiting for the alcohol to hit his system.

Mac cruised by, picking up the empty glass and giving the counter surface a flick with his white towel. "Where is Naomi tonight? Is she working?"

Toby pressed his lips together. Everything in him wanted to hurtle himself across the bar and strangle the life out of Mac for uttering Naomi's name. He lifted his chin slowly, leveling his gaze at Mac, his gaze cool. "Something like that."

Mac froze for a second as if he realized he was stepping into something that he didn't want to tangle with, gave Toby a quick nod and made his way down the bar, picking up a friendly conversation with two women, a blonde and a redhead, who had positioned themselves at the other end. Within seconds, they were laughing and joking around. It was exactly what Toby didn't want to hear at that moment. It felt like everyone around him was having a good time, everyone except for him.

Toby stared down at his hands, which he had folded on the edge of the bar. In his book, the day had been horrible — first, the Cornell project earned him not the accolades he was looking for, but the demotion everyone always dreaded. Then, looking for solace, Naomi had basically blown him off.

He didn't know what to think except that his life was spiraling out of control.

Everything that Toby had pinned his life on had come crumbling down, or at least it felt that way. His plans to propose to Naomi seemed ridiculous at that moment. And his interest in advancing at the firm were never going to happen given the way that Dan felt about him.

It was time for Toby to face reality.

He took a sip of the beer, setting the glass back down in the exact center of the square white napkin Mac had set it on. He stared at it, the coolness of the liquid seeping through the glass and into his fingers.

There were other pieces to the puzzle, pieces he could no longer ignore.

Toby fished a twenty-dollar bill out of his pocket and slapped it down on the bar, giving Mac a nod. He was still at the other end of the bar chit-chatting with the women. Toby knew the twenty would be enough to cover the alcohol and hopefully some of his bad attitude. He pushed his unfinished beer off to the side and stood up.

It was time to go. Spending time at the Tin Roof without Naomi only reminded him of the fact that she wasn't there.

Stomping out of the bar, he went to his car, slid inside, and started it up, stepping on the gas hard enough that the tires squealed on the pavement of the parking lot. He narrowed his eyes in the darkness, staring ahead of him. There was nothing he could do about work, at least not at that moment. But there was something that he could do about Naomi.

Toby drove through the center of Highmill, passing gas stations, a pancake restaurant that stayed open twenty-four hours, and a host of other stores and shops that were closed given the late hour. His headlights cut through the darkness. He could see the occasional patch of damp on the pavement in front of him, but it was nothing like it had been during the torrential rains of a couple of days before. There were a few stray branches on the side of the road from the storm that had passed through, but all in all, the city had weathered the rain like it always did — stalwart and solid.

If only Toby's life had that same quality. He was tired of things changing, tired of people taking advantage of him. He was tired of always being the victim of other people's whims. Didn't the people around him see he was special? Talented?

At that moment he wasn't even sure Naomi saw it.

She needed to. If anyone needed to accept who he was, it was her.

28

By the time Toby made it back to Naomi's house, all the lights were out. He imagined what was going on inside, Naomi curled up in bed, the sheets touching her soft skin. She might have her headphones on, listening to music, or even have her eyes closed, listening to one of the stupid meditation apps that she had loaded on her phone.

Toby knew the truth. She didn't need any of that. All she needed was to focus on him.

For a moment, Toby thought about driving away. He needed to talk to her. No, he needed to convince her that she was behaving badly. Ignoring him would be something she would regret for the rest of her life.

Feeling a pit of anger in his gut, Toby got out of the car, slamming the door closed. Convincing her wasn't going to work. He needed to tell her. He needed to do what he hadn't done at work — demand to be heard, demand to have someone take notice of him.

Taking control was the only answer.

Toby circled Naomi's house. He'd spent enough time there that he knew the weaknesses of the structure. In fact, he'd discussed them with her on many occasions. She had dreams about what she wanted to do to the house, improvements that she could make. It was one of the things that Toby loved about her more than anything else. The pairing of their talents was powerful. He had the design background, the creative genius to make a vision come to life. Naomi had the practical skill of being able to execute it.

Now he would use that to his advantage. Striding around the side of the house, Toby went to the back door that led into the garage. If he'd told Naomi once, he told her a million times to have the flimsy door replaced, but she hadn't. It was a contractor-grade wooden door with nothing more to secure it than a lock built into the handset. There was no deadbolt and no way to prevent intruders from making their way into the house.

Toby looked at the door, knowing it wouldn't take much to force it open. He lowered his chin and then wrapped his arm around the front of his body, ramming his shoulder into it, feeling the door pop open under the force of his body. He almost laughed. It didn't even take that much effort. Toby stepped inside, the dark of the garage surrounding him. He could smell the cooling engine of Naomi's SUV, plus the scent of gas and oil leaking from an old mower she had in the corner that she kept promising to have serviced before the grass started to grow again but hadn't.

He'd told her to take care of it. The fact that she hadn't was a disappointment.

In the darkness, Toby made his way across the garage, stepping carefully around Naomi's SUV and then up to the back door. Naomi never locked it. It was yet another thing he had tried to help her with that she hadn't done. The signs of rejection were mounting up around him. How had he not seen it before? Sure, Highmill was a quiet town, one that didn't have much crime, but all those things could change in an instant.

Couldn't she see he was trying to protect her?

Maybe it was good that she hadn't. Now Toby was using it to his advantage. When Naomi didn't meet him at the back door, a startled look on her face from the sound of the door being crashed in, he knew that she hadn't heard what had happened. He smiled. It was better that way. Naomi loved surprises, or at least she used to.

He grimaced, bile rising to the back of his throat. He wasn't sure what she liked anymore.

Toby strode through the house purposefully, walking up the steps to the second floor, not bothering to mask his entry at all. He knew Naomi didn't have any guns in the house. It wasn't like she was going to shoot him or something. Even if she had heard him, what was she going to do, take a swing at him?

That wasn't the Naomi he loved. The woman he loved was kind and devoted to him. Naomi had been that way until a few weeks before.

Then everything changed.

In the darkness, he made his way down the hallway. The door at the end of the hall was shut. His skin tingled. The fact that the door was closed meant Naomi was inside. He grabbed the door handle, twisting the metal so hard he wondered for a second if it would come loose from the door. Toby flung the door open. The glow of Naomi's phone lit up her startled face, a set of heavy earphones over her ears. She ripped them off. "Toby! You scared me to death! What are you doing? How did you —"

"Shut up!" he yelled, darting for the bed, yanking at her arm. "Get up! The way you talked to me earlier is unacceptable."

Even in the darkness, Toby could see that Naomi's eyes were wide and terrified. "What are you doing? Let me go!"

"No!"

Using his strength, he pulled Naomi out of her bed into a

standing position. He grabbed her wrist and pinned it behind her back, seeing that she was wearing sweatpants, T-shirt, and socks. It would be good enough for what he had planned. "You and me, we're going to go for a little drive and get things straightened out."

It was the first time all day Toby felt in control. As he shoved Naomi in front of him, he nearly smiled. It was time for Toby to put things right. This was just the first step.

29

Toby managed to drag Naomi downstairs without much of a fight. Why she wasn't kicking and screaming, he had no idea. Was that a good sign? Did she realize what she had done?

He gave her a moment to slide her feet into a pair of tennis shoes and grab a coat and then pushed her out the door, closing it behind them, dragging her by the elbow out to his vehicle. She complained about how hard he gripped her skin, that he was pinching her. He didn't care. Pushing her inside, he slammed the door behind her. Running around to the driver's side, he stared around him. Hopefully none of the nosy neighbors had one of those annoying doorbell cameras that picked up movement. Even if it did, he was a known quantity. He smirked. Everybody knew he and Naomi were a thing. In the dark, there was no way for them to see exactly what was going on anyway.

Not that it was any of their business.

Toby got in the car just in time to hear Naomi protest. "What are you doing, Toby? Where are we going?"

"Shut up! I already told you once we need to have a talk."

Naomi shrunk back in her seat. He heard her whimper as he drove out of her development. He was so angry at the noise, he raised his hand and threatened to backhand her, but stopped just short. She shriveled even more in the seat.

They drove the rest of the way in silence. Toby was seething with anger, and Naomi crying. Despite the emotional rollercoaster he was on, part of Toby found it interesting that when challenged, Naomi crumbled. She didn't fight back, she didn't argue. All she did was sit next to him and cry.

She knew the truth. She'd disappointed him. Now she'd have to make it up to him in a big way, but that wouldn't happen before he taught her a lesson.

Toby turned down a narrow road on the outskirts of town, marked with a small sign that said West River Marina. The road was pitch black, but Toby had been up and down it so many times that he almost didn't need his headlights, though they certainly helped. The long driveway widened into a parking lot, opening up on a branch of Henderson Lake. It was early in the season. Toby knew that with the time of day and the horrible weather the town had just gone through, that no one would be hanging out at the boat club. The lack of cars in the parking lot verified his theory. As he looked around him, he saw the blue-painted travel lift stood shadowed off to one side of the parking lot, the enormous machine standing sentry in the darkness, the straps used to lift the hulls of the boats off of their winter storage swaying gently in the nighttime breeze. The small building that stood next to the gas dock was dark and shuttered, the parking lot still filled with boats that were up on their jack stands, the white plastic that covered them from the winter still tight against their hulls.

But not all of the boats were still in dry dock.

All in all, Toby counted three boats that were ready for the season, one of them being his. The dock holders had only just that week gotten the go-ahead from the harbormaster to put boats in now that the dredging was done and the docks had been inspected for use. Toby had called immediately and had his boat put in the water. He paid a lot to keep a dock on Henderson Lake. There was no reason to delay in getting it in the water.

Not that the weather at that moment was all that conducive to boating.

Pulling up in front of his dock, Toby got out of the car and went to Naomi's side, grabbing her arm so tightly he knew he was bruising her skin. Part of him wanted to feel bad, but part of him didn't care. No one seemed to care about him. Why should he care about anyone else? "Let's go," he growled.

"Why are we here?" Naomi cried. "You aren't taking me out to the boat, are you? It's too cold." In the light that hovered above the parking lot, he could see that her face was tear-stained, the tip of her nose red.

"We need to set some things straight. You won't listen to me, so I'm going to make you listen to me."

"What?" Naomi stammered.

The fact that Naomi pretended to not know what had been going on infuriated Toby even more. Did she think he was blind? Did she think he hadn't noticed that it had taken her longer to respond to texts, that she'd become more resistant to spending time with him, and, God forbid he wanted to get close to her, all she seemed to do was push him away and claim she was too tired from work.

No. Dan had made a fool of him earlier that day at the firm. Naomi was not going to do the same.

Toby half-dragged and half-pushed Naomi down the dock, giving her a shove to get her across onto the boat. She nearly tripped as she stepped onto the back deck, catching herself at the last second on one of the rails.

Toby had bought the boat two years before as a gift to himself after a raise that he didn't feel was big enough. The boat was his consolation prize. It was a thirty-two-foot Wellcraft, an express cruiser, with a wide back deck with comfortable seats that were meant for sunset cruises and cocktails with friends. The bridge controls were off to the right-hand side, a small door on the left. Toby pulled the door open and stared at Naomi. "Go down below."

He knew that anyone in their right mind would be happy to get out of the weather.

Though the rain had stopped, it was still chilly, and Naomi wasn't exactly dressed for being out and about.

Naomi, still crying, walked down the steps and then turned around and faced him. Toby followed, using his body to block her ability to get past him up the narrow steps and down the dock.

"What now, Toby? Why are we here? What are we going to do, have some long discussion on your boat? I don't want to talk. I want to go home."

The words came out just as Toby flipped on the lights. "No. Not exactly."

In a single movement, Toby reached up, grabbed the back of Naomi's hair, gripping it tight to her skull. He felt her neck give way, her face forced upward as he pushed her toward one of the cabins. He shoved her inside, watching her collapse on one of the bunk beds. He stood in the doorway, staring at her. "Maybe if you spend a little time in here thinking, then we can have a discussion."

Naomi started to say something, her eyes red and puffy, her face blotchy. She grabbed at him, but he pushed her away. He could see her lips moving, streams of tears running down her face, but Toby couldn't hear her. The whoosh of blood in his ears was so loud at her rejection that he could barely contain his anger. She was lucky that the worst thing he had done was grab the back of her head.

He slammed the cabin door, grabbing a key from a drawer behind him and locking it.

As Toby turned away, climbing the steps out of the cabin down below, he could hear Naomi screaming and crying for him from inside the boat. He slid the door to the lower deck closed, calmly walked over to the bridge controls and flipped off the power to the boat interior. He watched the lights flicker and then go out.

Stepping off the boat, he looked at it one more time and then walked away.

30

Skye got up the next morning to find a text from Logan. He'd replied quickly the night before when she said she was ready to help him figure out who had killed Ian Dunn. But now, there was another text. "Any chance you could meet me at the station on your way to work? I want to go over a couple of things with you."

Skye closed her eyes and sighed. She'd been planning on going to the pool that morning. If Logan wanted her to stop by the station, she wouldn't have time for her swim. From her laptop in her home office she quickly checked her schedule for the day. As it updated, she noticed that her first counseling session that morning quickly blinked on the calendar and then disappeared. Apparently, her client, a woman named Helena, who had issues with just about everyone, including her husband, her kids, and the people she volunteered with at her church, wasn't coming in.

That was a break.

Other than meeting with Helena, Skye had only been scheduled to work on administrative tasks that morning. As the owner of the counseling center, she didn't take on many clients — at least not as many as she used to — only carrying a load of eight to ten each week. The rest of her days were spent recruiting new counselors and taking care of administrative tasks while her other counselors worked with the patients. How she'd ended up more on the business end of the practice, she wasn't sure. Correct that. She was sure. But that wasn't to say she liked it. She was the boss. She did the job of a boss.

Skye raised her eyebrows. The good news was that it gave her additional flexibility.

Given that Skye wasn't actually due to sit in an office with anyone and help them with their problems until after lunchtime, she quickly typed a text back to Logan, telling him that she could meet him at the office at eight AM. Skye checked her cell phone. It was just after six now. She glanced toward her bedroom door. Her bag of swim gear sat ready to go. "Flexible thinking is healthy," she muttered under her breath as she walked to one of her drawers and pulled out a pair of exercise tights and a tank top, quickly switching out of the leggings and oversized T-shirt she'd slept in.

Skye walked to the kitchen, filled up her water bottle, and made her way into the spare bedroom she used as a home office and exercise room.

Thirty minutes later, after completing an online bike workout that left her drenched, Skye jumped into the shower, quickly rinsed off and then got out, toweling herself dry. She wrapped a robe around her shoulders and twisted a towel over her long brown hair, trying to wring as much of the water out of it as possible.

Making her way into her closet, she chose an outfit for the day after consulting with the weather forecast. Slightly warmer in Highmill, the report read. "Springlike. High of fifty-two and sunny."

"Anything is better than that horrific rain," she muttered to herself, a shudder running through her body as if she was still cold from hiking out in the woods with Logan to find Bella.

Skye pulled a long knit black dress on as well as a pair of thick socks. The high would be fifty-two. It wasn't going to be that warm when she walked out the door, that she could be sure of. She went into the bathroom, quickly dried her hair, twisting it up in a clip and adding the slightest bit of makeup — just a little mascara, a touch of red lipstick , and a coating of concealer under her eyes to mask the black circles that she had accumulated over the last couple of days. She put on her glasses and added a black motorcycle jacket and a pair of thick-soled black boots to her outfit. Skye looked at herself in the mirror. She looked tough. Capable. Hopefully, she'd feel that way throughout her day. It was one of the techniques she talked to her clients about. "If you sit around the house in your sweats and never take a shower, you're going to look horrible. And if you look horrible, you are likely going to feel horrible. And if you feel horrible you are going to end up having to spend more time with me. So do yourself a favor, get dressed, take a shower, and put some real clothes on each day."

For herself and for her clients, she had discovered it had made a world of difference.

At exactly seven-forty, after checking and double checking her work bag to make sure she had everything, tossing in a load of laundry into the washer, and sending a quick text to her practice manager to let her know that she would be in later for her meeting, Skye slipped out of her house and went to her car, getting inside.

She'd been right to wear a warm outfit. While the weather forecast called for temperatures just over fifty later on that afternoon, it certainly didn't feel that way at the moment. Skye shivered as she got in the car, quickly flipping on the seat heater and tapping the console to raise the thermostat.

At seven-fifty-eight, Skye turned into the Highmill Police

Department, seeing an array of vehicles already parked out front. Police work was a twenty-four-seven job. As she slipped out of her car, she noticed a black pickup truck that looked like the one that had been parked at Logan's house the two times she had visited, parked off to the side. A Highmill police cruiser was just leaving the parking lot, the officer inside giving her a glance and then turning toward the road.

Skye pulled the front door open and stopped inside. She hadn't been in the station in a long time. Avoiding Chief Walsh had been one of the better moves she had made. The office still looked the same as the last time Skye had visited, though it had been a couple years — the same dusty plaques hung on the walls in the lobby, the same steel door preventing anyone from making unwanted entry past the lobby. The only difference was that the frosted glass window that used to separate the lobby from the offices and jail, which was reminiscent of her dentist's office when she was a child, had been removed, leaving the reception desk on the other side of the wall open and visible. A young woman with slicked-back black hair tied into a tight bun looked up from where she was working on a computer. Her name badge read Anita Manes. "Can I help you?"

"Skye Johnston here to see Logan Fletcher?"

"Come on in."

The door to Skye's right buzzed as the magnetic lock released. Skye pulled the door open and closed it behind her. She stood still for a second. Just like the lobby, not much had changed at the Highmill Police Department, even though Zara Walsh had been hired to come in and fix it up. As Skye followed the officer working at the reception desk toward the back of the building, Skye looked around her. She couldn't be sure, but perhaps the desks were new? Other than that, the taxpayers of Highmill should be happy that their police department wasn't spending any money on decor.

After following the receptionist toward the back of the building, she stopped in front of a door and pointed. "Here you go."

Skye gave a nod, holding her bag a little more tightly under her shoulder. "Thank you."

Skye peered inside. In front of her, there were two desks shoved together, a large whiteboard hung facing the doorway with printed-off images of people on it and scrawled handwriting. From where she stood, Skye couldn't read the handwriting, but she was relatively sure there was a picture of Ian Dunn hung on the board, one where his face was intact. In the corner of the office, there was a dog bed where Riggs was resting. He jumped up to greet her. Before she could figure out how to keep him away, Riggs was sniffing at her ankle. Satisfied she was a friend, he sat and looked at her with his big brown eyes.

"That's Riggs's version of good morning," Logan said, standing up from the desk.

Skye didn't move, staring at the dog. Riggs looked exactly the same as he had two days before when she'd seen him at Logan's house, save for the fact that he was wearing a thick leather collar around his neck and a vest that covered his back and sides, the white letters "Police" emblazoned on either side of it.

Logan, too, was dressed for work, wearing a black uniform from head to toe. Instead of the normal work pants that the Highmill police officers wore, Logan had on a set of cargo pants, a pair of thick-soled black boots, and a long-sleeved black shirt that had a single button open at the collar. He had on a heavy gun belt, his holster wrapping around his right thigh. Nearby, Skye saw a stiff tactical vest lying on a chair. She stared at it for a second. There seemed to be so many things attached to it that it looked more like a wearable tool chest than anything else.

Logan must have noticed her staring at the tactical vest. "Yeah, I don't wear that thing in the office. It's heavy."

"I can't imagine." Skye looked down. Riggs was still staring at her as if he expected her to offer a pat or a treat. She didn't offer either.

Logan gave a low whistle and then muttered something in a foreign language. Riggs gave her one last glance and then walked quietly away, curling up on his bed.

"What did you say to him?" Skye asked, setting her bag down near the door.

"I told him to go lay down."

"Not in English."

Logan smiled. "You noticed. All of our dogs respond to German commands. Most K9 officers are trained that way. German or Dutch usually. Dutch seemed harder, so I chose German."

Skye had heard about that but had never seen it in practice before. "Was it hard to train him in a foreign language?"

Logan sat down behind his desk, pointing to a chair nearby, inviting her to sit. "Hard? No. Riggs doesn't even know English. He has no idea whether I'm talking to him in English, German or Swahili. As long as I pronounce things consistently, he knows what to do. Still can't speak German though." Logan smiled and looked over his shoulder at the big dog. "We do that so if we're in a situation, someone can't call him off or encourage him to attack. That's reserved for me."

Skye frowned. "Attack?" She knew Riggs was a K9 officer but hadn't really thought through the attack capability he had. Knowing he was trained to bite made her even more leery. She stopped herself. What did she think Riggs was trained to do, carry a plate of cookies? "So." She decided to change the subject before she embarrassed herself any further. "You asked me to stop by. What's going on?"

Logan looked toward his computer and then twisted the

screen toward her. On it, she could see the images from the cave where they'd found Ian Dunn's body the other night. "Yeah. Thanks for coming. I'm glad you're willing to help me on this case."

Skye shrugged a single shoulder. "I'm sure you can handle it by yourself."

Logan arched an eyebrow. "You might be surprised. It's not like we get a lot of murders here in Highmill."

Skye conceded the point. It was one of the attractions of living in Upstate New York. The scenery was gorgeous, the crime rate was low, and the people were, in general, quite friendly. That said, as a psychologist, she knew that people could make bad decisions.

In fact, her entire career was built on helping people get themselves out of bad decisions. Someone had made a decision that was beyond bad when they'd killed Ian Dunn.

"Okay, so here's what we know," Logan said, leaning back in his chair and pointing at the screen, then at the whiteboard. "I've got a dead body on my property that doesn't belong there."

Skye furrowed her eyebrows. She knew that.

He continued. "We have the man's identity — Ian Dunn. We know he was killed elsewhere by the lack of bone and brain matter and blood found at the scene."

Grizzly but true.

"And there is the issue of his clothes."

"What issue?"

"You didn't notice that he wasn't exactly dressed for hiking?"

Skye lifted her chin. "Oh, yeah. That. Of course I noticed. He was dressed like he'd been at a meeting."

Logan nodded as if he was satisfied with her answer. "Correct. Not exactly what you'd be wearing to go out in a major rainstorm in Highmill, except that he was wearing a rain jacket. That says he was prepared to be out and about but not prepared to be in the woods. And then, there's the issue of the spiral fractures." Logan paused for a second and then looked at Skye. "When Dr. Chapman found those, that's when I knew I was going to need some help."

"Why's that?" Skye tilted her head to the side.

"Because people in Highmill don't get spiral fractures."

31

How long Naomi had been asleep, she had absolutely no idea. As she turned over on the bunk, memories began to rise in her mind.

She'd felt the boat wobble in the water as Toby got off. As if that wasn't bad enough, then he'd shut the power off. She'd screamed and yelled, pounding on the cabin door in vain, feeling the boat drift back and forth at its dock.

The cold had come next.

The temperature in Lake Henderson in the early spring was only in the forties, barely high enough to encourage the lake to thaw, nothing like it would be over the next few months as the summer sun warmed up the waters for families that loved to go tubing or people that wanted to water ski. The water was newly freed from its ice. And without the shore power, not only was Naomi in the dark, but she was in the cold.

And she wasn't dressed for it.

Tears streaming down her face, she pulled blankets off of the berth and sat down on the edge of the bed, wearing only the sweatpants, T-shirt and socks she'd had on in bed the night before. She wrapped herself in them, using the edge of the fabric to wipe her nose and her eyes. It was the best she could do without a box of tissues. She felt the boat gently bump against the dock then bump again. A wave of nausea ran over her. When she and Toby had taken the boat out in the summer before, he had tried to tell her that motion sickness was nothing. "It's all in your mind, Naomi," he claimed, looking over his shoulder as she sat on the edge of a seat nearby. That was easy for him to say. He'd been raised on the water. She felt like she was about to lose the very expensive lunch he had just paid for on the other side of the lake right over the edge of the boat.

"Just try to think about something else?"

It was easier said than done.

Now, in the dark, with only a small porthole where she could see outside, the motion was making her violently ill. She tried sitting up, she tried standing, she tried staring out of the small porthole. But in the darkness, her brain couldn't begin to process where the horizon line was. Finally, she laid down on the bed and tried to just take deep breaths.

Toby would come for her soon, wouldn't he?

At some point, hours later, Naomi woke up, a soft glow of light coming in from the porthole. She was still wrapped in the blankets she'd managed to salvage from the bunk beds. They smelled vaguely like mildew and chemicals from being stored all winter. The boat was cold. Not quite cold enough where she could see her breath, but definitely getting there. Naomi sat on the edge of the bed for a moment, trying not to move too quickly, waiting to see if the nausea that had chased her the night before had caught up or had left. She swallowed hard, staring at a single spot on the carpet and then lifting her eyes. For the moment, she was okay, just a bit queasy, but nothing like the night before. Turning slowly, she looked around her. The berth, the verbiage used for a bedroom on a boat, was small, not much bigger than her bathroom at home. It had a single door with walls made out of wood covered in rough fabric, something like burlap. There was a small nightstand next to the lower bunk with a lamp mounted on the wall. Blue carpet covered the floor, hosting a few stains from years past, which was expected on a boat that was a couple of decades old like Toby's was. On the wall in front of her was a picture of a sunset that had been screwed to the surface. Pink and blue patterned drapes covered the single porthole. Naomi peered out of this. From what she could see, it was a bright sunny morning, only the wisps of a few clouds passing by. There wasn't much to see from the tiny window, only a few empty docks off in the distance, a pickup truck driving slowly past them as if checking for any last signs of winter damage. She pounded on the window, yelling. "Help! Help!"

Why she bothered, she didn't know. The pickup truck was entirely too far away. There was no way the driver would hear her or see her waving frantically through the tiny, shadowed window. Frustrated and scared, Naomi plopped down on the edge of the bed. She had to get out. She couldn't just stay there and wait for Toby to come back.

There was no telling when he'd open the door or what kind of mood he'd be in. Naomi didn't want to have to wait to find out. She was cold and hungry.

With the blanket still wrapped around her shoulders, she began rattling at the door again. Then she stopped. She took a deep breath in, trying to keep her composure. Getting hysterical wasn't going to solve the problem. The only thing, she told herself, that would help is if she could get the door open. If she could, then she would be able to escape. From the time she'd spent on the boat with Toby, she knew the hatch to the back deck had a two-way lock, one she could open from either below or from the back deck. Where she would go or what she would do once she got free, she had no idea.

The reality was that none of it mattered unless she could get the door open.

She shook her head and stood back for a second. *Come on, Naomi,* she thought. She knew about construction. She knew how things are built.

That should put her at an advantage, right?

Naomi tried to think through her options. It wasn't as if she could take the door off the hinges. Not only was it locked, but the hinges were on the outside and she didn't have any tools. She pushed at the door tentatively, trying to think of options. The door swung toward her, so she'd be bucking the direction it wanted to go if she kicked at it. She tried a couple times anyway, half-heartedly, the door barely budging. Next, Naomi looked at the lock. Maybe she could take it apart?

After an hour of working at the door, Naomi sat down in a heap on the floor, curling herself up underneath the blanket. All of her moving around had made the boat rock at the dock. She was feeling sick again. She stared at the door in front of her. Would anyone at work even notice she was gone? Or would they be so overly concerned by Ian's death that they thought she had just run off?

Despair clouded over her, shrouding her in a fog that she couldn't see her way out of. She was locked in a cabin on Toby's boat with no way out, held prisoner by a man that just a few months ago she thought she might want to marry.

Was he just going to let her die there?

Naomi felt the bile rise in the back of her throat. Whether it was from the motion of the boat or the reality of the situation she was in, she had no idea.

32

"What's going on in here?"

Skye looked up from where she was seated next to Logan at his desk in time to see Zara Walsh standing in the doorway, her hands on either side of the doorframe, her body blocking the entrance.

Correction — Chief Zara Walsh.

Logan spun his chair towards Zara. "I asked Skye to come in and help me out with some of the details on the case. Figured it'd be okay with you. After all, she's the one that helped find Bella."

Skye looked over at Zara and then looked away, just long enough to see a disapproving glare from her. "Yeah, I suppose it's okay. We'll consider her your informant for the time being."

The way the words, "for the time being" landed didn't sit quite right with Skye. She turned toward Zara and stood up. "Look, if you don't want me here, I'd be more than happy to leave. I have enough issues to deal with without being dragged into this murder investigation."

Zara cocked her head to the side, a few strands of red hair escaping from the messy ponytail her hair was in. "I didn't say that. But if you're feeling uncomfortable, that's something entirely different. After all, police work isn't for everyone. Tough decisions have to be made. We aren't here to make everyone feel good about themselves."

It was a shot across the bow.

Skye wasn't going to take the bait. She'd seen too many people like Zara Walsh and knew exactly how they operated. They'd bait you, trying to get you to snap at whatever they offered and then hold their hands up in mock innocence, leaving the person they had baited swinging on the line. It was a classic passive-aggressive maneuver.

And if Skye knew anything at all about Chief Zara Walsh, it was that she was passive-aggressive.

Zara must have caught herself because she stood a little straighter and took a half a step back. "You're welcome to stay. But you're Logan's responsibility."

With that, Zara disappeared from the doorway, lumbering away. A minute later, Skye heard her barking at another officer about letting the coffee in the bottom of the pot burn.

Logan got up, scowling, and closed the door to the office. Riggs hadn't moved from his position on his dog bed, watching the interaction between the two women like a tennis match, as if he was waiting for Logan to tell him what to do.

There wasn't anything that could be done, at least by Riggs.

Logan sat down at his desk and leaned towards Skye, who was still standing nearby. She had her arms crossed in front of her chest. Things were definitely not good between her and Zara.

"You okay?"

"Yes," Skye said sharply. She didn't want to spend one more minute of her life on Zara Walsh. "Now, why am I here?"

"Oh yeah, that." Logan said it as if the tension between she and Zara had been enough to distract him from Skye's actual purpose for stopping at the office that day.

"Well, I have an order from the judge to go to Ian Dunn's house and poke around. See if I can find any clues as to why this happened and why he was a target. Was wondering if you would like to come along. I could use a profile. Figured his house would give us a good idea about who he is. Maybe even a clue about who would want to blow his head off."

If this was Logan's way of getting Skye out of the office, then she was all for it. Skye picked up her bag and hung it over her shoulder, tugging her jacket into place. "I'm ready when you are."

"I'll drive."

Skye eyed up Riggs. "I can certainly drive myself —"

Logan waved her off. "Don't be silly. Ian Dunn's house is on the other side of town. You'd have to pass the police station on your way back to your office anyway. Let's burn the department's gas."

Skye furrowed her eyebrows. Logan knew where her office was? She paused for a second, realizing it probably wasn't that illogical given the fact that they occasionally had a call from the office, someone who was out of control and needed to be transported to the local hospital or someone who was threatening to kill themselves. In either case, dispatch would send a police officer along with the ambulance in case the person got belligerent. "And what about Riggs?"

Logan raised his eyebrows. "Him? Oh, he rides in the back seat. You can ride up front with me. Don't worry," he said, gathering up a large black duffel bag and sliding into his tactical vest, securing the Velcro straps under each of his arms. "It's perfectly safe. As a matter of fact, there's no place in Highmill you could be safer than in a cruiser with me and Riggs." Logan reached down and scratched the back of Riggs' head as he attached the leash to him. "Isn't that right, boy?"

As Skye followed Logan and Riggs out of the office, she wasn't so sure.

33

In the car on the way over to Ian Dunn's house, Skye found she was sitting quite stiffly, her knees and ankles pressed together, her bag at her feet, her hands folded in her lap. She couldn't have been more prim if she'd been sitting at a lady's tea or in a stuffy church. If Skye had witnessed that body language from one of her patients, she would have quickly assumed that the person felt uncomfortable, defensive even.

Forcing herself to relax, Skye reached into her bag and pulled out a tin of breath mints. She offered one to Logan.

He smiled. "Is my breath bad?"

"No, of course not. I had coffee on the way over," she lied. "Thought maybe I had coffee breath."

Logan stared straight forward. "Seems fine to me."

Skye heard a sniffing from over her shoulder. As she turned to her left, she saw Riggs' black nose pressed up against the metal grate that separated the front and back seat of the cruiser as if he was sniffing for her mints.

"Does he always do that?"

"What?"

"Sniff like that?"

Logan chuckled under his breath. "In case you haven't noticed, Dr. Johnston, Riggs is a dog. Their whole life is sniffing. I read one time that a dog's sense of smell is about a thousand times more sensitive than ours."

Skye let that fact settle in for a second. A thousand times? She couldn't even imagine what he was smelling then. Good thing she had taken a shower after her workout.

"One of the department's dog trainers told me that a dog can smell its owner from seven blocks away. Makes you wonder, doesn't it?"

Skye wasn't sure exactly what to make of that.

The rest of the drive over to Ian Dunn's house, Logan asked Skye a few questions that covered the basics — how long she'd lived in Highmill (the last ten years), how she was feeling about the weather (she liked it a little warmer) and if she had any favorite restaurants (she did, but pretended she didn't).

In return, Skye asked Logan a few questions, carefully darting around the issue of his wife's death a few years before. Overall, Logan seemed friendly and open, but there was a way he gazed off in the distance that spoke of being haunted, of someone who seemed like they'd been through a great deal of trauma.

Skye knew that look. It was one she saw nearly every single day at work.

Luckily for her, before things got too serious, they pulled up in front of what she could only assume was Ian Dunn's house. It was exactly where Logan had said it was — on the outskirts of Highmill, in a development with large homes that she estimated were probably at least three thousand square feet. Logan pulled up in front and threw the car into park. Skye stared at him. "How exactly are we going to get into the house?"

Logan grinned. "This is the fun part. We get to break in."

"And what if he has an alarm system?"

"I already checked. He does."

Skye cleared her throat. "And what if said alarm system goes off?"

Logan slipped out of the car, grabbing Riggs's leash from where it was resting on the console between the two front seats. He leaned back inside. "Well, the alarm company can call the police department all they want, but then, oh yeah, I am the police department. Come on. Let's go, Dr. Johnston. We've got work to do."

Skye spent another few seconds in the car, debating about whether to bring her bag in with her. It seemed strange to leave it in the police cruiser unattended, but then again if someone had the nerve to steal something out of a police cruiser, then they were going to be in for a bigger problem than just taking a few credit cards. From inside, she pulled her phone and stuck it in the pocket of her motorcycle jacket, just in case she needed it.

For what, she had no idea.

By the time Skye got out of the car, Riggs and Logan were already halfway up the walk. She trotted along behind them, tucking her jacket tighter across her frame in the cool morning air. The outfit she had on would be perfect for working in the office but not necessarily for traipsing around outside. At that moment she wished she had grabbed a heavier coat.

When they got to the front door, both Logan and Skye stopped. Logan looked at Riggs, held his hand out and lifted it straight up at which point Riggs sat down. Logan then made his hand look like a stop sign in front of Riggs's face. Riggs didn't move.

"Hand signals?"

"Yep. We use them all the time." Logan fumbled in a pocket of the tactical vest he was wearing. Even with the heavy equipment on, Skye could see the muscles ripple under the sleeves of his shirt. From what Skye could tell, Logan was someone who was probably as committed to his fitness routine as she was. She wondered why he worked out. Every single person she'd ever met that was committed to their fitness fell in one of two camps — either they wanted to function better, or they wanted a way to manage their anxiety. She knew which camp she fit in, but did he?

But that was a question for another time.

It took just a few seconds with a lock pick set for Logan to get the door open. He keyed up the radio that was attached to his shoulder. "Dispatch, one-fifteen."

"One-fifteen, go ahead."

"I'm at the Dunn House. I'm getting ready to open the door. Be ready for the call from the alarm company. You can advise them I'm on scene with a court order."

"Copy that one-fifteen."

Logan looked at her, his eyes bright. He looked like he was having fun. "Ready?"

For what exactly, she wasn't sure. "Yup."

Logan pushed the door open. The alarm panel began to buzz at the side door. Logan popped the cover off, pulled a set of wire snips from an invisible pocket in his vest and began snipping at random wires as the alarm started to blare. When there was one wire left, he snipped it. The panel finally went dark and the alarm went silent. He shook his head. "It's always the last one."

Pocketing the tool, he tightened up his hold on Riggs's leash and then gave him the command to sit. Bending over, Logan unclipped the leash from Riggs's collar. Skye watched as the dog tensed. Logan reached for his gun, drawing it out of the holster and holding it low. A shiver ran down her back. What was he doing? Why was he drawing his gun? And if he was, why was she in the house with him and not safely in the cruiser?

As another shiver ran down her spine, Logan looked at her.

"We need to do a quick search just to make sure there's nobody hiding in here. Stay put."

Skye stood frozen near the door. She was suddenly feeling nervous at being in the house of someone who had been murdered, even though she had a trained police officer and his dog with her. They were going to leave her at the door? What if the murderer was hiding in the house?

Logan looked down at Riggs, muttered something that Skye couldn't understand and watched as the powerful dog took off, his head low, his ears forward. She could hear the scrape of his toenails on the tile floor, panting coming out of his mouth.

Logan walked forward about ten feet and stopped, listening.

At least Skye wasn't alone.

It was less than a minute later when Riggs reappeared. He ran right for Logan and sat, turning himself and facing the same direction as Logan was facing. Logan bent over, praising his dog and scratching him behind the ears. Logan turned towards Skye. "All clear."

Skye didn't move. "How do you know?"

"Because Riggs just told me."

Skye shook her head. "What?"

Logan shrugged. "It's all about the training, Skye. If Riggs had come back and laid down in front of me, I would know there was something I needed to look at. But if he comes back and sits next to me, then he's telling me that everything is fine. There are no moving targets in this house. Nothing we need to be concerned about."

"Okay. If you say so."

Logan continued. "Believe me, if there was a person in this house, he would have smelled them already."

"If you think so." She shrugged, "Oh yeah, the nose thing."

"Yup, the nose thing." Logan holstered his gun and looked at Skye. "Alright, now it's your turn to do your thing. I'm gonna have a look around the house too. I'm gonna have Riggs follow you. Just ignore him."

Skye frowned. "Are you concerned about something?"

"No, but having a one-hundred-fifty-pound German Shepherd on your heels should make you feel more confident that you're safe, and he needs to practice his follow command. So, do me a favor and just go about your profiling business and ignore him." Skye didn't like it. She still was leery about the big dog, but she agreed. "Okay."

"Meet you back here in five?"

"Sure."

Skye stood, her arms crossed in front of her chest. Whether that was because she was cold or because she was concerned about Riggs nipping at her fingers as she walked, she couldn't tell in that moment.

Both, maybe?

Skye sucked in a deep breath. If she was hoping to figure out anything at all, she needed to ignore the fact that Riggs was behind her. She needed to relax. It wasn't that she had a problem with dogs in general, just one in particular. When Skye was a kid, a German Shepherd named Boomer had escaped and managed to bite her sister Christy right through the nostril. Ever since then, Skye had been leery. No permanent damage had been done to her sister. Once she was a teenager, Christy, against the wishes of their parents, decided to have her nose pierced to cover up the scar. Skye hadn't cared about the nose ring, but it had led to a weeklong battle between her parents and Christy.

It was one of the many wonderful memories Skye had of her sister.

Skye pushed the thought away. The last thing she needed to do was have her judgment clouded by thinking about her own family issues. Something horrible had happened to Ian Dunn, something that represented a deep well of anger. That she knew for sure. Thinking back to the crime scene from a few nights before, all Skye could think about was the violence with which Ian Dunn had died. Whoever had killed him was experiencing focused rage in a way that Skye wasn't sure she had ever seen before. Multiple shots to the face spoke of someone so angry they wanted the other person to disappear. And the spiral fractures that the coroner had found spoke of force.

There was no doubt about it, whoever had killed Ian Dunn was angry. Now the question was, was the murderer angry at Ian specifically, or was Ian's murder just a crime of convenience?

Skye knew that was part of the reason they were at Ian Dunn's house. Logan was right. It would be helpful to get to know Ian a little bit better. There was no better way to do that than to search someone's private space.

Logan had disappeared. Skye looked around. She was alone in the small foyer in the front of the house. It was time to get moving and she took a few tentative steps forward, hearing the click of Riggs's nails on the tile. She did as Logan asked, ignoring the fact that there was a police dog on her heels.

Through a doorway on the right there was an office with a desk and built in bookcases, the kind that looked custom, not the kind that Ian Dunn would have purchased at a store like Ikea and put together himself. On the shelves were a myriad of books and awards, the subjects ranging from construction management and pricing to business management techniques and even an entire shelf on presidents, biographies on everyone from Washington to Eisenhower to Bill Clinton. Skye cocked her head to the side, thinking. Part of her wanted to start opening his desk drawers, but part of her didn't want to intrude on the privacy of the dead, not to mention that she didn't necessarily want to get caught up in the finer details of Ian's life. Logan had asked her for a profile, not necessarily anything deeper than that.

As she was walking out of the office, Logan appeared from around a corner. He pulled a dog treat from a pocket on the side of his pant leg and handed it to Riggs, who gobbled it down quickly. "Just checking in on you. This isn't the crime scene."

"How do you know?" Skye asked as he walked off, restating his command to Riggs to follow Skye.

"No blood, no guts," he called over his shoulder.

Skye rolled her eyes. "Of course. Silly me. How did I not think of that?"

The tap of Riggs's toenail continued to follow her as Skye made her way into the dining room, flipping on the light. Just like the office, there was nothing of interest there, just a long wooden table with matching chairs, the surface containing nothing but a thin film of dust. It hadn't been used in a while. Did that mean that Ian didn't entertain at home, that he didn't care much about the condition of his house?"

Skye wasn't sure.

Continuing to walk, she discovered the rest of the first floor contained a kitchen and a family room. Skye spent a considerable amount of time in each of them, flipping through Ian's mail, which contained no bills — she assumed he paid those online — a few trade magazines, including *Professional Builder* and *American Construction Trends*.

Pulling the door of the refrigerator open, she noticed that Ian had recently purchased food. This wasn't someone who was thinking their life was just about to end. There was a bag of oranges, a gallon of unopened milk, a six-pack of chocolate pudding cups, two bags of salad, and three individual bags of different kinds of lunch meat. Skye chewed the inside of her lip. This was someone who wasn't making gourmet meals at home. This was someone who was running in, grabbing a quick snack before bed and then hitting it, trying to be ready for the challenges of the next day.

Typical bachelor behavior.

After finishing her tour of the first floor, Skye walked upstairs, hearing Riggs still on her tail and doing her best to ignore him. The upstairs of Ian Dunn's house contained four bedrooms and three full bathrooms, one of them an en suite attached to the master bedroom, one located off the hallway and the final one perched between two bedrooms.

Taking a quick glance into the three bedrooms, she noted that two of them were completely empty, the third having a short stack of boxes — probably no more than a half a dozen — jammed up against one wall. The empty bedrooms gave the house the feel of someone who had just moved in or someone who was just about to move out.

At the end of the hallway was the master suite. Skye walked in, half expecting it to be nothing more than a sheet and a thin blanket tossed onto a mattress. Ian Dunn didn't seem like someone who spent much time at home. The house itself was nice, and she could tell it was well constructed, but it wasn't lived in. It was a house, not a home.

The bedroom didn't reveal much more than the fact that she had underestimated Ian Dunn's need for comfort. There was a king-sized bed with a mahogany headboard pushed up against the long wall of the bedroom, matching nightstands with two heavy ceramic lamps perched on each of them. There was a stack of books on one of the nightstands next to a bottle of water that had been capped after being half consumed.

The bed itself, covered in a dark gray comforter, had been made, the pillows neatly stacked. "So, Ian, you weren't here much, but when you were, you liked to be neat," Skye muttered under her breath.

Skye turned to the closet, finding Ian's clothes hung, but not in any particular order. The dirty ones were tossed into a hamper at one end.

Shaking her head, Skye walked down the steps, Riggs still

on her heels. She ran into Logan at the bottom who was waiting for her in the foyer. She shook her head. "I'm sorry to say, but there's not a lot here. Looks like he was either just moving in or just moving out."

Logan raised his eyebrows. "Did you go in the basement yet?"

"No."

He grinned. "You gotta see it."

34

Logan waved for Skye to follow him down to Ian Dunn's basement. The lights were all on. He had already gone through it once. What he saw, in his mind, was telling. He glanced over his shoulder, watching Skye make her way down the steps, Riggs still on her heels. He made a mental note to reward Riggs. His follow command was coming along well. He wasn't sure what he would use it for. But it might come in handy someday. He glanced over his shoulder. "Wait 'till you see this. It's like the bat cave down here."

Skye scowled. "What do you mean?" She had barely gotten the words out of her mouth when he heard her suck in a breath. "Oh."

Logan stood and took in the basement one more time. He guessed that Skye had noticed exactly the same thing that he had — the main floor of Ian's house was sparsely furnished, if at all. It looked like he was hardly ever there, as though he was either in the process of moving in or moving out. The basement, though, was something completely different.

On his initial walkthrough, Logan had discovered three main areas to the basement. The first one was pretty standard

— a place for the mechanicals — the furnace, hot water tank, things like that. The second area was a workout room outfitted with two flat screen monitors on the walls and pretty much every piece of gym equipment someone could need to work out at home with, including a set of weights, mirrored walls, padded floors, a treadmill, an elliptical, and a bench press set up. The third area was a home office, but it was very different than the office that was upstairs. There was a set of built-in bookshelves that looked identical to the ones that were upstairs and an enormous custom-made desk, at least fifteen feet long, built into one of the walls. A rectangular box had been constructed to match the desk. The top end of it was open, with what looked like a dozen rolls of blueprints standing upright inside. The desk itself was littered with papers and supplier catalogs, a large desktop computer at the corner with an oversized monitor that had a screensaver that showed what Logan guessed were some of the Pearce Construction projects alternating with their logo.

"Well, this looks a little different than his office upstairs now, doesn't it?" Skye stood in the doorway, her arms crossed in front of her chest, a frown on her face.

"What do you think?"

Skye sucked in a breath. "I'm not sure." She looked over her shoulder. "This is very strange to me. Ian has clearly invested a ton of money in his basement. He's a bachelor. Why not put all this stuff on the first floor?"

Logan shrugged. "Maybe he didn't have enough space to do what he wanted to?"

"No. I don't think that's it." With that, Skye wandered away.

Logan walked past the cluttered desk that had belonged to Ian and stared at the paperwork on it. There were printouts of requisitions for construction materials — everything from structural steel to bricks to an order for fifty thousand drywall screws to be delivered to a job site. Logan pulled open the drawers on the desk and was into the third one before he found anything interesting. "Hey, Skye, take a look at this," Logan yelled to her.

She appeared in the doorway a second later. "What did you find?"

"I'm not exactly sure." Logan handed the stack of papers he'd found at the back of the drawer to Skye.

She set them down on the edge of the desk, pulled the rubber band off and started flipping through them. "They're all notes and cards written in the last month."

"What do they say?"

"Not much, to be honest. 'We shouldn't do this.' It's signed with a heart."

Logan watched Skye. Her voice sounded strange, as if she had put something together. "What is it?"

"It's just that I can't say."

"You can't say?" Logan scowled.

"I heard something at work, but it's covered by client privilege."

Logan closed his eyes for a second, taking a deep breath. This case was frustrating enough. Now Skye was saying that she had no way to help him, even though she could? Why was she here then? Logan tried another tactic. "Okay, let's talk hypothetically."

Skye's face brightened. "I can do that, hypothetically, of course."

"Great. So, hypothetically, is it possible that Ian was having a relationship that maybe he shouldn't have then?" He started with a softball, an easy question, hoping that would get Skye talking.

"Yes. Given the evidence here, that's not hypothetical. If someone sends a note saying, 'We shouldn't be doing this,' that's a pretty good indication something is going on."

"All right, so, we have Ian involved with someone he shouldn't be involved with."

"Yes."

"Anything else you can tell me?"

"Hypothetically speaking?" Skye cocked her head to the side.

"Of course."

"Well, I can say that work romances can cause lots of problems. I can say that in general as well. I've seen that over and over again in my practice. There are issues when people try to transition from being work colleagues to romantic partners."

Logan smiled. He pulled his phone from his back pocket, pulled up the website from Pearce Construction and looked at their "about us" page. There were loads of young women listed on the page, ones that a guy like Ian Dunn might be in a relationship with. Even though he'd just met Skye, he could tell that she was the kind of woman who wouldn't violate her work boundaries. She was held to a code of conduct, just like he was. As much as Logan wanted to demand that she tell him, he knew it wasn't fair. Even more so, it wasn't legal.

Logan put his phone back in his pants pocket and looked around. He hooked his thumbs into the top of his tactical vest and looked at Skye. "All right. What do we know?" It was driving him crazy how slowly and methodically she worked, but then again, she was the one who had figured out where Bella was hiding. Maybe she would also be the one that could help lead him to figuring out who killed Ian Dunn. How exactly his relationship with a coworker was related, he wasn't sure. The only thing he could assume at this point was that whoever he had been involved with was one of Skye's clients.

Skye's voice interrupted his thoughts. "Well, what we know is that Ian is the kind of guy who likes to keep things quiet. He's a mover and a shaker but not the kind of guy who's going to show it."

"As evidenced by the sparse décor upstairs and the extensive work done here?"

"Yeah. People's environments are really telling when it comes to their psychological profile and status. For instance, I have clients who have been able to solve many of the problems with their anxiety by decluttering their house. Streamlining and simplifying a physical environment did exactly the same for their mental and emotional state. The brain is weird that way."

"And you're seeing the same kind of phenomenon here."

"Yeah. What I don't know is if it is secretive on Ian's part, or was," she corrected herself. "Or if he had another reason for keeping his personal space in the basement — for instance, he's in construction, so maybe he's worried about resale value, or perhaps he was in a serious relationship when he purchased the house. I'd imagine that the woman he was with would furnish and decorate the main floors, so maybe he kept all of his stuff in the basement."

"Like a man cave?"

Skye nodded. "Yeah, for lack of a better phrase. It is strange that he kept those personal notes bound up and hidden in the back of a drawer, especially given the fact it's in his basement. From the looks of it, he didn't do much entertaining, but even if he did, it's not like they were out on the kitchen counter for someone to see. He intentionally kept them but hid them in a random drawer in his basement."

Logan paused. He hadn't thought about it that way.

Skye looked at him, her face getting more serious. "But none of this tells us exactly why he was killed or where, does it?"

"No, it doesn't. Not even close."

35

Skye sat in her car for a minute, her hands gripping the steering wheel. Logan had just dropped her off at her car. She was still sitting in the police parking lot after going to Ian Dunn's house. Guilt nipped at her heels. She had said a lot of things hypothetically to Logan. She was only trying to help out, but the idea that she may have broken any of her client's confidences ate away at her like acid on metal.

As she was saying goodbye to Logan, she looked back at him. He had gentle eyes, she realized, despite all that he had been through with his first wife. Part of her desperately wanted to help him, not only to solve Ian Dunn's murder but to find joy again in his own life.

She looked at him, trying to distract herself from the rush of feelings she was having. "One more hypothetical issue to consider."

Logan grinned as if he was amused by their hypothetical conversation. "And what would that be? Hypothetically speaking, of course."

Skye fought off the urge to sigh. What had seemed funny a second ago now seemed old and stale, like watching two middle schoolers repeat the same joke over and over again to each other. "If there was a third party involved, that could make things very complicated."

Logan frowned, as if he was trying to put together the pieces. "Another person? Like a love triangle? Like one of them was already in a relationship?"

"It's just something to consider." Skye shut the cruiser door before Logan could ask her any other questions and walked away. Thinking about it as she sat in her car, her gut lurched. She felt some responsibility for Naomi. She had never met her boyfriend Toby, but just the stories about him scared her. He seemed demanding, unrelenting, as if he wanted something from Naomi. Actually, it wasn't a part of Naomi he wanted. The way Naomi told it, Toby wanted all of her. A month before, Naomi had told Skye about a date night Toby had put together. Toby had curated the entire experience — down to exactly what Naomi had to wear. When she showed up without the jewelry he'd chosen to go with her dress, he'd sulked.

Talk about controlling.

Skye sniffed as she drove to her office, trying to ignore the fear nipping at her gut for Naomi. Skye knew a thing or two about possessive men. It never ended well, that was for sure. Once Skye got settled in at work, her routine took over. She still felt a nag of frustration and guilt nipping at her heels, but she pushed it away. She hadn't revealed any information she shouldn't have to Logan, she decided. She had only tried to help set him on the right track to figure out who had brutally murdered Ian Dunn. There was no point in feeling bad about it. It was over.

She needed to let it go.

The first two hours at work Skye spent going over financials, interviewing a new potential therapist to add to the practice over a video conference, having a short conversation with her office manager and then a more lengthy one with her accountant.

Starved, Skye ordered food out for lunch and had it delivered to the office. She had left in a hurry that morning on her way to meet Logan and hadn't bothered to pack anything. Twenty minutes later, a delivery person from the sandwich shop down the street brought her a salad and a wrap sandwich. She picked at it for a few minutes, tugging a couple of pieces of turkey and bacon out of the wrap and taking a couple bites of soggy lettuce, then tossing the whole lot of it into the trash.

Stopping in the bathroom, she washed her hands, reapplied her lipstick, and went out to the front desk to collect the file for her next client. Her gut clenched. It was for Naomi. Skye cocked her head to the side, wondering why Naomi was back on her schedule. Hadn't Skye just seen her?

"Maria, why is Naomi back? She was here yesterday."

Maria, Skye's office manager, a short woman with dark hair and a round face, blinked. "She's in some sort of crisis. Said she needed to get in to see you. Hope that's okay?"

"Yes, of course."

"I'm not sure if she's here yet."

"I'll check."

Clients were forever adding sessions when they had a crisis. If Skye had to guess, she had found out about Ian Dunn after their last session and was grieving. It was a fair response in Skye's mind.

Skye walked down the hallway, expecting to see the door closed as if Naomi was already there. She always was. Since they started working together two years before, Naomi had never missed a session, had never canceled, had never rescheduled, and was never late. She was the ideal client in terms of showing up. Getting her to make changes in her life had been a different story, though.

Just as she sat down in the chair to wait for Naomi to arrive

— Skye realized she was a couple of minutes ahead of schedule — she heard her phone buzz in her pocket. She pulled it out and stared at it. Christy again. What did her sister need? The answer was the same as always. Nothing. She was just coming to cause havoc in Skye's life, just like the last time when Christy had wanted Skye to invest in a business Christy wanted to start.

There was no way Skye wanted to be tied to Christy. Not in a relationship and not in business.

Skye rejected the call, a lump forming in her throat. Two calls in a short duration could only mean one thing — Christy needed something, and she was out to try to extract another pint of blood out of Skye, as if she hadn't done enough damage already. Years of her demanding behavior made Skye wonder if their parents had died from a stress-induced illness. If Christy's behavior hadn't caused their deaths, it had certainly contributed to them.

Skye stared up at the ceiling as Maria walked by carrying a sheaf of files in her arms.

"Are you okay?" she asked.

"Christy is calling again."

"Are you kidding?"

A few of the employees of her practice who had been there for long enough knew that Skye had ongoing issues with her sister. Most of them did not. But Maria, who had been one of Skye's original employees, had lived through the nightmare with Christy appearing in Skye's life more than once. Maria waved it off. "Ignore her, Skye. You know no good is going to come from whatever it is she wants." She quickly stopped, correcting herself. "I mean, I don't want to decide for you, but —"

Skye nodded. "I know, Maria. Believe me, I know." Skye stared at her lap for a second, waiting for her phone to ping to let her know there was a voicemail. It didn't come. She wasn't sure if that was good news or bad news. Frowning, Skye looked up. "Hey, did Naomi Fraser call?"

"No, why?"

"She's always on time and she's not here."

Maria shook her head. "I don't know. I don't remember that she called to cancel. But let me go check the system again. Maybe she made a change online and it didn't come through to the scheduler? That darn thing. Trying to get it to cooperate..." Maria muttered as she walked away.

A second later, she was back. "Sorry, no info from Naomi. I checked the messages. There's nothing from her. She should have been here by now."

Skye sat holding her file in her hands and sucked in a deep breath. Was it just coincidence that Naomi hadn't shown up today after her boyfriend had been murdered? Skye's stomach lurched, a wave of bile surging and burning the back of her throat.

Or was it something else?

36

Logan, after their visit to Ian Dunn's house, dropped off Skye at her car and took Riggs into the police station. As soon as they were inside, Logan let him off his leash, refilled his bowl of water and gave him a couple scoops of food and a toy to chew on.

Logan sat down at this desk, thinking about what he'd found at Ian Dunn's house. It felt like something and nothing all at the same time. But then again, Skye had left him with a clue that he hadn't considered when she left the car. He stared at the images taped to the whiteboard, wondering how much Dr. Skye Johnston knew about these people that were involved in Ian Dunn's murder, or at least he wondered if they were.

The comment about a love triangle she made when she left was the most cryptic of all.

Sure, the idea that Ian was having a work romance was natural. People who worked together often developed feelings for each other. It had happened more than once at Highmill PD. Highmill wasn't exactly a large town. It could be hard to find someone to be in a relationship with. Who Ian Dunn had been involved with was still a mystery. The notes hinted to a work romance, but that could be a long list. Pearce was a big company and employed lots of people not only within its walls, but also with their contractors.

Logan pulled out his phone, looking at some pictures he'd taken of Ian's schedule. The computer in the basement hadn't been secured by a password, so he didn't need a court order to access it. Ian's online calendar had been there, front and center. Logan reviewed the last few months of dates on the calendar, looking for anything suspicious. There were no indications that he was in a relationship. Nothing really repeated on the calendar except for a networking luncheon every Tuesday afternoon. From the looks of it, unless it was just a placeholder appointment, it seemed like it was something that Ian did on the regular.

Logan quickly typed in the name of the networking group and pulled up their website from his desk at the station. The description was predicably inflated — "For executives wanting to build relationships in the community and next level their careers," the copy on the first page read. There was a man listed as the contact — Jerry Witnisky, the owner of an IT firm in the area.

Logan checked his watch. If he left now, he and Riggs could make the meeting or at least, the end of it. If Ian Dunn had been a regular, maybe Jerry, or someone else that was there, would know something about Ian and what he had been up to.

Five minutes later, after letting Zara know that he was headed out to see if he could find more evidence on Ian's murder, he headed out to the SUV, loading Riggs in the back of the SUV. Zara had always been good to him, but there was clearly still tension between her and Skye. Tension so thick that it could be cut with a proverbial knife. Skye had told him about her client and how she'd died. Her concerns had made sense, but he knew Zara operated in a way that was pretty black and white.

Logan cracked his neck as he drove. Whatever the ongoing problem was between Zara and Skye, he would deal with it later.

Then again, thinking about it, he wasn't sure that whatever problem there was between Zara and Skye was any of his business.

Arriving at an unmarked office building a few minutes later, Logan looked around. There were probably two dozen cars in the parking lot. How many of those were for the networking event and how many belonged to people who worked in the building, he had no idea. Logan pulled the cruiser into a reserved spot at the front of the building, grabbed Riggs's leash and clipped it onto the K9's neck before they went inside.

Logan paused at the front door and glanced back at the cruiser. He could have left Riggs in the car and gone in by himself, but not only was it good training for Riggs to be in a variety of new situations every single day, but it was also Logan's job. Riggs was Logan's partner. Logan was responsible for Riggs, and conversely, Riggs was also responsible for Logan.

At that moment, Logan was glad to have a partner he could depend on.

Inside of the office building, the lobby was empty, the heat from the furnace blowing right near the door as if it could keep the chilly spring air out. All it was doing was making the lobby steamy.

Logan looked around. Staring down a hallway, he noted a sign posted at the doorway to an open room just ahead of him. He could hear voices coming from that direction, a bit of laughter, and then saw a few people start to straggle out of the room, walking in pairs. The first two people walked past him, quickly made eye contact, and then moved to the other side of the doorway at the sight of the big German Sheperd with him. Logan walked toward the open door, seeing a sign on a placard outside that read "Executive Networking Event Here!"

Logan grimaced. Sounded like fun.

When Logan looked inside, there were a few people milling about in pairs or threesomes, chatting and talking, passing out business cards or typing things on their phones, a few smiles and handshakes all around. As soon as they noticed Logan, the tone in the room changed, as if they had just noticed a giant storm cloud on the horizon and needed to run for cover. It was nothing new. The arrival of law enforcement could cool a room like nothing else.

Within about a minute, the conversations had ended and the room had mostly cleared out, except for two people still standing and talking near the front of the room.

Logan recognized one of the men, the bald guy from the website named Jerry. "Are you Jerry Witnisky?"

Jerry turned and looked at Logan. "Ah, Officer. You're here to do some networking? If you are, I'm sorry. You just missed the event. We'll be here next week, though, if you would like to join us."

Who did this guy think he was? Officers didn't network at corporate events. "Not exactly," Logan answered dryly. "I have a few questions for you."

The woman standing next to Jerry was wearing a burgundy suit. She was dressed as if she was a lawyer or an accountant or something else. Logan's stomach tightened. He could only hope she wasn't an attorney. This wasn't a formal inquiry, just some casual questions, but lawyers had a tendency to make things way more complicated than they needed to be. "And who are you?" Logan asked.

"Me?" the woman pointed at herself.

Definitely not an attorney.

"I'm Beth Truby. I own Truby Insurance Services. You might have heard of us?"

"As a matter of fact, I have," Logan lied. "Nice to meet you."

Jerry stepped forward. "Well, what can we do for you, Officer?"

"Fletcher. Logan Fletcher."

"And who's this?" Jerry pointed at Riggs.

"This is my partner, Riggs." Riggs had taken up a position resting at Logan's feet.

"He seems very well-trained," Beth quipped.

Logan tried not to laugh. Did she think that they'd put a Kevlar vest on just any dog and call them a K9? If she only knew. "Do either of you know a man by the name of Ian Dunn?"

"With Pearce? Yeah, of course," Jerry responded quickly. "He's here every single week." Jerry cocked his head to the side. "As a matter of fact, this is the first time in a long time I haven't seen him."

Logan pulled a notebook out of a pocket in his vest. Apparently, word hadn't leaked out yet about Ian's death. That was good. That worked in Logan's favor. "I was just curious about the people that he hung around with when he was here. You said he was here every single week?"

"Yeah, but like I said, not today. I hope he's okay." It was clear by the hopeful expression Jerry was fishing.

It wasn't Logan's story to tell, so he ignored the comment and asked another question. "Can you tell me, is there anyone he was close to when he came to these meetings?"

"Close to? You mean like people he talked to on a regular basis?"

Logan instantly felt irritation at Jerry's subtle corrections, as if he hadn't used the right language for the networkers. "Yeah, you know, like colleagues, work associates?"

Beth blinked and then looked at Logan. "Well, there's always at least Ian and usually somebody else here from Pearce. It was usually Naomi Fraser. But then again, I didn't see her today either. Maybe they had a meeting or training or something. Pearce is pretty intense, from what I heard."

Logan felt his stomach lurch. Naomi Fraser. Jerry had just identified a female from Pearce Construction that Ian was at least friendly with. That was something.

Jerry continued. "Yeah, it always seemed like Ian and Naomi got along really well. Nice to see it. Work colleagues don't always get along that well. I know I saw them talking to that same guy every week. I can't ever remember this name."

"Toby Graham," Beth finished.

Jerry snapped his fingers. "Yeah. That's it. Toby Graham. He's an architect in the area. Kinda uptight and hot-headed, I think, but I don't know him well. They usually all sit together since they're in the same industry. I know Toby's firm and Pearce have worked together on a bunch of projects. Makes sense if you think about it. Toby draws up the project. Ian and Naomi build it. It's a natural pairing. That's what this group is all about."

Beth raised her eyebrows, staring at Jerry. "But you know that Toby and Naomi have been dating for like six months, don't you, Jerry?"

Jerry's mouth opened. "What? Are you kidding? How did I miss that?"

Beth hung her head as if she was embarrassed for him. "Jerry is very smart about business, but when it comes to relationships, not so much. We had a couple of guys nearly get into a brawl here about six months ago over a client they were both competing for. Got pretty ugly. Haven't seen either of them since."

Jerry chuckled. "That was probably for the best. You know, people get a little crazy when it comes to money. Me, I'm just all about people getting together and helping each other out."

Logan let Jerry ramble for a second, taking notes, then he interrupted. "So, just to make sure I have this correct, Ian hung around with Naomi, who he worked with, and a guy named Toby Graham, who is an architect. Anybody else you can think of?"

Jerry shrugged. "Well, Ian and I have had coffee a couple of times. His firm is thinking about installing a new software system that would be custom code. That's what my firm does so we've met. He also hangs out with another guy here." Jerry looked down at the ground for a second. "Yeah, his name is Jesse McLane. He's a restaurant guy. They own restaurants all over the country but are based here in Highmill. I know Ian has spent a bunch of time with him too. I think they were getting ready to start construction on a project for Jesse's company, but I can't be sure." Jerry threw his hands in the air. "Listen, my job is to provide the place for the introductions to be had. Whatever business happens after that is up to them."

Logan looked up at Jerry and Beth. "Thanks. The two of you have been very helpful."

As Logan walked away with Riggs at his side, he could only wonder if one of those introductions had managed to get Ian killed.

37

Skye was sitting at her desk, still frustrated by the fact that Naomi hadn't bothered to show up or call that afternoon, working her way through updating patient files when the phone rang.

Logan.

"Hey. What's going on?" From the noise in the background, Skye could tell that he was driving.

"You have time to take a ride with me?"

"A ride?"

"Yeah. I did a lot of digging in the last couple of hours and found a connection between Ian Dunn and a gal named Naomi Fraser. According to my source, she works for Pearce too. But she has a boyfriend. It's a guy named Toby Graham."

As the words came out of his mouth, Skye mouthed the name at the same time. She gave a nod. Good. He figured it out, so she didn't have to connect the dots. "How did you figure this out?"

"I went to a networking event — it was one of the few things that I found on Ian's calendar that was a recurring event. I talked with the guy that runs it."

Skye cocked her head to the side. "I didn't know you accessed Ian's calendar?"

Logan chuckled. "I can't let you in on all my secrets. Grabbed a few images of it from his computer while we were at his house. Anyways, the guy that runs the event, Jerry Witnisky, and this other woman named Beth Truby spilled the beans. They said that this Toby Graham, who's an architect in the area, he's been dating Naomi for about six months. But the thing is, they told me he's a little hot-headed, on the temperamental side." Logan paused for a second. "And guess who else goes to that same networking event."

"Ian Dunn."

"How did you know?"

"Because you said you accessed Ian's calendar."

"Oh, yeah. That. So, anyway, I ran all of their financials looking for overlap. I found out that Toby recently rented a hotel room."

"Well, if he was involved with Naomi, then maybe that makes sense. Maybe they were meeting for some sort of romantic retreat." Skye shook her head. Naomi hadn't said anything to her about that actually being the case, but it was a likely explanation. Clients didn't often tell their therapists everything, especially if they felt the therapist wouldn't approve. It wasn't actually Skye's job to approve or disapprove decisions people made in their lives, but people didn't always understand that.

"Well, that remains to be seen. Like I said, you want to take a ride with me and Riggs?"

"I guess." Skye looked at her desk, which was covered in stacks of papers that needed to get done. Her last two clients of the day had rescheduled — both of them had sick kids. What she should have done was hunker down in her office, get ahead of her paperwork so she could go home and have a quiet evening. "I can maybe drive over to the station in an hour or so?"

"I'm in your parking lot right now."

Skye stopped. It was a little presumptuous of Logan to think that she would be available and willing to go on another wild goose chase with him.

"I don't know. I —"

"Come on, Skye. Highmill doesn't have a detective unit. I don't have anyone else to help me on this case except for you and Riggs."

Skye found that strange. What was he talking about? "What do you mean you don't have anyone else? You have a whole department filled with trained officers."

"Well, it's not that I don't have *anyone* else. It's just that everyone else has their own work to do. Zara gave me the case and she expects me to solve it pretty much on my own. If I want to become the next official detective for Highmill, then I've got to do it on my own."

All of a sudden, the pieces fit together. Logan was being tested. Skye frowned. It was very Zara-like to put Logan in this position. In her opinion, it was almost cruel, given the fact that Logan was probably still grieving the loss of his wife. It had only been a couple of years. Grief took a lot out of people and took a long time to heal from. But then again, Zara was a cold customer.

"All right. I will be right down."

"Thanks."

After updating Maria at the front desk about what was going on, Skye grabbed her bag and ran downstairs. Their offices were on the third floor, so she tried to take the steps as much as possible. Given all the sitting she did every single day, the extra exercise was helpful.

As she emerged from the building, Logan stepped out of the car and smiled. "Your chariot awaits, ma'am."

Skye tried not to laugh. She was surprised. Logan was corny. She couldn't decide if it was irritating or endearing. As soon as she got into the car, she saw Riggs's black nose pressed up against the screen as if he was giving her a hello in the form of a sniff. Logan looked over at Skye and then at Riggs as he fastened his seatbelt. "He's glad to see you."

"How can you tell?" Skye grumbled.

"I don't know. I just can." He shrugged.

Skye stared at him for a moment and then looked away.

Eighteen minutes later, after a brief ride on the freeway, Logan pulled into a hotel that was on the outskirts of Highmill. Given the proximity to Henderson Lake, it was aptly called the Henderson Lake Hotel. Skye leaned forward and stared at the building. It was a two-floor building with exterior entrances and a flat roof. "This doesn't exactly look like the place for a romantic retreat."

Logan raised his eyebrows. "I was just thinking the same thing."

Skye got out of the car, the tension gathering in her shoulders. Logan met her in front of the vehicle, Riggs on his leash. It was hard not to notice that Logan had a tight grip on the dog. Logan's body language let her know that he was concerned about what they were about to find.

"Let's go to the office first. We can get a passkey once we figure out what room Toby rented."

Skye nodded but didn't say anything, tugging her jacket tighter around her body as she followed Logan and Riggs. Every few steps, Riggs checked behind him to make sure she was still there.

The lobby of the Henderson Lake Hotel was as outdated or more so than Skye expected. There were faded dark-green couches in the lobby along with a dusty ceiling fan that was circling lazily, even though the air circulation probably wasn't needed given the cool outdoor temperatures. The fans looked like something that someone had turned on years before and simply had forgotten to turn off or it had been so long no one could find the switch. There was a reception desk to the right, an older guy with flyaway hair sitting behind it, playing a book of Sudoku puzzles. "Can I help you?" he asked, sounding bored.

"I'm here to check a room that someone may have rented."

He seemed to barely notice the fact that Logan was in uniform and had Riggs with him. "What's the name?"

"Toby Graham."

The man put down the book of puzzles, sticking his pencil in the crease so he didn't lose his place and turned to the computer system. From the size of the monitor, Skye guessed the machine was at least a decade old. The man behind the desk shook the mouse and grunted. When it didn't wake up as fast as he wanted it to, he gave the monitor a slap. "Darn thing is on the fritz again." He coughed. "Keep telling the owners we need a new system, but they don't listen to me. Haven't for the last fifteen years. Not sure even why I'm here anymore."

By the looks of things, Skye couldn't agree more. The man coughed again and then looked at Logan and Skye. "Yeah, Toby Graham. I see it here. He rented the room three days ago for two weeks. Paid by credit card. Told us he didn't need any cleaning. That he would take care of it himself. We've just been putting towels outside his door. That was until yesterday, when he didn't pick them up. Why? Is he complaining? Did he call the cops on us?" The man set his jaw. "These people! They are always complaining. Can't ever do nothing right for them. This isn't the Taj Mahal. Can't they see that?"

Neither Skye nor Logan answered. Logan looked at the man. "I need a passkey and the room number."

"Do you need a court order?"

Logan narrowed his eyes. "Stand up, why don't you? I want you to see something."

The man jutted his chin out. "What are you gonna do, arrest me? I didn't do nothing, man. This is harassment."

Logan leaned over the counter. "Stand up. Now."

Skye took a step back, wondering what was going to happen next. The man behind the desk stood up and peered over the top of it, spotting Riggs. Riggs lifted his lips, showing a set of perfectly white teeth, a low growl coming from deep in his belly. "No. I don't need a court order. I need your cooperation. Now give me the room number and the passkey or I will arrest you for obstructing justice. My partner here will help."

The man shriveled back behind the counter for protection. "Yeah, yeah. Of course, Officer. Sorry, didn't mean to accuse you of anything."

Skye shook her head. Logan hadn't. But now she could see why Riggs was such a valuable partner. Talk about a way of encouraging compliance. A moment later, Skye and Logan had the passkey they needed. As they headed out the door, Logan cocked his head. "Well, that was interesting."

"Let's hope that's the end of the things that are interesting today."

38

Skye had never been on this kind of hunt before. Every nerve in her body tingled. What did Logan hope to find?

She followed him upstairs to the second level of the Henderson Lake Hotel via an exterior staircase. Following Logan and Riggs, she decided the hotel would have been more aptly named a motel. According to the apologetic man at the reception desk, Toby Graham had rented room 212.

As they passed room 208, Logan looked over his shoulder and stopped. "I want you to stay here, Skye. If anything crazy happens, I want you to run to the steps and go back to the cruiser. Do you understand?"

Skye was about to protest that she should go with him, that she would be safer that way, but decided not to. To date, Logan had been careful around her, even protective. It was a good feeling. She looked at the ground and then whispered, "Yes. I've got it. I'll stay here."

As Logan approached the door, she saw him look back at her as if ensuring she was doing what he'd asked. He gave her a nod, his expression serious. She nodded back. He unclipped

Riggs from his collar, used a few hand signals, which put the dog in a sit-and-stay. A moment later, she saw Logan pull his gun from his holster. It wasn't down low. He was holding it up in front of his face as if he was ready to fire. With his left hand, he had the passkey. As he slipped it in the door, she heard him say something in German. Riggs sprung up and charged into the motel room ahead of Logan.

Just seeing Logan and Riggs enter the room that way terrified Skye. What if someone was inside waiting and hurt one of them? Would she ever be able to forgive herself for not telling Logan everything she knew from the start?

Skye plastered herself near the door of room 208, fighting the urge to run down to the room Toby had rented. She gripped her hands into fists, trying to get her thinking back under control. What was she thinking about her not being able to forgive herself? It wasn't as though she was the one that was forcing them to go into the room. That was Logan's decision. Not hers.

Skye's heart pounded in her chest. She stayed exactly where Logan had told her to. It seemed like time stood still. She couldn't hear any noise coming from the motel room Logan and Riggs had entered. Her mouth became dry. A moment later, Riggs ran out of the room and headed toward her. A second later, she heard Logan shout her name. "Skye!"

She hurried down to the room, Riggs following. As she rounded the corner, she found Logan, holstering his gun. Riggs ushered Skye back into the room and then laid down in front of Logan, looking up at him. Wasn't that the sign that Riggs had found something? From inside his pants pocket, Logan produced a treat for Riggs and then clipped on his leash again, telling him to stay.

"What happened?" Skye asked.

"We found something." His jaw was set, his expression dark.

"What?"

"Take a look for yourself."

Skye moved forward through the small motel room, the smell a combination of mildew and something sour Skye couldn't place. As she did, Logan flipped on the lights. It was a typical dated motel room. The bed was covered with a quilted dark-green bedspread. Skye shuddered. God only knew how many different bodily fluids had soaked into it over the years. There was a dingy-looking, dark brown carpet and a couple of cheap fake brass light fixtures bolted to the walls next to the bed, probably so that the people who were staying there wouldn't steal the lamps. In the corner, a small refrigerator hummed. On top of it there was a coffeemaker and a few packets of coffee grounds.

Skye made her way to the back of the room where the bathroom was. There was no luggage in the room and it didn't look as though the room had been really used. So why then had Toby Graham rented it? As she turned into the bathroom, she understood why. Along the back wall of the bathtub, where the shower curtain had been pulled aside, there was a spray of blood and bone. She drew in a sharp breath.

From behind her, she heard Logan. "Sorry, I probably should have warned you."

Skye stood with her hand covering her mouth. "No, it's okay," she mumbled. She'd already seen Ian's mangled face. Now she'd seen where he'd been killed.

Logan keyed up his radio. "Dispatch, this is one-fifteen."

"Go ahead one-fifteen. I show you at Henderson Lake Hotel."

"That's correct. Room 212. Send Dr. Chapman and the Chief, please."

"Copy that."

Skye turned away from the grisly scene in the bathroom and walked back out into the main space of the motel room. Feeling numb, she wanted to sit down on the edge of the bed, but didn't dare knowing what might be on it. It was just one more thing to be squeamish about.

She rubbed her forehead. The whole scene — the tactical entry, the dingy room, the bloody bathroom — left her feeling a little light-headed. It was certainly different to watch blood and guts on television or at the movies than it was to see it live. The scene — clearly where a murder had happened — was real, visceral, the place where a person had lost their life. Was there a struggle? Had Ian been afraid? A wave of emotions covered her.

Then there was the smell.

She couldn't quite place it. It smelled vaguely like a combination of raw meat and metal, as if the iron in Ian's blood had somehow floated into the air, the last trace of his body smeared all over dirty linoleum and tile.

Logan came out of the bathroom a second later. Riggs was still guarding the doorway. As Logan approached her, she felt his fingers on the back of her elbow, guiding her out of the room. After seeing the bloody mess in the bathroom, she felt numb.

"Let's get some fresh air. The chief and the medical examiner are on their way."

"Oh, great." Skye's comment was half agreeable and half sarcastic. After what she'd seen, she wasn't sure that visiting with Zara was on her list of favorites.

Skye went outside and leaned against the balcony. She drew in a deep breath, forcing her shoulders to relax. Maybe she should have stayed at work after all. "So, this is where Ian Dunn was killed?"

"Well, I think it's a logical conclusion, although we'll need Dr. Chapman to confirm that the blood type and DNA matches Ian's."

Skye frowned. "I thought those DNA tests took a long time."

"Used to. They don't anymore. The new rapid testing procedures can get us results back in eight to twelve hours. Luckily, Highmill, for what reason I have absolutely no idea, was one of the test sites for some new tech that was being rolled out by Homeland Security."

Skye winced. "Hard to think Highmill is on the cutting edge of anything."

Logan chuckled. "I know."

Skye wrapped her arms around herself. She wanted some certainty that this was where Ian was killed. Whether that was so she didn't have to see another murder scene or because she wanted something that would tie Toby to Ian's death, she didn't know. "So does that mean that Toby killed Ian since he rented the motel room?"

"It's plausible. I would like to think so, but until we have a murder weapon to prove the connection, all we have is that Toby rented a motel room where Ian's blood and brain matter ended up."

Skye's mouth fell open. "Are you kidding me?"

Logan looked down at the ground and then back up at her. "I wish I was. It's one thing to know what happened in a crime. It's something else completely different to be able to prove it. And right now, any defense attorney worth half their salt would tear this case apart as circumstantial. Toby could easily claim that someone stole his credit card and used it in order to book the motel room and kill Ian."

As soon as he said it, Skye understood exactly what he was saying. Her job didn't require any of the evidentiary precision that Logan's did. He had to be able to prove things. Skye was just along for the ride, using her expertise as a guide for people who were lost. It was a different way of handling problems. Very different.

Just as Skye's heart rate was returning to normal, she saw a blue Highmill Police Department SUV pull up, followed about ten seconds later by a white van. Zara and the coroner.

Skye glanced Zara's direction and turned away. As she did, she noticed Logan's eyes on her. "That bad?"

"What?"

"Your relationship with Zara?"

"It's pretty bad. After what happened, I don't trust her." Skye didn't have a chance to say anything else, at least without running the risk of being overheard. She watched as Chief Zara Walsh ambled her way to the steps and then made her way up them slowly, definitely favoring her right leg.

Logan mumbled behind her, "She needs a knee replacement."

Skye blinked. Maybe that explained why Zara was always so crabby. Or maybe it was just a relationship hangover as a result of the problems she and Skye had experienced. There'd been no resolution, no recognition of the damage done, and definitely no apologies.

As the chief made it to the top of the steps, Skye noticed she was wearing a pair of faded jeans, old tennis shoes, and a Highmill Police Department jacket. Her red hair was hanging around her shoulders — it looked as if it hadn't been brushed — and her face was devoid of makeup. Skye bristled. Everything in her wanted to tell Zara to maybe put a little effort into how she looked. She was, after all, still a woman.

Then again, with how she was feeling about Zara, she could have shown up in a gown and a tiara and Skye was sure her internal dialogue would have found some way to criticize her.

The problem wasn't how Zara looked, it was how she behaved. But that was a problem for another time.

As Zara made her way to the motel room door where Logan and Skye were standing with Riggs, she gave each of them a brief nod, only addressing Logan. "You think this is the crime scene?"

"Yes, ma'am. Have a look for yourself."

She glanced at Skye with cool eyes. "I will."

Dr. Chapman followed next, carrying something that looked like a tackle box used for fishing. "Good afternoon!" he bellowed. "Well, this weather is far superior to the horrendous rain we had the other day, wouldn't you agree?"

Skye fought off the urge to say, "Indeed." Instead, she just nodded. How someone who dealt with death all the time was so upbeat and positive, she had no idea.

At least his patients didn't complain.

A moment later, Zara emerged from the motel room, shoving her hands into her pockets. Her expression was calm, as if she'd seen a million bloody bathrooms. "Yup, looks like a crime scene to me. I'll stay here, Logan. Let's get it taped off and you can take Skye back wherever she came from."

Wherever she came from? What did that mean?

Skye pressed her lips together and sucked in a sharp breath. Who was Zara Walsh to talk to her that way?

Logan nodded, straightening. "Sure, Chief."

Skye was just about to respond when she felt Logan's hand on her arm, giving her a squeeze. "Come on," he said. "Let me get you back to work."

39

Skye was seething the entire way back to the office. Logan tried a couple of times to start up a conversation with her, but she barely answered. Skye sat, staring out the window, her jaw set. Part of her was waiting for Logan to apologize for putting her in a position where she'd have to interact so closely with Zara, but he didn't. She was glad about that, which showed he knew that he didn't need to take ownership of the problem between her and his chief.

It was one the two of them needed to figure out.

As they drove back to her office, Skye's mind was circling in a million different directions — the sight of the blood and brain matter spattered all over the white walls of the dingy motel where Ian had presumably been killed, the fact that Naomi had missed her appointment today and now was linked to the whole mess, not to mention the fact that the bloody motel room that they had looked at was registered to Toby Graham, Naomi's boyfriend. A shiver ran down her spine.

Where was Naomi?

Skye almost said something about it to Logan, but she was still too angry about the way Zara had treated her. Any words she said, no matter how well-intentioned, wouldn't come out the way she wanted them to. She and Zara needed to work out the problems between the two of them. But now was not the time, and it certainly had not been the time to air out their dirty laundry in front of Logan and the overly chipper coroner, Dr. Chapman.

As they pulled into the parking lot of her office, the cruiser stopped. Skye looked at Logan. "I know we can't be sure, but do you think Toby did it? Killed Ian Dunn?"

Logan shook his head. "Honestly, I don't know. There are too many moving parts here. Is he a suspect? Absolutely. Is he my prime suspect right now? Absolutely. I don't have anyone else to look at. But I have too much experience to believe that I'm going to pin all my hopes on Toby Graham as the perp right now. I've seen too many of these cases twist in a completely different direction. I have to follow the evidence, not how I feel. It's a little different than the way that you work."

Skye scowled. Was it? As a psychologist, she followed the evidence of what she saw in her client's behavior as much as their feelings. It was just evidence of a different kind, the kind that was sending shivers up and down her spine. But she didn't have the energy at that moment to argue with Logan. She slipped out of his cruiser and gave him a wave.

He rolled the window down as she closed the door. "I'll give you a call when I find something else. Thanks for your help today."

Skye shrugged and walked away.

Maybe it would be better if he didn't.

Three hours later, Skye found herself still sitting at her desk working on updating patient files. She had taken a late appointment that another therapist couldn't accommodate and that, plus the field trip to the motel, had put her way behind in the work she needed to get done for the day. Despite the fact that she was feeling restless, she decided that staying at work was the best plan. Given what she had seen at the motel room, she wasn't surprised by her reaction. The office was safe. It was her space. She sighed and stared back at her computer but didn't move her fingers, still feeling slightly numb. It wasn't every day that someone like her got to experience a bloody crime scene. As much as it was a relief to find where Ian had been killed, it was also horrific.

The idea that Ian Dunn had lost his life in the tiny, dirty bathroom at the Henderson Lake Hotel was something that Skye was having a hard time dealing with. It was the intentionality of it. She knew that people who were sociopaths, narcissists, and psychotics sat as judge and jury over people. They felt that they had the power to decide who won, who was allowed to live and who needed to die. No matter how they justified it, it was nearly impossible for her to rationalize, even if mental illness was factored in.

By eight o'clock that night, Skye was exhausted. She'd made a dent in her paperwork, but that was all. She knew she wasn't being effective.

It was time to go home.

There was nothing more that she wanted but to take a shower, do laundry, and clean her house. She knew what it was about. It was her attempt to get her life back under control again, to feel safe. She quickly packed up her bag, shut off the lights in her office and walked out into the lobby. Everything had been closed up for the night, Maria having said her goodbye several hours earlier, the last sessions of the evening wrapping up more than an hour before. She was the only one left in the office.

Grabbing her car keys, Skye decided to take the elevator down to the first floor. The stairwells were unsecured. Was that some paranoia talking? She sucked in a breath as the doors opened on the first floor.

Skye, you are safe. You are fine.

Emerging out into the parking lot, Skye walked towards her car, holding the fob in her hand. She'd left her car in the same spot it always was, at the back of the lot where she would be forced to take a few extra steps. It was part of the transition she designed for herself to go into work and come out of work, a way of leaving the day behind after carrying everyone else's problems.

The parking lot itself was dark. Only a couple of cars were left in the lot. She turned around, looked at the building. From inside a yellow glow was coming from the windows. It looked like she wasn't the only one that was burning the late-night oil, unless it was just the cleaning service moving through the offices. The innocent camaraderie of knowing that other people were grinding away as hard as she was made her feel slightly better.

Skye looked around and then stared at the ground, walking slowly to her car. The night had stayed relatively comfortable, though she was glad she had her jacket on. The weather was warming in Highmill. At least that was something to feel good about. By the smell of the air, spring was in full swing. She realized the balmy summer months filled with humidity and mosquitoes were just ahead of them. With it came the inevitable turn of events at her office. Skye stared at the ground. Her clients' problems were as seasonal as anything else. Soon, she would be dealing with summer loves, kids going off to college, kids coming back from college, marriages that were falling apart because the kids are no longer in the house, job transitions and, by mid-summer, the stress, or relief, of getting the kids back into school. She shook her head as she walked.

It never ended.

Skye had worked endless hours to build her practice up. But it was hard to go home at night and be all by herself. She was gone too many hours of the day to have a dog like Riggs, and relationships had never really worked out for her, not after the one she had had when she was first in college. Just thinking about it made her heart race.

As she made it to her car, she pressed the fob to unlock it. She felt a breeze touch the side of her cheek, then the hair stood up on the back of her neck. Skye whipped around, fully expecting to see nothing there. But for once, she was wrong. In front of her stood a blond man, his face leering at her. He had his hands stuffed in his pockets, his head tilted to the side, his eyes narrowed. "Do you know who I am?"

Skye's heart thundered in her chest. "Should I?" Skye tried to keep her wits about her. She knew from her training that men like the one that was approaching her were bullies. Usually if their victim was strong, they would be left alone.

"I'm Toby Graham, Naomi Fraser's boyfriend."

Skye could barely breathe. She'd guessed that, but she wasn't going to give Toby the satisfaction of being that important. "What can I do for you, Mr. Graham?" She felt like her lungs had been frozen in place. Her lips started to tingle. There was no one around.

"My girlfriend Naomi, she's your patient. What? She hasn't talked about me?" Toby seemed insulted.

Skye needed to try to de-escalate the situation so she could get into the car and drive away. "I can't talk about my patients, Mr. Graham. If you know who I am, then you should know that."

As she reached for the door handle, Toby lunged in front of her, blocking her path and slammed his palm down on the roof of her car hard enough that she was sure it left a dent. "I don't care about your rules and regulations, Dr. Johnston. I want to know what Naomi has said about me."

Skye took half a step back away from the car. Toby was clearly coming unglued. What story he was telling himself about Naomi, she could only guess. Her hands shaking, Skye dropped the fob and quickly scooped it up from the ground, trying to look like she was calm. She was anything but. "You know I can't talk about that, Mr. Graham. Maybe you and Naomi can schedule a couple's session."

"A couple's session? What? You think there is something wrong with me? No, Dr. Johnston. I'm not leaving until you tell me what I need to know." It was then that Skye saw his intention in his expression. The narrowed eyes, the muscles rippling across his jaw, his clenched fists — this was a man who would do whatever was needed in order to get what he wanted.

Including physical violence.

Skye looked down at the ground as if she was trying to figure out what to do, buying a moment to think. Hiding the key fob in her pocket, she quickly pushed the panic button. She recently had it connected to the alarm system at her house. If she pressed the button, it would alert the alarm company to immediately send help. She could only hope it would work.

If it didn't...

Skye held her hands up in surrender. "All right, all right. What is it that you want to know?" Skye knew she had to get him talking. She had to buy time for help to get to her. She pressed the button a couple more times, hoping that the system was working. She heard her phone ring. Everything in her wanted to dig into her bag and scream into it to get help, but she didn't move. Panic rose in her body.

"I already told you what I want to know. What did Naomi say about me?"

Skye froze. How should she answer that question? "I don't know, Mr. Graham. I can't give you specifics. I don't write those down. I see dozens of clients every single week. If I said something, I might be misstating it, and I don't want you to be mad at Naomi."

Toby whirled around, rubbing his hand through his hair, then turned and stared at Skye, leaning so close to her she could feel the warmth of his breath on her face. "Are you kidding me? From what Naomi has said about you, you remember everything."

"Well, I don't about that..." Skye tried to stall. Her mind was racing. If help was coming, would they use their sirens?

"I know you remember. Tell me." The words came out cold.

"Like I said, I..."

Skye didn't have a chance to finish her sentence. Toby took a half a step back reaching around behind himself. A second later, he pulled a gun. Skye backed up so fast, she banged into her car, nearly falling. Toby grabbed her arm, dragging her to a standing position. "You are not driving away from me, Dr. Johnston. You're going to tell me what you know about my girlfriend right now."

"I, I don't know anything..." Skye stammered.

What she didn't know was how she was going to survive.

40

Logan was late leaving work. The paperwork on the Ian Dunn case was mounting. Luckily, Kevin's wife, Beth Ann, had been able to pick up Bella from kindergarten and had taken Bella back to the Mills's house to play with Kevin's twin girls.

At this point, he was even late for picking Bella up.

Shaking his head, he pulled his pickup truck out of the station's parking lot, heading for Kevin's house. A call went out over the radio. "All units, we have a distress call at 7292 Highmill Road. The alarm company reported it's coming from a key fob that is equipped with a distress button. No other details."

The back of Logan's neck instantly tightened. He knew that address. That was where Skye Johnston's office was. He stepped on the gas, glad he'd left his radio on. He picked up the walkie-talkie and hit the call button. "Dispatch, this is one-fifteen. Show me as en route." The powerful engine of his pickup truck revved as Logan hit the gas. He glanced at Riggs in the backseat, his long pink tongue hanging out. "Hold on, boy. I might need you."

Two minutes later, Logan turned the truck tightly around

the corner at the address he had been given by dispatch. He could see the silhouette of a woman and a man in the parking lot, the woman backed up against her car, the man just inches from her face. Logan set his jaw. From the silhouette, it looked an awful lot like Skye. He gripped the wheel even tighter. Had one of her patients gone nuts on her?

Logan slammed on the brakes near Skye's car and hopped out. He could hear the man shouting at Skye. He was holding something in his hands. Was it a gun?

Logan didn't have time to think. He opened the back door to the truck. Riggs leaped out, taking off towards Skye, immediately putting himself between her and the man with the gun.

For a second, the man looked startled to see the enormous dog appear out of nowhere. He let go of the hold he had on Skye, glanced in Logan's direction, and then ran for his car. Logan drew his gun. "Stop! Police!" At the same time, he yelled in German for Riggs to stay where he was in case the man circled back toward Skye.

Logan sprinted toward the man, trying to stop him, but somehow, he was able to get around the truck and back into his own vehicle. A second later, Logan heard the tires squeal and the engine rev. He jumped out of the way as the BMW hurtled past him.

Logan stared at the car for a split second as it retreated into the distance. He was out of breath from the adrenaline surging in his system. He quickly holstered his gun and ran over to Skye. "Are you okay? What happened?"

Skye's mouth was open, her eyes wide, her skin the color of a pale porcelain doll. He saw her start to wobble as if she couldn't keep her balance. He held out his hand. "Here, sit down." He pointed toward her car. "Sit inside and try to take some deep breaths. Do you need an ambulance?"

She stared at the ground. "No. No. I'm okay."

Riggs had positioned himself right by her leg as if he was

telling Logan that no one was going to get to Skye. Logan reached into the pocket of his work pants and tossed Riggs a treat. Logan watched as Skye's fingers inched down off of her lap, her hands shaking, her fingers reaching for Riggs' fur. "You saved my life. Your dog, he saved my life."

Logan raised his eyebrows. The admission was sweet. "That's what he's supposed to do." Logan knelt in front of her. He looked up at her face. She was beautiful even when she was in shock. He pushed the thought away. "Skye, you need to tell me what happened. Do you know who that was?"

"It was Toby Graham. He had a gun. I think he was going to kill me, or at least take me somewhere, but I pressed the button on my key fob." She was rambling. It was a sure sign of shock.

"Yes, I know. That's how we found you. I'm glad that you had that. What did he say?"

"He wanted information about Naomi."

Just then, a Highmill cruiser pulled up, lights flashing. Another officer, Mitch Leiland, ran towards them. "Fletcher? You okay over there?"

Logan nodded. "Yeah. We're okay. She's shaken up. You can call off the cavalry, but we're gonna need to take a report."

"Copy that."

Logan looked back at Skye. She was shaking violently. "I was going to try to fight him off, Logan. Really, I was. Like I did last time, but he had a gun. I didn't know what to do. I don't know what to do when there's a gun. I froze. I shouldn't have, but I did."

Logan's expression went slack. "Last time? What are you talking about, Skye? What do you mean the last time? Has Toby threatened you before?" Questions started to run through Logan's mind. If she'd had a run-in with Toby, why hadn't she said that to him before?

She shook her head. "No, I'm sorry. I can't explain it. I'm just not myself right now. I need to go home." She twisted her legs in her car, as if she was going to drive away.

Logan shook his head. "Oh, no, you don't. You're too shaken up to drive. Give me your keys. I'll drive you home."

Skye looked slightly relieved. "But what about my car?"

"I will get another officer to bring it to us." He held his hand out. "Let's go. I'm going to get you home."

41

"Are you okay? Are you sure that was Toby Graham? There's no chance it was another patient?" He needed to be sure. Logan put his hand on Skye's back. She'd made it out of her car, but now she was bent over, her hands on her knees, staring at the ground. Even through her jacket, he could feel her chest expanding and contracting. She was out of breath. Clearly, whoever had attacked her had scared her pretty good.

Skye stood up and stared at Logan. She closed her eyes for a second and then sucked in a sharp breath, looking at him. "Yes. I'm sure."

"What did he want?"

"He wanted to know what Naomi had told me about him." Skye looked up and then settled her gaze back on Logan. He could see from the headlights of his truck on the scene that her expression was strained. "I shouldn't tell you this, but I guess client privilege is out the window since he just attacked me."

Finally. Maybe now he'd get some answers. "It's okay. Take your time."

"Naomi Fraser is one of my clients. I've seen her for years. She's been working through what to do about Toby."

"What do you mean?"

"He's suffocating her. He wants all of her attention, all the time. Basically wants her to marry him, help him start a business, then quit her job and stay at home with their kids once it's off the ground."

"And I'm guessing she doesn't want that?"

"No. And here's the strange thing. Naomi didn't show up for her session today."

"Is that unusual?"

Skye nodded. "Very unusual. I don't think I can remember a session that Naomi missed. She's been working hard and making lots of progress. And there's one other thing."

A lump formed in Logan's throat. Clearly Skye knew a lot more about what was going on. Now it seemed it was all coming out at once. Logan felt anger and relief at the same time. He couldn't protect her if he didn't know what was going on.

"She and Ian Dunn have been seeing each other."

The lump that had formed in Logan's throat dropped to his stomach. Naomi, Toby, and Ian were all connected, but it wasn't just work. It was romantically. "Why didn't you tell me this earlier?"

"You know I couldn't. And you said you figured out that Ian and Toby knew each other. In my mind it was just a hop, skip, and a jump to figure out that Naomi was part of the calculus. She's the third in the love triangle."

Logan's face reddened. He felt foolish and frustrated. "I had no idea that Naomi didn't show up today. How could I know that if you didn't tell me?"

When he looked back, tears were running down Skye's face, the glint of them showing in the headlights of his truck. He frowned. "What is it?" Everything in him wanted to wrap her in his arms and tell her that everything was going to be okay. The feeling surprised him. It was the first time he'd had a thought like that since Rachel had died. The urge was so strong, he moved away from her. He looked at Riggs. Riggs apparently had developed feelings too. He laid protectively at Skye's feet, resting his head on her shoe.

"It's just that Toby... He reminded me of —"

It was as if Skye was choking on the words that were trying to come out. Her face was twisted in a mask of grief and anger. Logan waited for a beat. He knew that sometimes people needed a moment to process before the words would come out. He'd seen it over and over again at a scene. Something horrific would happen. The first officers that arrived would demand a complete accounting of what the person had experienced, except that wasn't possible in the tension of the moment. The person was still going through the trauma. Sometimes they just needed a few minutes. Other times it was hours or days later when finally the whole story came out. He could only hope that it wouldn't take Skye that long to tell him what was going on. He had a sinking feeling that lives depended on it — maybe even theirs.

"It's just that the same thing happened to me in college."

"What?"

Skye looked at the ground. "When I started at Cornell, I was an Economics major. My freshman year, my first class was with a professor I thought was amazing. He was everything a girl could want — handsome, accomplished, intense. I started going to see him for help that I actually didn't need. It was just an excuse to be alone with him. One day, things escalated. He kissed me. We started seeing each other on the side. I'd sneak off to his office at all hours of the day and night. He didn't want anyone to know. He was worried he might lose his tenure. And then things turned. Nate became possessive and controlling. Tried to tell me where I could go and how I could spend my time. Called me a pig. And that was the nicest of the names he called me. Two weeks later, he became violent. Broke my jaw and my arm." She stopped talking.

"Then what happened?" His voice was quiet. Maybe too quiet.

Skye met Logan's gaze. Her eyes were hard, made of steel. It was a strength that Logan hadn't seen in many people before.

"I got smart." She cocked her head to the side. "I ended up at the hospital. A social worker came in to talk to me. I think they knew I'd been attacked and expected that I was going to stonewall them. Said a man was in the waiting room. Wanted to see me but they wanted to check and see if it was okay. I was in a lot of pain, even with the medication they'd given me. I couldn't even talk. I opened my phone and showed them a picture of Nate and I together. The social worker said, 'Yeah, that's him.'" Skye blinked. "It was one of the most frightening moments of my life, Logan. If I had let him in, there was no telling what would have happened next."

"What did happen?" Logan's mouth was dry. It explained a lot about her.

"I asked for a piece of paper and wrote with my good hand 'police.' The next thing I knew, there was a security guard standing in front of my door. A few minutes later the cops arrived. I gave a full statement as best I could with a broken jaw. Spent a week in the hospital. Had to have surgery on my jaw and arm. My teeth were wired together for six weeks."

Hearing the story, Logan shook his head. How any man could touch a woman like that, he didn't understand. There was a ball of anger in his gut the size of a grapefruit. Only a coward would go after a woman like that. "So, when we found the spiral fractures on Ian's arm —"

Skye nodded. "I knew exactly what you were talking about. Sure, they can be from torture, but they can also be from a quick twisting motion. That's what happened to me." She rubbed her arm as if she was remembering the pain. "The long and the short of it is that Cornell found out. Professor McCord was fired and arrested, not in that order. I testified at his trial. Turns out I wasn't the only one. Three other girls came forward when I did. All of them had been abused in one way or the other. I started going to therapy based on the recommendation of the social worker from the hospital."

"And that's when you decided to become a psychologist?"

"Yeah. To help people like me."

Everything in Logan wanted to take Skye home, get her situated on his couch, make her some soup and rub her feet to make her feel better. Instead, he looked away. "And you're worried the same cycle is repeating itself with Naomi?"

"I am."

"Well, then I think we better go see if your patient is okay, don't you?"

42

Skye felt relieved that all of the information she had been hiding from Logan had finally come out. Though with Toby Graham coming after her and Naomi Fraser missing, Skye didn't think she had broken any confidentiality rules at that point by sharing what she knew, there was a part of her that didn't care. Confidentiality was a double-edged sword. A psychologist she'd gotten her PhD under, a woman named Laura McKinney, had said, "If people would just be direct, we'd be out of a job."

There was truth to that theory in this case. There was clearly something going on. Naomi's boyfriend, Toby Graham, was unhinged. What exact form of mental illness he was suffering with, she wasn't precisely sure.

But then again, at that moment, she didn't care.

Part of her wanted to care. She was a psychologist, after all. Wasn't it her job to care for people who were struggling with their thoughts and emotions? It was, she realized as she slid into Logan's truck, hearing the door close behind her as he got her safely inside. She leaned her head against the seat, closing her eyes. The problem was her job wasn't to try to heal somebody like Toby Graham. Not after what he had done to her. Accosting your girlfriend's psychologist outside her place of work was taking things to the next level.

And it had brought up a bunch of painful memories.

Skye tried to push the thoughts of Professor Nate McCord out of her mind. But it was hard. She saw him in her head, as she had the last time she'd seen him, during his trial. He'd sat smugly at the defendant's table wearing an expensive suit, flanked by his attorneys, his face sneering at her as she provided testimony to the court the week before. She'd also been there a few days later when the trial had ended, and the jury came back with a guilty plea. His sneer turned into rage as the bailiff put handcuffs on him and dragged him away, bellowing that the women wanted him and he hadn't done anything wrong. Skye hadn't seen him since. The judge had given him the maximum sentence of twenty-five years for first-degree assault. The charge, described as "reckless and intentional harm" by the judge, fit. All Skye could do was imagine him sitting in jail somewhere, his hair and beard all grown out, long and scraggly, wearing an orange jumpsuit.

She could only hope orange was his color.

Logan's voice interrupted her thoughts. "Do you know where Naomi lives?"

Skye nodded. "I can find out." She tapped her phone and opened the app that they used for client management. She showed Logan the address, her hands shaking so badly she could hardly keep her phone still. He typed the address into the navigation system on his truck. "I think I know where this is, but we'll use the GPS just to be sure."

Skye leaned back in the seat, grateful for the heat blasting in the truck. Riggs had positioned himself as the third person in the front seat, though his body wasn't entirely up front. If he had been, he was so big he would have taken up all of the space. He perched with his front paws on the console between the two of them, his big head just off of Skye's left shoulder. She looked up at him. The big dog looked down at her, resting his chin on her shoulder for a second, then glancing at Logan as if he was embarrassed by his affection for Skye. Logan smiled. "I think he likes you."

"I think I'm kind of starting to like him too."

As the words came out of her mouth, Skye was trying to figure out if she meant the dog or Logan.

It didn't take them long to get to Naomi's house. Naomi lived in a house that was about the same size as Skye's, only it looked like it had been built more recently. Logan parked the truck at the curb, cut the engine, and looked at Skye. "I'm going to leave you here in the truck. Riggs and I will go check it out."

Skye pressed her lips together. This was a place that was familiar to Toby. She didn't want to be alone in the truck where he could get to her while Logan and Riggs were inside. Was Logan thinking about that? A shudder ran through her body. "No, that's okay. I can come with you."

Logan frowned. "Are you sure? You're going to have to stay behind us."

He apparently hadn't picked up on the fact that she didn't want to sit by herself in the truck. "That's okay. I won't be any trouble."

Logan grinned. "You never are."

Skye looked down at her lap. "You don't know me that well yet."

There was a pause. She waited for a second to see if Logan would say anything else, maybe even reach out and touch her arm. But he didn't. She drew in a long breath. Given how raw her emotions were at the moment, that was okay.

Skye saw the back door of the truck open, heard Logan utter a few commands in German and then watched Riggs jump out of the truck. Skye slid out, standing by the truck, watching and waiting. Logan went around the back, opened a steel storage box with his keys and pulled his tactical vest out of his truck. He slid it on over his head, then reached for his gun, pulling it from the holster and checking to make sure it was loaded and ready to fire. Just watching him go through his preparations made Skye nervous. It wasn't the fact that Logan had a gun. He was a police officer. That was completely reasonable. What wasn't was the fact that he was checking it to make sure it was ready to face the man that had just attacked her.

A lump formed in her throat. The situation was becoming a nightmare.

By the time Skye looked back at Logan, he'd reached back into the box one more time and pulled out a brown dog vest that read "Police" in bright white letters and snapped it on over Riggs's back. Skye looked at him, feeling curious. He must have read her thoughts because he looked at her. "The vest is what signals Riggs that it's time to work. Dogs are smart. They pick up on visual and behavioral clues."

"But he protected me without having his vest on?"

"I know. We can do that in a pinch, but it's better for him in the long run if we do things by the book."

Skye nodded. "You need to call this in or something? Let Zara know where we are?"

Logan shook his head. "The only person that I would let know would be dispatch. But I'm off duty at the moment. If we find something, I'll let them know."

Skye wondered if any of it had to do with Zara. Either way, she was grateful.

Logan twisted the leash around his spare hand and started toward the house. She followed, staying as close to them as she dared. She didn't want to get in their way, but she most certainly didn't want to be left behind, not with Toby Graham on the loose.

She hated the feeling. It was one she'd worked hard to

replace in her life after Nate. Now one bad interaction and she was back to where she started — living in fear.

As they approached the front of the house, Skye pushed the thought away. Everything was dark. There were no lights on inside, no indication that Naomi was home. Even if she had been home sick, Skye expected she would see the glow of a television on inside, or perhaps even a light on in the kitchen.

But the house was dark, like it had been abandoned.

Logan and Riggs charged up the driveway and went to the front door, Logan using a flashlight to inspect it. "Nothing here." He rattled the door. "It's secure."

Skye felt her heart thump in her chest. What exactly were they hoping to find? Had something really happened to Naomi? Maybe she was just out of town and had forgotten to let Skye know?

But that didn't explain the terrifying interaction Skye had just had with Toby, then, did it?

As they walked around the front of the house, Skye noticed that Riggs was sniffing the ground and stopping every few feet. Then he'd look up, as if he was processing a whole bunch of sensory details all at once — the smells, the sounds, the movement of critters in the grass around Naomi's house. Skye was amazed by Riggs's demeanor. He was focused, but he looked like he was enjoying the challenge.

As they rounded the front of the garage, Logan turned and made his way down the side, heading for the backyard. He passed the side door and then stopped, taking two steps back. "Wait," he whispered. He directed his flashlight beam on the back door.

Before Skye could say anything, Logan had drawn his gun, positioned his flashlight underneath it and dropped the leash, uttering something to Riggs in German, whose entire body had become taut like a spring at the command.

Skye felt her mouth go dry. "What is it?"

Logan looked over his shoulder. "Someone busted this door open."

Skye's stomach clenched into a knot. Thoughts cascaded through her mind like water rushing over a waterfall. Was it Toby? Someone else? Was Naomi inside? Would they find her in the same state as Ian Dunn?

Skye fought back the coil of fear that was wrapping around her. She needed to follow Logan and Riggs. That was her only job at the moment. What they'd find inside, she had no idea. She only hoped it would include finding Naomi in time.

43

Logan shot a look at Skye. "Stay here!" he hissed. Skye stood frozen behind Logan and Riggs. By the looks of Riggs's body language, Skye could tell the powerful dog was ready to get to work.

"I can't."

Skye's entire body had started to shake. She knew what it was. It was a PTSD flare-up from the trauma her body had sustained at the hands of Dr. Nate McCord, brought on by Toby Graham. Her mind was clear, but her body was reliving the fear it had felt so many years ago.

"Fine but stay right behind me. Grab a hold of my belt. When I move, you move. That way I know exactly where you are. Clear?"

Skye almost sighed in relief. She nodded and reached awkwardly forward and grabbed Logan's belt with her left hand, gripping it tightly. She could feel the warmth of his skin on her knuckles.

It would have been awkward if she wasn't so terrified.

Logan looked back at her. "Let's go," he whispered.

Under his breath, he whispered a command to Riggs that

Skye couldn't make out, who emitted a low growl, his lip curling. Logan started moving through the doorway. Skye stayed with him, holding on as he walked slowly forward into the house.

Inside the garage, it was pitch black. A little light from the sky outside cast inky black shadows across the garage. As they passed Naomi's car, she felt Logan's body hesitate in front of her and then stop. He used the back of his hand to touch the hood of Naomi's car. "It's cold. She hasn't driven this in a while."

"Maybe she's somewhere inside," Skye whispered.

Logan nodded and started moving again.

After passing the car parked in the garage, they made their way to the back door, the three of them in a tight pack, Skye still trailing close behind Logan, Riggs off to his left side. Riggs sat below the three steps that led up to the interior of the house, quiet whines coming from inside of him. Logan held his hand up after clicking off his flashlight. He leaned over, unhooked the leash from Riggs's collar and pushed the door open, whispering another command.

Like a shot, Riggs ran ahead of Logan and Skye into the house. Skye could hear his toenails on the floor, then heard them grow softer as the dog ran up the steps and came back down a minute later. When he returned, he sat right next to Logan. Logan shook his head. "Just like at Ian's house. There's no one here."

"Are you sure?" Skye lifted her hand from Logan's belt.

"My partner says so. And I believe my partner."

Skye wasn't so sure she had as much confidence in Riggs as Logan did, though he did just go after Toby on her behalf. She stood frozen, staring inside the house.

Logan flipped on a light then looked at her. By his response, he must have noticed Skye's stiff expression. "It's okay. Riggs and I are here. Let's take a look and see if we can figure out what happened to Naomi."

Was it that obvious she was still freaked out? Skye sucked in a breath, willing the pounding of her heart to stop. If she had only left the office when everyone else had, none of this would be happening, she realized.

And then she realized she sounded just like someone she knew.

Her clients.

Realizing that if she hadn't been at the office, Toby would have found her somewhere else, Skye blew out a breath, trying to calm her nerves. She was rationalizing. The reality was someone like Toby would have found her no matter where she was. Shaking the thought from her head, she followed Logan as he flipped on a few more lights. It was time to focus on finding Naomi. Skye swallowed and took a deep breath. If she was there, the least she could do was try to help. Blinking, she took a few tentative steps forward.

Skye had never been to Naomi's house. It wouldn't be right if she had. She would have crossed boundaries in a way that wouldn't be appropriate while Naomi was in treatment.

But she was there now. And hopefully, she and Logan were in time.

The house itself was neat. There was a white sectional in Naomi's living room, a thick blanket tossed over the corner of it, and colorful throw pillows tucked against the back, brightening up the space. A few pictures had been hung on the wall. From what Skye could see, they looked like pieces that Naomi had picked up at an art show or a flea market. They certainly weren't expensive pieces, although they were nice and highlighted the way the room looked.

On the other side of the room, there was a bookshelf with a few pictures on it. Skye walked over and looked at them. The images were a chronicle of Naomi's life. There was a picture of Naomi in between two older people — probably her parents, wearing a black cap and gown. Graduation. Skye knew from their sessions that Naomi had been one of only three women to graduate from the SUNY Buffalo Construction Management program the year she finished her degree, one of the top fifty programs in the nation. It was something she was intensely proud of. Skye could relate. She was proud of what she'd accomplished in her practice too. It was something the women shared.

A second later, Logan's voice cut across the family room. "Skye? In here."

As if helping things along, Riggs trotted over to her and then followed her in the direction of where Logan's voice had come from.

When Logan saw the sight, he chuckled. "Looks like Riggs is feeling responsible for you. He's herding you."

Skye wasn't sure how to answer. "What did you find?"

Logan's face became stony. "Take a look at the way the kitchen was left, and you tell me."

Skye sucked in a deep breath, trying to calm herself. The kitchen itself was outfitted in what looked like custom wooden cabinetry with a granite island. Skye thought back to a session she'd had with Naomi where Naomi had told her that when she redid her kitchen, she used cabinets and materials from a project that had been rejected by the homeowner. "Their scraps are better than anything I'd buy on my own," she had quipped at the time, a grin on her face.

Now Skye knew exactly what she was saying. The kitchen was beautiful. Cabinets with thick white doors were outfitted with long black door handles and a wide vent covering a six-burner gas stove. White granite or marble, Skye couldn't tell the difference, covered the counters. In all, it looked like something out of a magazine.

Then Skye started to look a little closer.

There were a few dishes in the sink, a little bit of coffee left in the coffee maker. On the counter were a few bags of groceries that hadn't been unpacked, plus a phone, Naomi's wallet, and a bag that had her laptop in it.

"She would never leave her wallet and cell phone if she went somewhere," Skye said, a sinking feeling in her gut.

"That would be my guess too."

"So where is she?" Skye's eyes widened.

Logan shook his head. "I have no idea."

44

"Well," Logan said, shoving his hands in his pockets and looking at the tile work in Naomi Fraser's kitchen before glancing at Skye. They'd searched the house, but Naomi wasn't there. Her bed was unmade, there were spoiling groceries on the kitchen counter along with her cell phone, wallet, and work bag, and a busted back door. "Toby Graham is clearly a person of interest in Ian's death."

"But what about Naomi?"

Logan rubbed his jaw. It was a question he was afraid that Skye was gonna ask. She was sharp. Maybe too sharp for her own good. And now that he knew what she'd been through, he could understand her unease around people, especially men. "Technically, there's not a lot I can do. She could be out with friends and decided to leave her stuff at home. No one has filed a missing person's report, and given the fact that Highmill doesn't have a —"

"For God's sake, I'll file it, Logan!" Skye yelled, waving her hands in the air. "There's no way she would leave her phone and her purse here. And after what happened to me today with her boyfriend, what other explanation is there? Toby Graham has to be responsible."

Logan shook his head. "I wish it was that easy, Skye. But the State of New York has a firm policy. Anyone over the age of eighteen has to be gone for twenty-four hours with a filed missing person's report before any department goes out to look for them."

"Even if they're in imminent danger?"

She had to play that card, didn't she? "I get where you're going—"

Skye's eyes flashed as she stared at Logan. "Do you? Do you remember the terror you felt just the other day when Bella was missing?"

Logan set his jaw. "Don't bring my daughter into this."

Skye didn't back down. "But you know that feeling, don't you? What if Naomi is feeling that right now? What if all she needs is someone to come after her, to make sure she's okay? Are you just going to turn your back on her?"

"There's not a lot I can do."

"Sure there is. We're here, aren't we?"

"This is like a wellness check."

"Well we haven't exactly determined whether she's well or not, have we? Couldn't you try to locate her as a witness or a corroborating source for my attack? Toby came after me. She's his girlfriend. Doesn't that count for something?"

Logan paused for a second. Clearly Skye wasn't going to give up. Not that he disagreed, but sometimes trying to match what the law was capable of doing with what needed to happen was a little challenging. Scratch that, it could be a lot challenging.

He looked at the ground, then reached over and clipped the leash back on Riggs's collar. "I know what you're saying."

"You know I'm right."

Now Skye was just pushing him, trying to make her point. "I

hear you, Dr. Johnston. You don't have to beat me over the head. I agree that there are questions about where Naomi Fraser is." He stopped to calculate for a minute. How far was he willing to run this investigation based on Skye's hypothesis? His mind flashed back to the state that Ian Dunn's body had been left in the cave, the enormous damage to his face, the way his body had just been dumped in the back of that cave, as if whoever had left it there was hoping a bear or a coyote would smell the rotting carcass and devour it, scattering bones all over the woods.

Worse yet, it had been on *his* property.

That part, although it made him angry, he was relatively sure was inadvertent. What criminal would want to dump a dead body on land owned by a police officer? Criminals were stupid, but were they that stupid?

Toby Graham sure wasn't, at least from what he could see.

"Alright. What's your theory about what's really going on here? Is there anything else you haven't told me, Skye?"

Logan waited for a beat, searching her face. Her expression was stony, as if she was fighting an inner battle.

If there was something else she knew, it was time to speak. Time wasn't something Logan thought they had a lot of, at least not before another body dropped.

45

Skye crossed her arms in front of her chest. Logan was stubborn, maybe more than she'd like, but she understood what he was saying. There were police procedures that he had to follow, but there were also lives on the line. Couldn't he see that? Who exactly was he protecting? Himself? Zara? The department? That didn't change the fact that Naomi was out there, somewhere.

"My theory? I bet every dime I have that Toby Graham has Naomi somewhere."

"Why?" Logan's voice sounded calm, curious even.

When she looked up at Logan, she realized by the relaxed expression on his face that he wasn't challenging her, he was genuinely interested in what she thought. She felt heat rise to her cheeks as if he was looking into her soul. It had been a long time since someone had listened to her that way.

She turned away, running her finger along the cool granite countertops, starting to pace. "From what Naomi has told me about Toby, he's a classic narcissistic controller. Now, I can't be completely sure about a personality diagnosis given the fact that I have only now met him one time, and he was obviously not in a good headspace during that interaction, but what I can tell you about what she has said of his behavior is that he has great dreams and aspirations for their life together. He talked to her about starting their own architectural and design firm, with him as the head of the architecture side and her as the head of the construction side, until they had children, of course."

"Did she want children?"

"No, not really."

"Did she tell Toby that?"

"No. That was one of the things we had talked about. She was afraid to tell him a lot of things."

Logan scowled. "Afraid? Why?"

Skye thought back to a few sessions before when Naomi had come in visibly upset. She'd said that Toby had gotten very angry at her, angry in a way that she didn't know how to deal with. "He was manipulating her with his anger. The minute that she didn't do something the way that he wanted to have it done, he would get furious. Naomi had said that his mood was getting worse. He kept flying off the handle for no reason. Something about work stress."

Logan shook his head. "Yeah, the guy at the networking event said that Toby hadn't been there. He'd been working on some big project. Hadn't seen him in a while."

Skye nodded. "That fits. If Toby was under additional work stress, then that would explain why he was leaning harder on Naomi."

"Safe port in a storm?" Logan raised his eyebrows.

"Exactly. And if Naomi gave Toby any friction about his requests —"

"Then there would be consequences."

Skye stopped pacing for a second and looked at Logan. "Is that enough information?"

"Almost. One other question. How does Ian Dunn fit into

this? What exactly was Naomi's relationship with Ian? Do you know anything more than you've told me?"

It was a pointed question and a fair one. Skye couldn't blame Logan for asking after how she'd behaved. She'd withheld information up to that point. If she'd been anyone else with any other job, Skye knew that she probably would be in cuffs as an accessory to whatever crimes Zara planned on charging Toby with, but she was covered by doctor patient confidentiality.

At least for the moment.

"Naomi was having an affair with Ian."

"You mentioned they were part of a love triangle already. Were they intimate?"

Skye nodded. "As far as I could tell, yes. And don't be mad. Technically, I couldn't tell you. Honestly, I probably shouldn't even be telling you this now. She's still my client. I guess she and Ian had started seeing each other about a month ago from what I can tell. Things were moving fast."

"So those notes that weren't signed, that were left blank that we found at Ian's house?"

"I'm pretty sure those are from Naomi."

Skye leaned the palms of her hands on the kitchen counter, waiting, a heaviness covering her. There wasn't anything else she could do at that point. Would there be consequences for what she'd said, or conversely, what she hadn't? She didn't know.

When she looked up, Logan was running his hand through his hair, staring off in the distance. It was the classic posture of someone who was trying to sort through information. "Well, Naomi's disappearance increases the likelihood that Toby killed Ian, in addition to assaulting you."

"Is it enough to try to find Naomi?"

Logan shook his head. "It isn't, but it is enough to try to find Toby."

46

As Toby fled the parking lot where he had found Dr. Skye Johnston, he felt two things — rage and frustration. Dr. Johnston, or Skye as Naomi called her, was one of the people responsible for the damage done to his relationship. He'd wanted answers.

He hadn't gotten any. Not one.

Toby pounded the steering wheel with his fist. He'd just needed a minute more, just a little bit longer to get the information he needed out of Skye so he could put things back together again with Naomi.

But then, somehow, the police had miraculously arrived.

Naomi. His thoughts drifted to her. He'd left her on the boat, all alone. He'd stopped earlier that day, let her out to use the bathroom and given her two bottles of water and a couple of protein bars and turned the shore power back on so at least there was heat. When he saw her attitude, Toby shoved Naomi right back into the cabin where he'd put her the night before without saying anything. He'd been hoping that when he showed up, she'd be grateful, would throw her arms around him as if somehow the time spent on a dark, cold boat would have made her aware of what she was doing to their relationship, but it hadn't. She struggled and fought against him, elbowing him hard in the gut. He'd almost punched her but stopped just short. This was the woman he loved.

Toby glared into the darkness. But Dr. Johnston was another issue entirely. He would have had no issue punishing her for what she'd done.

The set up was perfect. He'd waited for two hours for Dr. Johnston to make her way out of the office. Two other times, he'd thought he'd spotted her, but it was just someone else leaving. Then finally, she came wandering out the front door, wearing a tough girl outfit — a black jacket, black dress, black motorcycle boots.

All Toby could do was try not to laugh. She wasn't nearly as cool as she was trying to look.

It was then that he decided that Dr. Skye Johnston was nothing more than a wannabe. She was no different than his boss , Dan, or Caitlyn, the girl that had stolen his Cornell project. He'd gotten several calls and emails from coworkers at the firm with questions on projects, including one from Dan. He hadn't bothered to answer.

Toby refocused on the road in front of him. No, he'd give Naomi one more chance. He'd go back to the boat, have a conversation with her and try one more time to get their relationship back on track.

And if he couldn't.

Well, he had experience killing people now.

And with what he was planning on doing to Naomi, no one would ever find her again.

47

Skye tapped her fingers on the edge of the counter in Naomi's empty kitchen. Logan had walked into the other room. He was on the phone with the department. Everything in her wanted to follow him, to yell in his ear, or better yet, steal the phone from him and tell Zara to get her act in gear, something that would spur them on to take action, but she didn't. Skye sighed. Riggs had taken up a position nearby, resting on his stomach. He was relaxed, his big head resting on his front paws on the floor near the doorway. Riggs had an expression on his face that made Skye wonder if he had any idea what was going on.

Or was he still guarding her?

At that moment it didn't matter. Though she wasn't much of a dog person, Riggs was beginning to grow on her, especially after he had gotten Toby away from her in the parking lot at her office. Skye walked over to the refrigerator and opened it up. She looked around and found a piece of cheese. Dogs could have cheese, couldn't they?

She set it on the counter and opened the cabinet doors looking for something she could put water in. Dogs needed water. And she guessed by the size of Riggs, probably a lot of it. A minute later, she found a plastic bowl. "This will have to do, buddy," she said, looking at him. Seeing her move around the kitchen, Riggs had picked his head up, his ears. Skye ran the water in the sink for a second and then filled the bowl up halfway, setting it down near where Riggs was resting. She pulled the wrapper off a slice of American cheese she'd found at the bottom of the deli drawer in Naomi's fridge and fed him a few bites. She started by putting them on the floor. Seeing how gently he picked them up, she tried holding it with her fingers, hoping he didn't bite her. She was surprised to find how tentatively he took the cheese from her.

"Gentle, Riggs," Skye heard Logan behind her.

As she turned around, she saw that Logan had a crooked smile on his face. It was cute. "Are you trying to corrupt my dog?"

"No, why?"

"American cheese isn't exactly in the approved diet for canine officers."

Skye shrugged. "Well, consider it a thank you for saving my life."

Logan chuckled. "Well, in that case, I guess we can let it pass." He stood watching as Riggs drank almost half of the water that Naomi had offered him. "I'm guessing you think Naomi would be okay with Riggs sharing her food and water?"

Skye stopped. She hadn't even really thought about what Naomi's response would be to Skye taking food out of her refrigerator and using a bowl for a dog that she probably used for food. She blinked, surprised at her own behavior. She was crossing boundaries left and right. She straightened. "I think Naomi would be grateful that someone was looking out for her, so I don't think she would mind," she said stiffly.

"Fair enough."

Feeling guilty, Skye picked up the plastic bowl, poured the

rest of the water in the sink, used some soap and washed it, quickly drying it and putting it back in the cabinet where she found it. "No harm, no foul," she muttered under her breath.

With everything back in place, Skye turned toward Logan and asked, "What are we gonna do now?"

"We?" Logan asked. "I'm going to drive you back to your house to make sure that you get home safely. After that, I'm going to see what I can do to find Toby Graham."

Skye almost said, "Not Naomi?" But she bit her tongue. "I don't want to go home."

"Why?" Logan said, frowning.

"You know." Skye looked at the ground.

"What do you propose?"

"Well, I'm already involved in the case. You may need a mental health professional to help you with Toby."

"If I don't shoot him first."

Skye pressed her lips together and raised her eyebrows. "As a psychologist, I can tell you that there are many better ways to deal with someone who is having mental issues."

"And as the woman he tried to attack an hour ago?"

"Either you pull the trigger, or I will."

It was Logan's turn to raise his eyebrows. "Remind me to never mess with you."

"So noted."

"So what you're saying is you want to ride along with me and Riggs?"

Skye stared at the ground. She was almost afraid to admit that was what she wanted to happen. "If it's okay."

When she looked up, she saw Logan with his fingers buried in the fur behind Riggs's neck. "What do you think, boy? Is it okay if Skye rides along with us?"

The big dog looked up at Logan and then at Skye and then sat at Logan's feet. Logan shrugged. "I'll take that as a yes. But only under one condition."

"What's that?"

"That you remember that you're not law enforcement. You have to do exactly what I tell you to do when I tell you to do it."

It sounded like a reasonable request. Skye could tell that Logan was a natural protector, a police officer who was far less concerned about the power of the position and more concerned about the role of protecting people who were in harm's way. She liked that about him. She studied him for a second. Despite his sharp jaw and short beard, his eyes were kind and soft. She'd seen him look at Bella with a mixture of love and protectiveness that she'd never experienced in her life. She wondered what his expression had been like when his wife had died. Had it been pained? Filled with love? Both?

Rachel had been lucky. Logan seemed like one of the few good guys left out there.

48

Logan honestly didn't know if he should be amused or infuriated by Skye's demand to go along with him. There was a third option — empathy.

Based on the story that she told him about Dr. Nate McCord, her broken jaw and arm, and the way that Toby had nearly dragged her away, Logan couldn't blame her. Skye was a conundrum, that was for sure, he thought.

Skye was strong and tough, yet vulnerable at the same time. It was clear she was wounded in her own way, but then again, so was he. Logan could tell that somewhere underneath all the pretty outfits, bluster, and psychological talk, that her own heart had been broken, maybe even more than once. It made sense, especially given the fact that she had decided to become a psychology major after the abuse. At the time, she was probably as much seeking help for her own issues as she wanted to help other people.

Either way, it was admirable in his book.

Logan straightened. "Alright, before I get everyone else involved, any ideas where Toby would have gone?"

"No."

"Okay. I think our next stop is going to be his house."

As they walked out to the truck, Riggs leading the way, Logan pulled his cell phone out of his back pocket. He dialed Zara. They were a small enough department that she preferred to be in the loop on anything big.

"This better be good news."

"Do I ever call you with bad news?"

"All the time."

"Fair enough."

"What do you want?"

Logan smiled. Zara's harsh banter was the product of years of working in a male dominated industry. Law enforcement, for all the progress they had made, was still a boy's club for the most part. Logan ignored her tone. She didn't mean anything by it. Down deep, Zara had a heart of gold. She was intensely loyal to her officers, especially those that worked hard and were loyal to her.

"I've got a little problem I need some help with." Logan went on to describe how he'd responded to the call for Dr. Johnston, managed to chase Toby Graham away, at which point Skye had revealed that Naomi was her client and that she was involved in a three-way love affair with her current boyfriend, Toby Graham, and a guy from her office, Ian Dunn.

"And I'm guessing this is the same Ian Dunn we found in a cave with Bella?"

"Correct."

"And I'm guessing, based on the attempted assault of Dr. Johnston, you'd like to take a run over to Mr. Graham's house and have a word with him."

"Correct." Logan had learned that with Zara if you simply answered the question she asked you, things went far more smoothly.

"And am I also to assume that you would prefer to do this with a little backup?"

"Given the way he went after Skye, yeah. I mean, I have Riggs and all, but —"

"Done. Let me radio dispatch and have them send a couple cars over there."

"Thanks, Chief."

"You're welcome. Be careful and keep me posted."

Despite the tension between Skye and Chief Walsh, Logan had no doubt that by the time they pulled in over at Toby Graham's house, there would be other cruisers there ready to assist.

Eight minutes later, when they pulled down Toby Graham's street, Logan realized his assumption had been correct.

Logan watched as Skye got out of the car and stood near the front bumper of his truck while he went and talked to two other officers who had arrived on the scene. A minute later, he walked back toward her. "We need to go check the house to see if Toby is inside." He handed Skye the leash to Riggs. "How about if you take care of Riggs for me while I'm in there?"

Skye looked down at the big dog. He was so tall next to her petite frame that his head hit her at about mid-thigh. He looked up at her and then at Logan as if he was trying to figure out what was going on. "I don't know, I don't know how to —"

Logan held his hand up. "All you need to do is tell him to sit, Skye. You can handle it. He'll keep you safe while I'm inside with the other guys. If anything happens just let go of the leash. He'll know what to do."

Logan didn't wait for any other questions from Skye. She was the kind that would fuss and argue with him for way too long. And if they had any hopes of finding Toby, and hopefully Naomi, he needed to move quickly. The fewer questions the better.

By the time he got to the front door, two other Highmill police officers had joined him there. They were all dressed in matching tactical vests, their guns pulled, aimed for the ground. Officer Hauser, one of the youngest guys in the department, held something that Logan called the gizmo in his hand. It was an electronic lock picker, something the department had just purchased. As much as Logan wanted to snatch it out of his hand, Zara had sent Hauser to the training, so he got to use it until the rest of their order came in.

The premise was simple. Stick the prongs in the door lock, wait for a second while, a little computer moved pieces of metal around until it found the correct combination to pop the lock open, and voila. No damage done to the door and almost instantaneous, silent entry.

Almost.

Logan gave a nod and Officer Houser shoved the gizmo in the door. There was just the whisper of whirring, then the light turned green. Officer Houser turned the handle on the gizmo to the right and the door popped open as if they had some sort of a magic key.

Hauser grinned.

Logan didn't stop to give him an atta boy. If they waited and Toby was home, even the slightest noise could give him a tactical advantage. Logan held two fingers up in the air and pointed inside. He led the way. He knew Hauser and the other guy dispatch had sent, Caden, would fan out behind him. They'd done this drill a million times during training, if not more. Highmill, New York, might be a sleepy town, but Zara had been good about investing in ongoing training for her team. She said it kept them sharp and safe.

And at that moment, Logan couldn't agree more.

Within a minute or two, the three men had managed to clear the house from top to bottom. As they emerged outside, he saw that Skye and Riggs had moved up the driveway. He jogged over to where they were standing, taking the leash from Skye. "I thought I told you to stay by the truck."

"I tried, but Riggs was whining. He kept pulling. He's really strong." Skye raised her eyebrows as if she was trying to play the innocent.

Logan wasn't buying it. Riggs was too well-trained for that. "I bet you could have stopped him if you wanted to."

"Well, maybe," Skye muttered under her breath.

Logan raised his eyebrows.

Skye looked away for a second like a kid who'd gotten their hand stuck in the cookie jar, and then back at Logan, her expression hard. "I take it he wasn't in there?"

"No. We're ready for you to walk through. Think you can do that? Maybe give me some insight as to what makes this guy tick?"

Skye stayed silent but nodded.

Without saying anything else, Skye started walking up the driveway, her arms folded in front of her chest. Whether it was from being nervous or being cold, Logan had no idea.

He followed Skye into the house, Riggs right on her heels. As they got to the door, Hauser and Caden stepped aside, letting Skye through.

Skye stopped and looked around. She turned and stared at Logan. "A full profile of this guy could take me weeks. The best I can do is some impressions right now like I did with Ian's house."

"I'll take what I can get."

As Skye started to move away, Logan put Riggs in a sit and then unclipped his leash from his collar. Logan looked at the big dog and whispered, "Follow," giving him the same command they used earlier at Ian Dunn's house. Logan knew that the house was clear. But he also knew that Skye needed the comfort of feeling protected if they had any hope of getting good information out of her. She was still rattled by what had happened earlier. It wasn't as though he could blame her. Being involved in an attack could take hours to recover from even on just a physical level.

He shook his head. What most people didn't realize is that many times the law enforcement officers were the ones who suffered the most when there was an incident. He'd seen more than once when an ambulance was called for an officer whose blood pressure had skyrocketed from the adrenaline jump of a chase or an arrest. As a rookie, Logan remembered a time when an old sergeant had a massive coronary at a scene and had died. It had been a shock. They'd lost a good cop that day. Logan hadn't had that problem — at least not yet…

But at that moment, the best he could do for Skye was to send Riggs with her.

She returned to where Logan was standing near the front door chatting with Hauser and Caden a few minutes later. "I didn't spend a lot of time looking through his stuff. But his closet tells a very interesting story."

Logan grabbed her by the arm and guided her away from the other officers. Given what Skye had been through, he thought she might need a little space. "What's that?"

She scowled. "Everything is perfectly arranged. It's almost to the level where I would suspect he has some sort of OCD. You know what that is, right? Obsessive compulsive disorder."

"I've heard of it."

"It's a way for people to manage anxiety. They attempt to overly control their physical environment in order to overcome other things they're anxious about."

"Like those people that wash their hands all the time?"

"Yes. That's one manifestation of it, but it's more complex than that."

"Okay, so what does that have to do with his closet?"

Skye glanced toward the direction of Toby's bedroom and then back at Logan. "Every article of clothing is organized by color and by shirt sleeve length. It looks like a men's clothing store up there. Honestly, I've never seen anything like it. The bathroom looks exactly the same. I bet if you opened any cabinet or drawer in this house, you would see a high level of organization, like something you'd see on one of those home renovation programs on television."

Logan walked into the kitchen. He could hear Riggs's nails on the floor behind him. That meant Skye was following. He opened a cabinet door and saw exactly what Skye was talking about. All of the food that was in that cabinet was organized by category, neatly arranged as if Toby was running some sort of a store or expecting Martha Stewart to stop by at any moment. Logan closed the cabinet door and then opened a drawer, finding exactly the same thing. "Oh jeez, you're right. Now I really feel like a slob."

Skye shook her head. "Don't. This is the level of organization that signals a neurosis — a pretty serious one. People like this have a need to control every single aspect of their life. And when they can't, they can come unglued, and in a big way."

The pieces were starting to fall together. "Like what we saw with Toby and you earlier?"

Skye paled slightly at the reference. "Exactly. This is someone who is spiraling. He's grasping for a way to get back in control again."

"What would have triggered him?"

"That I can't tell you for sure. I believe that part of it was Naomi's waning interest."

"Do you think he knew about Ian Dunn?"

"I don't know. We had talked about her breaking up with Toby, but she hadn't said anything about actually telling Toby about Ian before it happened. Now, seeing this, that would have been the last thing I would have recommended."

"And if Toby found out about it on his own?"

"That, kind of combined with work stress that you described earlier? Yeah, that would be enough to cause him to spiral out of control. No question about it. Anything Toby would have considered a deception would have thrown him even farther out of feeling in control."

Logan shook his head. "The only problem is I don't know where he's gone. Do you think Toby took her?"

"It's likely, though I can't be sure. If he thought their relationship was on the edge, he might have grabbed her and taken her somewhere to try to get control again. He was very focused on what she and I had said about him."

"He didn't ask about her or what she was feeling?"

"Not per se. He got in my face and demanded to know about himself."

"That's strange."

Skye sighed. "Actually not so much. People with anxiety driven OCD are often concerned with how they appear to others — whether they've been found to be less than."

"So you think he grabbed Naomi? She didn't leave willingly?"

"No way. Leave her wallet and phone? Who would?"

Logan had to agree. There was just too much evidence for him to think otherwise. "Where would he take Naomi? Did she give you any clues of things they liked to do together?"

"No. We didn't really talk about their dates in great detail," Skye said, wrapping her arms across her chest. She grimaced and then her face brightened. She pointed. "Wait, I might be able to help with that."

Logan followed as Skye walked out of the kitchen and back into the family room. There was an antique writing desk pushed up against the wall. Logan noticed the beautiful woodwork and how it was polished to a high sheen. Toby's OCD or not, it was a gorgeous piece. On it were a series of photographs. They were all in matching frames of different sizes. Skye pointed.

"See that picture?"

Logan bent over and stared at it. It was of a man and a

woman. The man looked identical to the one that he'd almost caught in the parking lot at Dr. Johnston's office. "What about it?"

"That's Toby and Naomi. It's at a marina. I wonder if Toby has a boat?"

Logan nodded. "Good thinking. Let me have the office run the records."

49

Skye paced nervously back and forth outside while she waited for Logan to talk to Hauser and Caden, the other officers that had shown up to help him clear Toby's house. Logan had sent her out with Riggs, holding the leash. "All you gotta do is walk. He'll follow. He knows what to do."

Why Logan kept sending the dog with her, she wasn't sure. Riggs wasn't exactly a therapy dog, though it did give her some comfort that he was nearby.

Or maybe she did. Riggs was a trained K9 officer. He'd already protected her once. Maybe Logan thought it would make her feel more comfortable after what she'd been through.

Glancing down at the top of Riggs's head, she realized it was something, at least, she thought, a kind gesture that she couldn't help but appreciate. She pushed the thought away. Relationships were something she was good at helping other people sort out. Her own relationships were another issue entirely, one that scared her.

By the time Logan had come out of the house, doing a final search of his own, the other two cruisers had left. Where exactly they'd gone, Skye wasn't sure, though she had heard their radios going off. Most likely, they probably had some other call they had to attend to. Highmill was filled with bars and restaurants, not to mention families in domestic disputes, robberies, and pretty much anything else you could think of. Small towns weren't immune to serious crime, no matter what a romance novel would lead people to believe.

A minute later, Logan emerged from the house, jogging toward her. His expression was serious.

"Anything else happen inside while I was out here?" Skye realized she was happy to be outside. After what had happened with Toby, she didn't have the stomach to stay in his house any longer than she had to.

Logan shook his head, his lips pressed together. "No. Nothing yet."

"Where did the other guys go?"

"They probably had a call." Logan turned up his radio for a second and listened to it. He nodded. "Yeah, they got a call. Drunk and disorderly over at the Valley Inn."

Skye was only half interested in where Officer Hauser and Officer Caden had gotten off to. She felt impatience start to nip at her gut. "What are we doing now, Logan?"

"Waiting for a minute."

The waiting thing wasn't working well for her. "Waiting for what?"

"For a call back from dispatch. They're running some records for me. It should be just a minute. You don't have to be anywhere, do you?" He grinned.

At this time of night? After getting attacked by Toby Graham? Other than sitting in her house alone with Toby on the loose, Skye had nothing going on, but she wasn't sure she wanted to admit that. "I guess not."

The truth was that Skye didn't have anywhere else she needed to be. Other than occasionally meeting friends or colleagues for drinks or dinner, she never had any activities in the evening. She didn't belong to any clubs, any groups, preferred to shop online, and was pretty much comfortable in only two locations — her home and her office. The fact that Logan had picked up on it either so quickly or so inadvertently, left Skye with a queasy feeling. She wasn't sure what to think. Should she be embarrassed or relieved?

Before she had a chance to say anything else, Logan's phone rang. He put it on speaker. "Hey, Chief."

"Fletcher, I have news. I heard the call for background on Toby Graham's assets. Is that right?"

"Yeah. Why are you calling me back? I called dispatch. Didn't want to bother you again."

"Bother me?" Zara said dryly. "It's my department."

Logan rolled his eyes. "Did you find anything out?"

"Maybe. There's a boat down at West River Marina that's registered to him."

"Any idea what kind of boat it is?"

"From what I can tell from the title work we pulled, it looks like a thirty-two-foot Wellcraft. You know, one of those go-fast boats with a cabin in the front part of the hull?"

Logan nodded.

Skye watched the conversation with amusement. Logan had put Zara on speaker but hadn't bothered to tell her that Skye was standing right there. She sucked in a breath like she was going to say something and then, seeing the cautionary look on Logan's face, decided to stop.

"Okay, thanks. I'll check it out."

Skye raised her eyebrows. *I* will check it out? He was going to go alone?

As Logan ended the call, he looked at her. "Feel like going for another drive?"

Anything was better than going home, at least until Skye had a better idea where exactly Toby had gone. "Yeah, sure."

50

"You really want to go? You sure you don't want me to take you home?" Logan pulled Skye's key fob out of his pocket. "Oh yeah, Hauser gave this to me. They parked your car in front of your house for you."

Skye looked back at Logan as they headed for his truck. She knew what he was really asking her — was she ready to possibly face down the person that had just attacked her?

"Thanks, and yes, I do want to go." She didn't feel the question required any more discussion than that.

Logan gave a sharp nod and started the truck.

"Alright. Let's see if we can go find Naomi. If she's not there, then we're gonna have to regroup."

A chill ran down Skye's spine. What if Naomi wasn't there? Skye didn't even want to consider the possibility. Men like Toby Graham were unpredictable when their control was threatened. There was no telling what he was capable of doing. Clearly his need for control was pushing him to aggression, possibly even violence. His little demonstration in the parking lot was evidence of that.

As they drove, neither of them said anything. Skye could

hear a few bars of country music playing in the background. Logan was the kind of guy that liked country? She wasn't sure she would have pegged him as someone who did, but then again, he had a daughter. It might be just what he played in the car while they were together. The only other sound was the soft panting of Riggs from the back seat.

Skye glanced over her shoulder. Riggs was lying down, his head resting against the seat of the truck. His eyes were alert, yet calm, clearly enjoying all of the time running around as best she could tell. Skye had never been a dog person. She'd never been raised with them, but now she could kind of see why Logan was so attached to his partner. Riggs was powerful and calming. It was a good combination.

As Skye looked in the back seat and then turned her head toward the front, she caught a glimpse of Logan's profile. He was tapping his fingers on the steering wheel as if he was marking time before they got to the marina. Part of her wondered if he'd been on calls there before. Henderson Lake was a beautiful place in the summertime. The tree-lined lake filled with cottages and small marinas where families would come for a weekend to enjoy being out on the water after a long winter.

But Henderson Lake had a darker side. It was a favorite place for suicides. By her count, Skye knew that anywhere from two to four people each year took their life out at the lake, the beauty in the summertime becoming eerie and ghostly in the winter, large sheets of ice moving silently across the surface of the water, ready to take anyone who dared enter it into a state of hypothermia almost immediately. Most incidents involved someone jumping from the bridge into the water. Skye couldn't imagine the last moments for someone who was teetering on the edge of the ironwork, their terror, their grief, the waves of depression and exhaustion covering them. It would take all of that to make someone jump into the dark, icy waters below, knowing they'd never come up again.

She rubbed her chin. Henderson Lake was both beautiful and tragic at the same time.

Hopefully, today wouldn't end in another one of those tragedies.

Skye stared out the side window. She had a vague idea of where they were — somewhere trailing along the southern edge of the lake — but she didn't know specifically where they were. The thought caught her by surprise. How had she built up that level of trust with Logan that she didn't feel the need to know exactly where they were so fast? Was it just that he was a police officer? She shifted in her seat. People that worked in law enforcement weren't immune to bad behavior. A lump formed in her throat and then quickly subsided.

She glanced over at him again wondering if he was single or dating someone. When she'd been at his house, she hadn't seen any evidence of a woman in his life. There was no hand-wringing girlfriend worried about him or Bella when she'd disappeared and no texts that Logan seemed to be focused on responding to. Maybe he was single? Part of Skye wondered if Logan was open to a new relationship, from a professional perspective, of course, she told herself. It would be good for Bella.

Or maybe it wouldn't.

Skye shook the thought from her head. It was hard to believe she was even thinking about Logan's relationships. Hers never worked out. Not once. Skye bit her lip. She needed to get her thinking under control. Yes, he had come to her rescue. Yes, he had been a good companion for the last two days, but she had her work to focus on.

Skye straightened in her seat. *C'mon Skye. You are here to help with the case and find Naomi. That's all. After that, it's back to work and swimming. Focus.*

"We're almost there."

"Okay." Logan's voice cut through her thoughts. She realized her mouth was dry. Her mind had run away with her, which was fine while she was in the truck with Logan and Riggs.

It wouldn't be fine if she couldn't regain her focus to try to help find Naomi.

Skye gripped her hands into fists, feeling her nails bite into the palms of her hands. She glanced for a split second at Logan and then turned to the window as they pulled into the marina.

"I'm ready."

51

Skye leaned forward in her seat as they passed through the gate of the West River Marina. There was a blue sign out front that was desperately in need of painting, plus a metal gate that had been left open. Apparently, no one was too concerned about trespassers this time of year.

The shadows were long on the driveway as Logan's truck made its way towards the lake. After following the road as it curled to the left and then back to the right, Skye heard the tires of the truck as they hit gravel. Up ahead, the headlights cut through the darkness, lighting up a series of muddy puddles filled with water from the horrendous rains of the two days before. Skye reached for the dashboard to steady herself as the truck rocked back and forth on the rough driveway.

"Sorry," Logan muttered, glancing in her direction. "This driveway is a mess."

"It's fine."

Skye wasn't as fragile as maybe Logan thought.

Or maybe she was.

In the chilly spring weather, the puddles could take weeks

to dry up. Trees edging the driveway were still naked of their spring leaves, the ends of their branches just starting to swell with running sap and new life that would cause all of Highmill to be painted in shades of verdant greens in the coming weeks. Skye knew that it wouldn't take too long before spring actually looked like it sprung in their area of New York.

The driveway widened out as they passed through a second gate. This one was also open, a keypad set off to the side that seemed to be hanging by a few wires, as if someone had started to fix it and then stopped.

Skye focused on what she was seeing ahead of her. There was a wide parking lot in front of them, a stretch of empty docks jutting out into the darkness. The majority of the boats at the West River Marina were still up on their jack stands, many of them still shrouded in stark white shrink wrap to protect them from damaging winds and snows of winter. A few of them were uncovered, maybe half a dozen by Skye's estimation, ladders left abandoned off to the side of the hulls, evidence of the fact that their owners had been out to start their summer preparations but hadn't had their boat dropped in yet.

The massive blue-painted travel lift stood off to the side, the straps used to lift the hulls off the stands and drop them in the water swinging gently in the night breeze coming off the lake. Ahead of them, Skye could see just a handful of boats in the water — only three boats by her count. Two of them were small, one of them a little longer in size. Probably early spring fishermen as she had to guess by the size and style of their boats.

"Any idea which one is his?"

"Zara said it's a thirty-two-foot cruiser." Logan pointed.

"Do we know if it's in the water yet?"

"Dispatch was trying to get ahold of the guy that owns the marina, but they haven't gotten back to me yet." Logan stopped the truck. "I'm guessing if he's here, his boat is in the water. If it was up on stands, he'd have no power. He'd also have to get Naomi to climb a ladder to get inside."

"Sounds logical."

Logan pointed. "If that's the case, it has to be that one over there. The other two are too small."

Skye's stomach knotted. There was a long boat with a pointed bow at the far end of one of the docks. It was tied off by itself, gently bobbing up and down on the current in the lagoon. It looked peaceful, but if Toby had Naomi inside, it would be anything but.

Logan checked his phone. "Zara just texted me."

Skye's stomach lurched. "What did she say?"

"She said, 'Backup is on the way.' She wants me to wait."

Skye raised her eyebrows. "And are we gonna do that?"

Logan grinned. "Probably not."

Skye liked the way he was thinking. As she slid out of the truck, she expected Logan to get Riggs out as well.

He didn't.

"Riggs isn't coming with us?"

"No. Don't know exactly what we're going to find out here. It could be close quarters on a boat. We haven't done a lot of training near the lake. Don't want him to fall in and then I've gotta fish him out. He'll be safer here. He's a big dog."

"I hadn't noticed."

"Very funny." Logan's face became serious. "We'll walk down there and see what we can see, then wait for backup."

Skye nodded. Part of her was glad that Logan didn't want to wait for backup to arrive to go see the boat and check it out. If Naomi was on there, then every moment mattered not only to her physical health but to her mental health as well. But part of her was concerned. If Riggs didn't go, then Skye was Logan's backup.

And she wasn't exactly a police officer.

And she was wearing a dress.

The thought of Skye being Logan's only backup didn't seem to impact Logan whatsoever, at least not by the expression on his face. As Skye walked around the front of the truck, Logan met her near the bumper. He pulled his gun from his holster, pulling the slide back ever so gently while it was pointed at the ground. "I'm locked and loaded. You ready?"

Skye fought off the urge to shake her head at his comment. "Sure. Let's go."

"Follow me."

As they walked, Skye followed behind Logan. He clicked on his flashlight as they made their way from the truck down to the edge of the docks. The air smelled murky, as though something had been dredged up from the bottom of the lake nearby. Skye tried to ignore the smell, figuring it was either a dead fish or something else.

Then she realized that a dead fish would be the best option at that moment.

The minute they walked onto the dock, Logan clicked his flashlight off. The darkness surrounding them was absolute, the murky water below them seeming to absorb any extra light that was available. It took everything Skye had to keep her feet moving forward. It was cold and pitch black. Without Logan's form in front of her, navigating the docks, she was sure she would have fallen into the water.

The only sound around them was a gentle lapping of the water against the dock posts and their footfalls on the wooden dock planks. For some reason, as they walked, Skye felt like the boat got farther and farther away, though it didn't. Whether it just an optical illusion or the feeling of something sinister, Skye couldn't tell, but everything in her wanted to turn and go back to the truck.

She kept walking.

As they got closer, she could see a light on from a subtle glow from a porthole in the bow of the boat. She frowned. This wasn't the kind of boat that had a lot of living space. It looked like one that had just a small area in the front of the bow. The back was completely open. From what she could see as she followed behind Logan, there was no one sitting back there, though she didn't take long to look. It was so dark she was trying hard to concentrate on where she was walking. She felt like the dock was wobbling under her boots, though it was fixed. What was happening to her? Maybe vertigo from the darkness? Skye walked quicker, catching up to Logan. Falling into the cold waters of Henderson Lake that time of year would lead to almost instant hypothermia. It wasn't the kind of distraction that would help them get Naomi back, that was sure.

Though it felt like it took a long time, the walk from the edge of the parking lot out to the boat probably only took a minute or two. As they got closer, she noticed that Logan's posture stiffened. He stopped in front of her, pulling his gun from the holster and grabbing it with both hands. "You see those lights on?" he whispered.

Skye nodded.

"Somebody's on that boat. I'm going in."

"This is a bad idea. We should wait. Isn't that what Zara said to do?"

As the words came out of her mouth, she couldn't believe she was actually taking Zara's side.

He glanced back at her, his face serious, his jaw set. "I'll go myself, Skye. You can go back to the truck. If your friend Naomi is on that boat, she's down there with a madman. All the pieces fit. The love triangle gone bad, Toby's controlling personality, the affair with Ian Dunn. It all fits. I know he's the one that's responsible for the murder and Naomi's disappearance. I can feel it in my gut. Heck, if I hadn't rolled up on you as fast as I did, there's no telling what would have happened to you."

Skye shivered. She didn't doubt his assessment, she was doubting herself. "Okay, I'll stay with you," she breathed. "Just remember, I'm not Riggs."

"No, you're not," he glanced at her and gave her a wink. "You're much cuter."

52

Skye didn't have a chance to process Logan's comment. He took off in front of her, walking quickly, closing the distance to the boat with the lights on. His posture had completely changed. Holding his gun up in front of his face, he walked with bent knees, rolling his feet heel to toe. He looked like someone who was in full battle mode, like one of the thriller movies Skye watched late at night on television that featured a SWAT team.

As they got to the back of the boat, Logan stepped on board, holding his hand up and waving Skye forward. She stepped from the dock onto the boat, staying hidden behind him. Why he brought her with him, he wasn't sure. She wasn't a cop, didn't have a gun, and wasn't exactly dressed to help.

What she did have was a working knowledge of the people involved. That could be the difference in how the case turned out, he realized.

He held a finger up and then pointed at the back hatch door. The glow of light was coming from there. "I'm going to have to move fast. Stay with me or stay out of the way."

"Okay."

Logan lowered his chin. "And whatever you do, don't get in front of my gun."

Skye licked her lips. The last thing she wanted to do that night was get shot. "Sure. Right," she managed to mutter.

Logan took a couple of steps forward. Skye knew that if anybody was down below, they knew by now that someone else had gotten on board. They'd feel the boat dip to one side.

They were out of time.

Logan crossed the back deck in a single step and approached the hatch door, tugging it to the side and staying in the darkness. Skye could barely breathe. She stood back, trying to get a look down below. She couldn't see much from her vantage point behind Logan, except that the space seemed small.

Logan disappeared ahead of her down a set of narrow steps. Skye drew in a sharp breath as she heard scuffling. The next thing Skye heard caused her skin to crawl. "Don't do it, Toby! I'm telling you, don't do it!"

Then there was silence.

A moment later she heard some low voices. They sounded strained. She couldn't make out the words. Was she supposed to stay put or go back to the truck? She was just about to get off the bobbing boat when Logan's voice cut through the darkness. "Skye? Can you come down here?"

Skye took two steps forward, her legs weak. She peered down below and started down the steps. The space was tight — probably not more than ten feet wide and about the same in length, most of it taken up by a built-in table and a short set of cabinets with a half-size refrigerator and a two-burner stove. His back to the steps, Logan stood with his gun up to his face, his finger on the trigger, his expression stony and focused. Not more than five feet in front of him was Toby. He had Naomi in front of him like a human shield, a closed door behind him, his arm wrapped around her throat, a knife touching her skin.

"Well, if it isn't Dr. Skye Johnston, the source of all of my grief," Toby's voice dripped with sarcasm.

As Skye made it down the steps, Logan motioned for her to stay behind him. She took up a position off his left shoulder, as close to the steps as she could manage. Her skin was tingling. She was within a few feet of someone who was holding a hostage. If she didn't stay calm, there was no telling what could happen.

Skye drew in a slow breath, trying to keep her voice even. "Hey, Toby. You wanna tell me what's going on here?"

Toby narrowed his eyes. "Oh, now you wanna talk? You want to use some of your theories on me, Dr. Johnston, now that you know I've got your girl here?"

Skye felt her heart thundering in her chest. She sucked in another slow, deep breath. "No, Toby. You're too smart for that. I just wanted to check on my patient." Skye looked at Naomi. "Naomi? Are you okay?"

It was the dumbest question in the world. Skye could tell by how Naomi looked that she was definitely not okay. Her cheeks were sunken, there were black circles under her eyes, and her lips were pale, almost the same color as her face, as if either shock or the cold had gotten to her. Skye stared at her for a second and gave her a slight nod, one that she hoped Naomi interpreted as, "Hang in there, we're gonna try to get you out of this."

But Skye wasn't sure that was going to be possible.

Logan took half a step back, lining up his sights on Toby. "Listen, Toby, clearly we have a lot to talk about, but I can't really concentrate very well when you've got a knife to Naomi's neck. How about if you drop it and we'll have a man-to-man discussion and see what we can resolve?"

"Resolve?" Toby chuckled. "There's nothing to resolve here, Officer. You have trespassed onto my boat. Me and my girlfriend, we are just hanging out, just dealing with a few of our issues. Oh wait, she's actually not my girlfriend anymore." Toby narrowed his eyes. "We've made it official. Show them what I gave you, baby."

Weakly, Naomi held up her left hand. There was a diamond ring on her fourth finger. "Just a little while ago I asked Naomi if she'd become my wife. She agreed. So now, you are interfering in a domestic dispute. Nothing to worry about here."

Nothing but the knife to her neck. Skye balled her hands into fists. What did Toby think was going to happen? Did he think that Skye and Logan would apologize and get off his boat? Certainly he wasn't that unglued from reality, was he? Skye stiffened. By the looks of it, time was running out. Men like Toby didn't do well when they were cornered.

And that was exactly the position he was in.

As the words came out of his mouth, Skye could see his grip on Naomi tighten. The knife began to dig into her neck, a few drops of blood running crimson toward her collarbone. Skye's mouth went dry. One false move and Toby could end Naomi's life with a mere tightening of the sharp blade against her carotid artery.

Skye cleared her throat. "Toby, you know this isn't right. Naomi has told me what a gentleman you are. I'm not seeing that. You're standing with a knife to your fiancée's neck."

"This isn't right? Who are you to judge, Dr. Johnston? From what I hear from Naomi, you don't have much of a personal life. What would you know about being treated well by a gentleman? Never been married, no kids. What do you know about relationships? And yet here you are trying to screw mine up. You're the one that caused Naomi to stray."

"Excuse me?" Skye furrowed her eyebrows together.

"Yeah, she told me all about it, how you are the one that told her she could do better. That's why she ran to Ian Dunn."

Skye watched as Logan shifted his position just slightly. "Tell me about Ian, Toby."

Toby laughed out loud. "Oh, and now our police officer wants to know what happened to Ian. I bet you do!" Toby spat, dragging Naomi backwards toward an open cabin door by a few more inches. "He's a loser. Sorry, *was* a loser. He was preying on the women in his organization, flaunting his success and his position. But it's okay, Naomi and I have talked about it. She knows that I'm not the kind of man that'll play second fiddle to anyone. And I protected her. I took care of Ian. He won't trouble anyone anymore, will he, honey?" As the words came out of Toby's mouth, he leaned toward Naomi, landing a kiss on her cheek.

A single tear ran down Naomi's face.

Skye felt like throwing up. In all of her years as a psychologist, she'd never run into someone as out of touch with reality as Toby. And the scary thing was, he was functional, the kind of psychopath that was loose among the rest of the population.

He was the most dangerous kind.

Skye saw the muscles in Logan's back tense out of the corner of her eye. They were in a standoff. If they didn't do something soon, people were going to die.

And maybe all of them.

53

Chief Zara Walsh spotted Logan's dark truck the moment that she pulled into West River Marina. She jumped out of her car muttering curse words under her breath as fast as her persistently sore knees would allow her to do so. The pain was an almost daily reminder that her doctor had told her to get knee replacements, and she had stubbornly put that off.

Logan had clearly not listened to her. Where had he gone?

As she checked for her gun at her side, an old habit from the police academy after one time she showed up to class without it and was embarrassed in front of the other recruits, she swore again, this time much louder. Was Logan's truck really dark? Was she seeing things?

She pressed her lips together. She could have his badge for defying orders. Trotting over to it, she only half expected to find him inside.

Only half because she knew how he was.

It was empty. Riggs was whining in the backseat. Zara opened the back door. "Did they leave you behind, Riggs?" Riggs whined and then barked staring toward the edge of the dock. Zara's stomach sunk. She'd attended enough canine training to know that something was going on, something that she wouldn't like, something that was a threat to Logan. "Come on, boy. Let's go."

Before Zara could say anything else, Riggs jumped out of the truck and took off, completely ignoring her shouts to sit and stay. He was down at the end of the dock before there was anything she could do.

54

The standoff had gone on for a good five to seven minutes by Skye's count. They were clearly in the realm of what could become a long-term standoff, save for the fact that they were in such a small space. Something would have to give, and soon. They couldn't maintain the status quo of Naomi being held by a knife for much longer.

Skye glanced at Logan after her next round of questions to Toby had failed. Logan's shoulders had to be fatigued from holding the gun up in a static position and the adrenaline surge. Skye's entire body felt tense. Nothing had changed except for the fact that Toby looked more angry and Naomi looked more scared. Every tactic Skye had tried to use on Toby, he seemed to be ignoring. She tried guilt, she tried negotiating, she tried suggestion, she even tried questioning his logic. All of it he managed to outmaneuver.

He was stubbornly insisting nothing was wrong while he was holding a knife to Naomi's throat. All Skye and Logan needed to do was leave and everything would be fine.

Toby had lost his mind.

The mere fact that Toby couldn't see what was going on

scared Skye. Skye was just about to put her hand on Logan's shoulder and encourage him to back up and to give Toby and Naomi a little bit more space, hoping to de-escalate the situation, when she heard a noise from behind her. She didn't have a chance to identify it before she saw Riggs out of the corner of her eye. In one smooth movement, he jumped down the steps and positioned himself in the middle of the fray, taking up a position in front of Logan and Skye, his teeth bared. Several sharp barks came out of him, a low growl following. As Skye looked toward Toby and Naomi, she could see the terror in their faces. The idea of being bitten by an animal pulled up a primal fear in people that was hard to explain. Skye's heart thundered in her chest. Now they were all at risk — Logan, Skye, Naomi, and even Riggs.

Something had to give.

Logan glanced over his shoulder for a second, giving Skye a look. What exactly it meant, she wasn't sure, but she knew she needed to be ready. Logan looked at Toby and said clearly, "Toby Graham, you are under arrest for the murder of Ian Dunn, for the kidnapping of Naomi Fraser, and for the attempted assault of Dr. Skye Johnston. Now let go of Naomi, drop the knife , and turn around with your hands up."

"Or what? You're gonna have your dog attack me?"

Something in the way that the words came out caught Skye's attention. Toby was afraid, probably for the first time.

Logan didn't give him a chance to answer. He yelled a command in German. Riggs jumped, lunging at Toby. He grabbed his right arm, his sharp teeth puncturing Toby's skin. Toby howled. As he did, Naomi fell off to the side. Skye grabbed her, dragging and pushing her toward the steps that led up and out of the cabin. She could hardly breathe. It all happened so fast. She had just helped Naomi get over the edge of the boat and onto the dock when she heard a gunshot. Skye stopped and looked, her heart sinking.

. . .

ZARA WAS HALFWAY down the dock when she saw two people emerge. She started running, looking over her shoulder to see Sergeant Kevin Mills and Officer Hauser joining the chase toward her. They were so focused on what was going on they didn't bother to acknowledge each other.

Then she heard the gunshot. Zara ran toward the two figures that had made it off the back of the boat. She squinted in the darkness. It was Skye Johnston and Naomi Fraser, the woman they had been looking for. Zara sprinted toward them on the narrow dock, ignoring the pain in her knees. As she dragged them away, she called into her radio, not seeing Logan or Riggs. "Dispatch, this is Chief Walsh. I need an ambulance at the West River Marina. Now!"

Zara looked at Skye as she wrapped her arm around Naomi. Naomi wasn't doing anything but shaking and groaning. Whatever she'd gone through on the boat had traumatized her. Zara looked at Skye, who was following close behind. "Are you okay?" Zara asked, glancing at Skye.

"I am. But Logan — he was on the boat with Toby."

Zara waved Mills and Hauser past her, herding the two women down the dock to safety. "It's okay, Skye. We'll figure it out. Just hang with me. Let's get the two of you out of the way."

55

It had all happened so fast. Leaving Riggs in the truck had been a tactical error, Logan realized later. Who exactly had let him loose out of the back seat, he had no idea, but he would definitely owe them a beer.

Logan heard a voice over his shoulder "Everything okay down here?" The question was coming from a voice he recognized — Kevin Mills.

Relief flooded over him. Backup had arrived. "We're okay. Come on down. I could use a hand."

Logan glanced over his shoulder, his gun still up in a firing position. Toby sat slumped against the wall in the belly of his boat, his hand up to his right shoulder. When Riggs had attacked, Logan was able to get a shot off as Riggs let go and backed away. Toby had lunged for Logan despite the bite to his arm, grabbing the knife off the ground.

At that point, Logan had no choice but to shoot him. Kevin stood next to Logan and nodded. "You can holster now, Fletcher. I've got this."

Logan didn't realize until that moment that he was frozen in his spot. He quickly reholstered and waited for Kevin to handcuff Toby and drag him off the boat. He called off Riggs, who was still standing near Toby, growling and showing his teeth.

Officer Houser came down below a moment later, surveyed the scene and shook his head. He offered Logan a hand as he climbed out of the living quarters below deck where Naomi had been held. Logan glanced down below and looked at Hauser, who was standing by, pulling on a pair of gloves. The boat was a crime scene now. "Better not to move anything," Logan said.

"Copy that," Hauser replied.

Logan walked off the boat, following Kevin, who had a hand on Toby's shoulder and another on the back of his cuffs and was pushing him down the dock, all the time Toby yelled, "You had no right to get on my boat! I'm gonna sue you for everything you're worth. You've ruined my life!"

The litany went on and on, Riggs following behind, occasionally growling as if he was warning Toby to behave.

As Logan was stepping off the dock into the parking lot, he saw Naomi sitting on the bumper of the ambulance that had just arrived. A moment later, the paramedics motioned to Naomi and got her settled on a gurney, covering her with blankets. Skye stood nearby, talking to her, leaning forward, holding her hand, a blanket wrapped around her as well.

Logan shook his head. Naomi was lucky to have someone like Skye in her life.

And now, so was he.

EPILOGUE

Skye had packed carefully for dinner at Logan's house. He said it was a thank you for all the help she'd given him over the last few days, first for helping him find Bella, then for her assistance in helping him figure out what had happened to Ian Dunn and Naomi Fraser.

Standing in her kitchen, she double-checked what she had packed — a new puzzle for Bella — puzzles were excellent for neurological development — as well as stopping to pick up an apple pie from the farmer's market. Logan had told her she was in charge of dessert.

The minute that Skye knocked on the door, it opened. Logan was in front of her, wearing an old pair of jeans and a T-shirt, a kitchen towel flipped over his shoulder, a wide grin on his face. "Come on in," he said, motioning her forward. "Here, let me take your bag for you."

"Okay, but there's one thing I need from it."

Skye reached inside and pulled out a big bag of dog treats. She'd spent twenty minutes in the treat aisle at the pet store trying to figure out exactly what to get Riggs. He'd helped them all that week. She figured he deserved a little reward as well.

Logan laughed. "Oh, so you brought him some treats? I guess you like dogs after all."

"Well, he did save me after all."

Skye ripped the bag open and fished a treat out, holding it gently for Riggs. Smelling food, he'd trotted over and sat dutifully in front of her, waiting patiently. He took it from her ever so gently as if he was trying to encourage her to give him more by his good behavior.

Logan shook his head. "I'm gonna lose my dog. You're gonna be his favorite."

Skye smirked. "I'm not already?"

Logan shook his head and walked off.

Skye followed. The house smelled amazing. The scent of garlic and basil filled the air. She took her coat off and draped it on a chair nearby. "Something smells good."

Before Logan could answer, Bella ran over, wrapping her arms around Skye's leg. Skye was a little taken aback by the five-year-old's demonstration. She wasn't used to people being so happy to see her, or at least not *that* happy. "Hi, Skye." Bella giggled.

Skye knelt down. "What are you giggling about?"

"Your name. It still sounds funny."

"That's okay. Do you know what?"

"What?"

"I brought you something. It's in that bag your dad took from me."

Bella slapped her thighs. "You did?"

Skye didn't have a chance to answer. Bella ran off before she could. A minute later, she came back squealing, "I love it, Skye!"

Logan called to her. "And what do you say?"

"Thank you!"

With that, Bella ran off to her bedroom. Skye stood in the middle of the kitchen and then decided to position herself on the other side of the counter from Logan. She and Logan were alone. There was a flock of butterflies flapping away in her stomach. Why, she wasn't actually sure.

Or was she?

Skye smoothed her sleeves. She'd changed her outfit three different times and finally settled on a pair of jeans and a red sweater. After blowing out her hair into soft waves, she'd added some cranberry-colored lipstick that nearly matched her sweater. She didn't want to look too overdressed, but also like she hadn't put any effort in either.

This was just a thank-you dinner, wasn't it? It wasn't like it was a date.

Maybe it was. Or, more accurately, maybe she hoped it was.

Skye shook the thoughts from her head. She pressed her lips together and then sucked in her breath. "So, what did you make for dinner? I'm starving!"

Logan had his back to her, stirring something on the stove. He looked her way, a big smile on his face. "Well, I've been off for the last couple days. Zara put me on administrative leave after the shooting. Thought I'd cook up something good. Hope you like Italian?"

"Of course." Skye knew Logan being on administrative leave was standard. They'd have to process the scene, process the reports, have Logan go see a police psychologist to determine if he was fit for duty, and then he would be back at it. She and Zara hadn't talked about their issues, but somehow in the face of the shooting, Skye's anger had dissipated. She would have preferred to talk through their issues, but somehow Zara's decisions didn't seem to matter anymore.

At least at the moment.

Skye focused on Logan, who was staring at a pot of water boiling furiously on the stove. Apparently, he was working off his energy by cooking.

"I hit up the market this morning while Bella was at school.

I made homemade spaghetti sauce and bought some fresh pasta. We've got garlic bread and meatballs and a big Caesar salad. Sound good?" Logan turned away, stirring his sauce again.

"It sounds delicious." She tapped her fingers on the kitchen counter. "Any news on the case?"

"Oh yeah, that," Logan said sarcastically. He wiped his hands on the towel and then walked toward her. Only a counter between them kept them apart. "Well, Toby has been transferred to a psych unit for an evaluation. I guess by the time they got him to Woodland Medical Center he was mumbling nonsense under his breath."

Skye nodded. In her mind that wasn't surprising. All of the foundations of Toby's life had been busted out from underneath him. Everything he'd been able to control — his job, his relationships, his freedom — had been pulled away.

"And how about you? Are you okay?"

Logan shrugged. "You know, it's never a good day when I have to pull my gun. It's even worse if I have to fire it. But, that said, I'm glad that Naomi is fine. I only hit Toby in the shoulder. He will be fine." Logan winced for a moment, as if the memories of the incident had surfaced. He stared at Skye. "Naomi is fine, isn't she?"

Skye nodded. Unlike Logan, who had taken time off from work, Skye had buried herself in it. Naomi had been in for a session every day for the last three days, working through the trauma and what had happened to her, seeing not only Skye, but another counselor on her staff that specialized in acute trauma therapies. After getting checked out at the hospital, Skye had tracked down Naomi's doctor and had them provide her with some anti-anxiety medication and anti-depressants she could use for the short term while she got her life put back together again. "She's doing okay. She's getting the help she needs. It's gonna be a long time before she trusts anyone again, I think."

Logan nodded. "I know how that is."

Skye looked down. The comment hit home. Would what Nate did to her ever go away enough for Skye to have a normal life? "So do I."

There was a heavy silence between the two of them for a moment.

Logan changed the subject, tossing his kitchen towel on the counter. "I think we're ready to eat. Bella!"

An hour later, after filling themselves with pasta, meatballs, salad, and garlic bread, all of which were some of the most delicious that Skye had ever eaten, Skye positioned herself on the floor to play with Bella and help her with her new puzzle while they waited for their stomachs to settle before dipping into the pie Skye had brought. Riggs was resting on his bed near the fireplace after licking pasta off of Bella's tomato sauce-stained fingers. As they were putting the final piece of the frame of the puzzle in place, Logan's doorbell rang. He came back a minute later, a confused expression on his face. "Skye, it's for you."

Skye pointed at herself. "For me?" No one knew she was at Logan's. Was this some sort of a joke?

"Yeah, for you."

Skye got up, her stomach sinking. Was Logan playing a joke on her? Something to lighten the mood? She walked to the door, pulling it open. As she did, she spotted a short blonde woman with wiry hair wearing a ripped flannel shirt over a T-shirt and a pair of stained jeans.

Her sister Christy stood in front of her, her hands shoved into her pockets. "Hi, Skye. It's good to see you. We need to talk."

∼

Skye's story continues in *No Idea Who,* available now!

If you'd like to join my mailing list and be the first to get updates on new books and exclusive sales, giveaways and releases, click here!
I'll send you a prequel to the next series FREE!

Join the KJ Kalis Facebook Reader Group here

Made in United States
Orlando, FL
03 March 2026

78981088R00173